Alexander
the
Great

Alexander the Great

Edited and Introduced by
Alexandra F. Morris

General Editor: Jake Jackson

FLAME TREE
PUBLISHING

This is a FLAME TREE Book

FLAME TREE PUBLISHING
6 Melbray Mews
Fulham, London SW6 3NS
United Kingdom
www.flametreepublishing.com

First published 2022
Copyright © 2022 Flame Tree Publishing Ltd

22 24 26 25 23
1 3 5 7 9 8 6 4 2

ISBN: 978-1-83964-994-3

The classic texts in this book derive from *Alexander the Great* by Jacob
Abbott, published by Harper & Brothers Publishers, New York and London,
1902, and *The Invasion of India by Alexander the Great as described
by Arrian, Q. Curtius, Diodoros, Plutarch and Justin* by J.W. M'Crindle,
published by Archibald Constable and Company, Westminster, 1896.

Printed and bound in the UK by Clays Ltd, Elcograf S.p.A

Contents

Series Foreword

STRETCHING BACK to the oral traditions of thousands of years ago, tales of heroes and disaster, creation and conquest have been told by many different civilizations in many different ways. Their impact sits deep within our culture even though the detail in the tales themselves are a loose mix of historical record, transformed narrative and the distortions of hundreds of storytellers.

Today the language of mythology lives with us: our mood is jovial, our countenance is saturnine, we are narcissistic and our modern life is hermetically sealed from others. The nuances of myths and legends form part of our daily routines and help us navigate the world around us, with its half truths and biased reported facts.

The nature of a myth is that its story is already known by most of those who hear it, or read it. Every generation brings a new emphasis, but the fundamentals remain the same: a desire to understand and describe the events and relationships of the world. Many of the great stories are archetypes that help us find our own place, equipping us with tools for self-understanding, both individually and as part of a broader culture.

For Western societies it is Greek mythology that speaks to us most clearly. It greatly influenced the mythological heritage of the ancient Roman civilization and is the lens through which we still see the Celts, the Norse and many of the other great peoples and religions. The Greeks themselves learned much from their neighbours, the Egyptians, an older culture that became weak with age and incestuous leadership.

It is important to understand that what we perceive now as mythology had its own origins in perceptions of the divine and the rituals of the sacred. The earliest civilizations, in the crucible of the Middle East, in the Sumer of the third millennium BC, are the source to which many of the mythic archetypes can be traced. As humankind collected together in cities for the first time, developed writing and industrial scale agriculture, started to irrigate the rivers and attempted to control rather than be at the mercy of its environment, humanity began to write down its tentative explanations of natural events, of floods and plagues, of disease.

Early stories tell of Gods (or god-like animals in the case of tribal societies such as African, Native American or Aboriginal cultures) who are crafty and use their wits to survive, and it is reasonable to suggest that these were the first rulers of the gathering peoples of the earth, later elevated to god-like status with the distance of time. Such tales became more political as cities vied with each other for supremacy, creating new Gods, new hierarchies for their pantheons. The older Gods took on primordial roles and became the preserve of creation and destruction, leaving the new gods to deal with more current, everyday affairs. Empires rose and fell, with Babylon assuming the mantle from Sumeria in the 1800s BC, then in turn to be swept away by the Assyrians of the 1200s BC; then the Assyrians and the Egyptians were subjugated by the Greeks, the Greeks by the Romans and so on, leading to the spread and assimilation of common themes, ideas and stories throughout the world.

The survival of history is dependent on the telling of good tales, but each one must have the 'feeling' of truth, otherwise it will be ignored. Around the firesides, or embedded in a book or a computer, the myths and legends of the past are still the living materials of retold myth, not restricted to an exploration of origins. Now we have devices and global communications that give us unparalleled access to a diversity of traditions. We can find out about Indigenous American, Indian, Chinese and tribal African mythology in a way that was denied to our ancestors, we can find connections, match the archaeology, religion and the mythologies of the world to build a comprehensive image of the human adventure.

The great leaders of history and heroes of literature have also adopted the mantle of mythic experience, because the stories of historical figures – Cyrus the Great, Alexander, Genghis Khan – and mytho-poetic warriors such as Beowulf achieve a cultural significance that transcends their moment in the chronicles of humankind. Myth, history and literature have become powerful, intwined instruments of perception, with echoes of reported fact and symbolic truths that convey the sweep of human experience. In this series of books we arc glad to share with you the wonderful traditions of the past.

Jake Jackson
General Editor

Introduction to Alexander the Great

Alexander the Great remains one of the most illustrious historical figures of the ancient world. He not only cultivated a mythological presence of sorts while he was alive, but his legend was further amplified after his untimely death. The facts and likely fabrications of his life have fascinated both scholars and the general public ever since. But can we ever know the true Alexander when histories and biographies often reflect the societal biases of the time in which they were written?

The texts that follow are revised versions of the classic *Alexander the Great* by Jacob Abbott, first published in 1876, and *The Invasion of India by Alexander the Great as described by Arrian, Q. Curtius, Diodoros, Plutarch and Justin* by J.W. M'Crindle, first published in 1893. These texts have been updated for improved accessibility and easier reading, such as changing names and geographic locations to their modern, more commonly known spellings, and adjusting numerical values to their modern equivalencies. Further changes reflect the inclusion of new scholarship and archaeological discoveries made since the works were originally published. It is important to periodically update older scholarship in order to see how the historical field has evolved and trace the origins of certain historical facts, misconceptions and ideas. For example, at the time these texts were written, Troy had not yet been discovered and World War I and the associated conditions of modern warfare had not yet happened, both of which have impacted historians' understandings and interpretations of Alexander's life and the world in which he lived. Historical updates can also expose and contextualize the cultural norms and biases of the period in which a work was created. In this particular case, it means that certain relationships and people in Alexander's life were deliberately omitted from or changed in these texts, as they did not fit neatly into the moral standards of the nineteenth century era in which they were written. This does not mean these older histories of Alexander are completely inaccurate; rather, they offer us glimpses into how his character and deeds have been viewed over time. Alexander the Great remains, above all, a timeless historical figure, who has gained both notoriety and immortality in death.

The Ancient Sources and Historians

From the earliest historical accounts of Alexander the Great, interpretations of his character have split into two factions, and this continues to be reflected in modern scholarship. Alexander is either viewed favourably, or he is made out to be a monster or a tyrant – or both. There are five main surviving ancient sources who wrote about Alexander the Great: the ancient historians Arrian (whose work we focus on in this collection), and also Diodorus Siculus, Curtius Rufus, Plutarch and Justin. None of them, however, were alive at the time the events happened, living up to two or three centuries after Alexander's own life, which ran from 356 to 323 BCE. They also had their own agendas and biases in writing these histories, so they are not always entirely historically reliable.

Arrian was a historian, born in Nicomedia, Greece, who lived during the time of the Roman Empire (c. 87–160 CE). In addition to being a historian, he served in the Roman Senate and was governor of Cappadocia, which points to him having a military background (in ancient Rome, serving in the military in some capacity was often an unofficial requirement for running for political office). Arrian wrote numerous histories, many of which still survive today, and his history of Alexander the Great covered seven books (books in ancient historical scholarship are often all the same work, but divided up into the scrolls they fit on to physically, rather than referring to separate works or subjects) which are collectively known as the *Anabasis*. Arrian deliberately modelled his histories stylistically on the work of the earlier Athenian historian and soldier Xenophon. This means that Xenophon's work served as the basis for Arrian's own, and influenced how Arrian approached his own work, with Arrian even naming his work *Anabasis* after Xenophon's *Anabasis*. Xenophon lived contemporaneously with Philip II, and died shortly after Alexander the Great's birth.

Curtius Rufus was a Roman historian who lived sometime during the first century CE. His only known surviving work is his biography of Alexander the

Great, known as the *Historiae Alexandri Magni*, or *Histories of Alexander the Great*. However, it only survives in partial form, with several books missing. Not much else is known about him or about his work, and his origins and the exact dates of his history are still debated by scholars.

Diodorus Siculus was a Greek historian, born in Sicily during the end of the Hellenistic Period (*c.* 90-30 BCE), several hundred years after the death of Alexander the Great. Like Arrian, he is known to have written extensive histories and many of them survive to this day. His monumental work was the *Bibliotheca Historia*, or *Historical Library*, of which fifteen of what was originally forty books survive. It was arranged geographically covering the entire known ancient world, and drew on the work of many other ancient authors. Diodorus's history ranges from mythological history before the destruction of Troy and continues up until *c.* 60 BCE. His history of Alexander the Great was contained in this work. Not much else is known about him.

Justin was a Roman author who lived sometime during the time of the Roman Empire in either the second or third century CE. His surviving work is the *Historiae Philippicae* or *Philippic History*, which spans forty-four books, and covered the kings of ancient Macedonia. Unlike the others listed here, Justin was not strictly a historian. Rather, he collected, excerpted and preserved the passages of an earlier work also known as the *Philippic Histories* written by Roman historian Gnaeus Pompeius Trogus during the reign of Augustus. Justin focused on excerpting those passages which he found the most interesting. Not much else is known about him.

Plutarch was a Greek and Roman historian who also lived during the time of the Roman Empire (*c.* 46–119 CE). He was born in Chaeronea to a wealthy family. This was the same Chaeronea where Philip II won his last major battle, and where Alexander the Great had one of his first major military victories, which may have influenced Plutarch to take up Alexander and Philip II as subjects for his biographies. Plutarch is also the historian we know the most about. Like Arrian, he had other jobs. He worked as a magistrate, ambassador, and later became a Priest of Delphi. He was also a Platonist philosopher, biographer and essayist. A large portion of his works still exist, and these range from biographies to essays to transcribed speeches. His history of Alexander was written as a biography and was part of a series of biographies of famous Greeks and Romans referred to collectively as the *Parallel Lives*, which were arranged in pairs to illustrate commonalities in virtues and vices of the selected individuals. Rather than being strictly historical, Plutarch's work focused on the character traits of the individuals he profiled and their influence on humanity in general. Alexander the Great's biography was paired with Julius Caesar.

These five historians' works were based on earlier ancient sources, including contemporaries of Alexander the Great. These included Alexander's friends, companions and eventual successors, Aristobolus, Nearchus and Ptolemy. They also included the historian Cleitarchus who worked in the royal court of Ptolemy at Alexandria, Egypt, once Ptolemy became pharaoh. Like the nineteenth-century historians they informed, these earlier sources also suffered from biases and personal agendas, which further complicates the issue of historical reliability in Alexander's biographers. The ancient Greek historian Arrian based his history on the works of Nearchus, Ptolemy and Aristobolus. Ptolemy also drew his history from the works of the royal court historian Callisthenes. Some of Callisthenes's later work might also be questioned because of his supposed involvement in the Pages' Conspiracy to assassinate the king, for which Alexander had him executed as a traitor. The Roman historian Curtius Rufus and Greek historian Diodorus based their histories primarily on the work of Cleitarchus, who primarily drew from soldiers' stories. The Roman-Greek historian Plutarch lies somewhere in the middle, drawing from Ptolemy, Aristobolus and Cleitarchus. As a result, we have never had a complete picture of Alexander the Great, and the truth about him most likely lies somewhere between extraordinary leader and monstrous tyrant.

Philip II, Ancient Macedonia, and Alexander the Great's Upbringing

Alexander the Great, also known as Alexander III, was king of ancient Macedonia. He was the son of King Philip II and his chief wife Queen Olympias, a princess from the Greek geographic region of Epirus. Philip II, however, had multiple marriages, most of them political in nature. These marriages were important because in ancient Macedonia assassinations and struggles for power within the royal family were fairly common (and continued after Alexander's death).

Philip II's other wives included Audata of Illyria, Phila of Elimeia, Nicesipolis of Pherae, Phillna of Larissa, Meda of Odessos and finally Cleopatra Eurydice of Macedonia. Philip's marriages gave Alexander a number of siblings, including his sister Cleopatra (who is not the same as the famous Cleopatra VII of Egypt, although that Cleopatra was a direct descendent of Alexander's friend Ptolemy), and half-siblings Cynane, Thessalonike and Philip III Arrhidaeus, plus more unnamed illegitimate brothers and sisters.

Alexander's relationship with both parents ranged from loving to volatile, mirroring in many ways the relationship they had with each other. However, when it came to his education, they agreed. Alexander was educated first by Leonidas of Epirus and Lysimachus of Acarnania, and later as a teenager by the famous philosopher Aristotle. Philip and Olympias's relationship was often stormy, fuelled in part by her ambition and desire for power, and his volatility and distemper. Alexander was sometimes caught in the middle of his parents' arguments, which resulted in Philip publicly trying to kill him while in a drunken rage after one such disagreement *c.* 337 BCE, forcing Alexander to go into exile with Olympias. On other occasions, Philip II showed pride in his son, such as young Alexander's taming of the un-ridable horse Bucephalus, and when Philip put Alexander in charge of part of his military in the battle of Chaeronea. Not much is known about Alexander's relationships with his siblings, but he apparently retained some affection for both his sister Cleopatra and his disabled older half-brother Arrhidaeus, who is mentioned in the ancient sources as having some unspecified intellectual impairment.

Philip's Murder and Alexander's Kingship

When Philip II was murdered at the marriage celebration of his daughter Cleopatra, twenty-year-old Alexander became king. The murder itself has been steeped in controversy since ancient times and historians still disagree over who, if anyone, was likely involved besides the assassin Pausanias. Theories range from Persian involvement to Olympias to Alexander himself. After his father's death, Alexander subjugated the parts of Greece which tried to revolt. He then went on to conquer much of the known world, creating, by the age of 32, an empire which ranged from ancient Greece to parts of ancient India. While

Alexander was a military genius in his own right, much of his success can also be attributed to the many military innovations introduced to the Macedonian army by his father, Philip II. These included doubling the size of the infantry and cavalry, the creation of the Macedonian phalanx (a unit armed entirely with *sarissas*, or long spears), increased discipline and training for soldiers, as well as promotions based on merit.

Alexander had plans to continue his acquisition of territory before his untimely death in Babylon at age 32. After his passing, his empire was split amongst his remaining companions, generals and relatives. However, this did not last, and war broke out between the remaining successors in a bid to control what remained of Alexander's empire. Arrhidaeus took the throne name Philip III Arrhidaeus and became co-regent with Alexander's as-yet-unborn son, Alexander IV, ruling for approximately seven years after the death of Alexander. Both Alexander IV and Arrhidaeus were assassinated in the ensuing power struggle between other relatives or former royal companions. Cleopatra, Cynane, Olympias and Thessalonike were also involved with, and ultimately killed in, the war of the successors following the power vacuum created by Alexander the Great's death.

Alexander's Relationships

Besides his siblings, Alexander is known to have had several relationships throughout the course of his short life with both men and women. His closest companion and most intimate relationship was with his childhood friend Hephaestion. While male lovers at this time in history were not uncommon, Alexander and Hephaestion being almost the same age was unusual. This influenced how the ancient sources interpreted their relationship, and later modern biases have also influenced how their relationship has been reported. All ancient sources indisputably agree, however, that Alexander suffered intense grief after Hephaestion died. Alexander is also known to have married Roxanne, the daughter of a Sogdian chief, who was the mother of Alexander IV, and his chief wife. Alexander followed his father's strategy of political marriages, and therefore also married the Persian princesses Stateira and Parysatis. He is also mentioned in the ancient sources as potentially having intimate relationships with the Larissan woman Campaspe, the Persian noblewoman Barsine, and the eunuch Bagoas. However, as Alexander's relationships have also been coloured by myth, it is likely that at least some of these were apocryphal. Campaspe is reported to have served as Alexander's mistress, and he possibly lost his virginity to her before she was given to the painter Apelles. Her story has been traced back to ancient Roman accounts by historian Robin Lane Fox, but Campaspe is not mentioned in any of the five major ancient sources on Alexander the Great. Barsine is mentioned by the five main ancient Alexander historians, but not as being intimately involved with Alexander. She is reported to have had an illegitimate son with Alexander named Heracles, who was later also killed in the war of the successors. Among others, Mary Renault, another Alexander the Great scholar, finds Heracles's origins as an illegitimate son of Alexander to be doubtful at best, questioning why, if this was the case, he was not chosen as a potential successor for Alexander until seventeen years after Alexander's death. Renault also notes that the name Barsine is how Stateira was referenced in the ancient Greek sources, calling the existence of another Barsine into doubt. Bagoas is mentioned in the ancient sources, but his relationship with Alexander was also subject to biases from both ancient and modern historians, with the ancient Roman historians being particularly critical of it and labelling Bagoas as the real power behind Alexander's throne. Another relationship mentioned primarily in the *Alexander Romance* – stories about Alexander most likely created during the Middle Ages – which is almost certainly fictitious, is Alexander's encounter with the Amazon queen Thalestris. Additionally, besides his relationship with his mother Olympias, Alexander is reported to have had motherly relationships with both the Queen Mother of ancient Persia, Sisygambis, and with Queen Ada of Caria. His relationships with strong women, starting with his mother Olympias, were a recurrence throughout his life and were reflected not only with her, but with Ada, Sisygambis, and with Roxanne as well.

Alexander's Sexuality

Today's terminology around sexuality cannot be applied directly to the ancient world, for they had different cultural understandings of what sexuality was than we do today. Therefore, it is inappropriate to label Alexander as either gay or bisexual, and either choice is not without controversy in the historical field. However, what can be said is that Alexander had relationships with both men and women, and did not seem, unlike some Greek men, to be exclusively involved with men. Bagoas remains Alexander's only historically documented homosexual relationship. Suggesting that Alexander was sexually involved with Hephaestion is still a controversial subject that splits the historical field almost as closely as the favourable versus unfavourable historical views of the great king, and may also be a reflection of modern cultural biases.

Alexander's Appearance

While we have some general idea of what Alexander might have looked like, his appearance, too, is debatable and surrounded by as much myth as the rest of his story. He has been described as having been short in an age where height was often seen as being a sign of good character. In fact, he is explicitly mentioned in one of the stories as being shorter than Hephaestion, resulting in Hephaestion being mistaken as king. Alexander is also said to have had curly light-coloured hair, resembling a lion's mane, although some accounts mention it as blonde and some as red. He is also described as clean-shaven, breaking with his father's traditional beard. Alexander is mentioned in some sources as being left-handed, and as possibly having heterochromia, or eyes which were two different colours, one blue and one brown. It is altogether possible that his eyes were blue, and the brown appearance was a dilated pupil caused after a battle injury he had sustained. We do have some surviving sculptures and portraiture of Alexander, but what survives is mainly later Hellenistic and Roman copies of earlier Greek statues, and they often vary widely in appearance. Frequently these portraits show him leaning to one side, but it cannot be definitely said if this was an actual defining trait (indeed some historians have tried to medically diagnose Alexander because of this head tilt), or an artistic convention which was not necessarily representative of reality. Alexander's favourite artist, who had the exclusive rights to make marble portrait sculptures of him, was Lysippos. By this arrangement, Alexander remained in control of his image from the beginning – meaning what we have is his idealized version of himself.

In many ways besides his military and political genius, Alexander the Great was one of the first people in history to realize the importance of actively fashioning his own historical narrative and public image. This, in turn, ultimately shaped how he has been viewed historically. In some ways it has even led to the debate on whether he was a visionary leader or a tyrant. In either case, he successfully did what no one else had done prior: conquering much of the known world with an extremely loyal army who could not bear to see him hurt. His empire, while short lived, united many different cultures and peoples under a common language and culture. A particularly culturally significant aspect of the study of the history surrounding Alexander is that it created for the first time in history an elite class of disabled people, as his war veterans were the ones left in charge of the cities and territories he conquered. This pattern was continued with the appointment of Arrhidaeus as co-regent after Alexander's death. It is tempting to speculate on what could have been had Alexander lived, but, regardless, he irrevocably shaped history, leading in part to the world we have today.

Alexandra F. Morris (Introduction), originally from South Salem, New York, is a PhD researcher in history and a Module Tutor at Teesside University, UK. Her doctoral research focuses on disability during the Hellenistic & Ptolemaic Periods in ancient Egypt and Greece. She also is interested in Ptolemaic Egypt, Alexander the Great and ancient Egyptian and Greek art, medicine, politics and religious practices. She has an MA in Museum Studies from New York University and an MA in Near Eastern Languages & Civilizations (Egyptology) from the University of Pennsylvania. Her BA is in Archaeological Studies, Anthropology and Art History with minors in Classics and history from SUNY Potsdam. She has cerebral palsy and dyspraxia.

Alexander the Great

 **THE FIRST PART** of this book is Jacob Abbott's *Alexander the Great*. Abbott (1803–1875) was an American maths and philosophy professor, school principal and religious pastor. He also became a prolific author of books written for the general public. These books included such subjects as histories, biographies, religion and popular science, as well as fiction.

Abbott writes in a highly readable style, but his characterizations of some of the relationships between Alexander and his father, Philip, are influenced by the morality of the writer's era. This led Abbott to omit Alexander's other siblings and Philip II's other wives. Abbott additionally frames Philip marrying Cleopatra Eurydice as a divorce from Olympias and a new marriage, when, from what we know historically, he never actually divorced Olympias, just took an additional wife. It also has led to Hephaestion being characterized as a close friend of Alexander rather than a lover. Abbott also has focused his history primarily on the work of the Roman historians.

Chapter I
His Childhood and Youth, BCE **356–336**

The Briefness of Alexander's Career

A LEXANDER THE GREAT died when he was quite young. He was but thirty-two years of age when he ended his career, and as he was about twenty when he commenced it, it was only for a period of twelve years that he was actually engaged in performing the work of his life. Napoleon was nearly three times as long on the great field of human action.

His Brilliant Exploits

Notwithstanding the briefness of Alexander's career, he ran through, during that short period, a very brilliant series of exploits, which were so bold, so romantic, and which led him into such adventures in scenes of the greatest magnificence and splendour, that all the world looked on with astonishment then, and mankind have continued to read the story since, from age to age, with the greatest interest and attention.

Character of Alexander – Mental and Physical Qualities

The secret of Alexander's success was his character. He possessed a certain combination of mental and personal attractions, which in every age gives to those who exhibit it a mysterious and almost unbounded ascendency over all within their influence. Alexander was characterized by these qualities in a very remarkable degree. He was finely formed in person, and very prepossessing in his manners. He was active, athletic and full of ardour and enthusiasm in all that he did. At the same time, he was calm, collected and considerate in emergencies requiring caution, and thoughtful and far-seeing in respect to the bearings and consequences of his acts. He formed strong attachments, was grateful for kindnesses shown to him, considerate in respect to the feelings of all who were connected with him in any way, faithful to his friends and generous toward his foes. In a word, he had a noble character, though he devoted its energies unfortunately to conquest and war. He lived, in fact, in an age when great personal and mental powers had scarcely any other field for their exercise than this. He entered upon his career with great ardour, and the position in which he was placed gave him the opportunity to act in it with prodigious effect.

Character of the Asiatic and European Civilization

There were several circumstances combined, in the situation in which Alexander was placed, to afford him a great opportunity for the exercise of his vast powers. His native country was on the confines of Europe and Asia. Now Europe and Asia were, in those days, as now, marked and distinguished by two vast masses of social and civilized life, widely dissimilar from each other. The Asiatic side was occupied by the Persians, the Medes and the Assyrians. The European side by the Greeks and Romans. They were separated from each other by the waters of the Hellespont, the Aegean Sea and the Mediterranean. These waters constituted a sort of natural barrier, which kept the two civilizations apart. The races formed, accordingly, two vast organizations, distinct and widely different from each other, and of course rivals and enemies.

Composition of Asiatic and European Armies

It is hard to say whether the Asiatic or European civilization was the highest. The two were so different that it is difficult to compare them. On the Asiatic side there was wealth, luxury and splendour; on the European, energy, genius and force. On the one hand were vast cities, splendid palaces and gardens which were the wonder of the world; on the other, strong citadels, military roads and bridges, and compact and well-defended towns. The Persians had enormous armies, perfectly provided for, with beautiful tents, horses elegantly caparisoned, arms and munitions of war of the finest workmanship, and officers magnificently dressed and accustomed to a life of luxury and splendour. The

Greeks and Romans, on the other hand, prided themselves on their compact bodies of troops, inured to hardship and thoroughly disciplined. Their officers gloried not in luxury and parade, but in the courage, the steadiness and implicit obedience of their troops, and in their own science, skill and powers of military calculation. Thus, there was a great difference in the whole system of social and military organization in these two quarters of the globe.

Now Alexander was born the heir to the throne of one of the Grecian kingdoms. He possessed, in a very remarkable degree, the energy, and enterprise, and military skill so characteristic of the Greeks and Romans. He organized armies, crossed the boundary between Europe and Asia and spent the twelve years of his career in a most triumphant military incursion into the very centre and seat of Asiatic power, destroying the Asiatic armies, conquering the most splendid cities, defeating or taking captive the kings, and princes, and generals that opposed his progress. The whole world looked on with wonder to see such a course of conquest, pursued so successfully by so young a man, and with so small an army, gaining continual victories, as it did, over such vast numbers of foes, and making conquests of such accumulated treasures of wealth and splendour.

King Philip – Extent of Macedon – Olympias

The name of Alexander's father was Philip. The kingdom over which he reigned was called Macedon. Macedon was in the northern part of Greece. It was a kingdom about twice as large as the state of Massachusetts, and one third as large as the state of New York. The name of Alexander's mother was Olympias. She was the daughter of the King of Epirus, which was a kingdom somewhat smaller than Macedon, and lying westward of it. Olympias was a woman of very strong and determined character. Alexander seemed to inherit her energy, though in his case it was combined with other qualities of a more attractive character, which his mother did not possess.

The Young Prince Alexander

He was, of course, as the young prince, a very important personage in his father's court. Everyone knew that at his father's death he would become

King of Macedon, and he was consequently the object of a great deal of care and attention. As he gradually advanced in the years of his boyhood, it was observed by all who knew him that he was endued with extraordinary qualities of mind and of character, which seemed to indicate, at a very early age, his future greatness.

Ancient Mode of Warfare

Although he was a prince, he was not brought up in habits of luxury and refinement. This would have been contrary to all the ideas which were entertained by the Greeks in those days. They had then no firearms or other technologically advanced weaponry, meaning that unlike today, combatants were required to be in close physical contact with one another. In ancient battles the soldiers rushed toward each other, and fought hand to hand, in close combat, with swords, or spears, or other weapons requiring great personal strength, so that headlong bravery and muscular force were the qualities which generally carried the day.

Ancient and Modern Military Officers

The duties of officers, too, on the field of battle, were very different then from what they are now. An officer now must be calm, collected and quiet. His business is to plan, to calculate, to direct and arrange. He has to do this sometimes, it is true, in circumstances of the most imminent danger, so that he must be a man of great self-possession and of undaunted courage. But there is very little occasion for him to exert any great physical force.

In ancient times, however, the great business of the officers, certainly in all the subordinate grades, was to lead on the men, and set them an example by performing themselves deeds in which their own great personal prowess was displayed. Of course, it was considered extremely important that the child destined to be a general should become robust and powerful in constitution from his earliest years, and that he should be inured to hardship and fatigue. In the early part of Alexander's life this was the main object of attention.

Alexander's Nurse – Alexander's Education – Lysimachus

The name of the nurse who had charge of our hero in his infancy was Lannice. She did all in her power to give strength and hardihood to his constitution, while, at the same time, she treated him with kindness and gentleness. Alexander acquired a strong affection for her, and he treated her with great consideration as long as he lived. He had a tutor, also, in his early years, named Leonnatus Leonidas of Epirus, who had the general charge of his education. As soon as he was old enough to learn, they appointed him an instructor also, to teach him such branches as were generally taught to young princes in those days. The name of this instructor was Lysimachus of Acarnania.

Homer

They had then no printed books, but there were a few writings on parchment rolls which young scholars were taught to read. Some of these writings were treatises on philosophy, others were romantic histories, narrating the exploits of the heroes of those days – of course, with much exaggeration and embellishment. There were also some poems, still more romantic than the histories, though generally on the same themes. The greatest productions of this kind were the writings of Homer, an ancient poet who lived and wrote four or five hundred years before Alexander's day. The young Alexander was greatly delighted with Homer's tales. These tales are narrations of the exploits and adventures of certain great warriors at the siege of Troy – a siege which lasted ten years – and they are written with so much beauty and force, they contain such admirable delineations of character, and such graphic and vivid descriptions of romantic adventures, and picturesque and striking scenes, that they have been admired in every age by all who have learned to understand the language in which they are written.

Aristotle – Alexander's Copy of Homer

Alexander could understand them very easily, as they were written in his mother tongue. He was greatly excited by the narrations themselves, and pleased with

24

the flowing smoothness of the verse in which the tales were told. In the latter part of his course of education he was placed under the charge of Aristotle, who was one of the most eminent philosophers of ancient times. Aristotle had a beautiful copy of Homer's poems prepared expressly for Alexander, taking great pains to have it transcribed with perfect correctness, and in the most elegant manner. Alexander carried this copy with him in all his campaigns. Some years afterward, when he was obtaining conquests over the Persians, he took, among the spoils of one of his victories, a very beautiful and costly casket, which King Darius had used for his jewellery or for some other rich treasures. Alexander determined to make use of this box as a depository for his beautiful copy of Homer, and he always carried it with him, thus protected, in all his subsequent campaigns.

Alexander's Energy and Ambition

Alexander was full of energy and spirit, but he was, at the same time, like all who ever become truly great, of a reflective and considerate turn of mind. He was very fond of the studies which Aristotle led him to pursue, although they were of a very abstruse and difficult character. He made great progress in metaphysical philosophy and mathematics, by which means his powers of calculation and his judgment were greatly improved.

He early evinced a great degree of ambition. His father Philip was a powerful warrior, and made many conquests in various parts of Greece, though he did not cross into Asia. When news of Philip's victories came into Macedon, all the rest of the court would be filled with rejoicing and delight; but Alexander, on such occasions, looked thoughtful and disappointed, and complained that his father would conquer every country, and leave him nothing to do.

The Persian Ambassadors

At one time some ambassadors from the Persian court arrived in Macedon when Philip was away. These ambassadors saw Alexander, of course, and had opportunities to converse with him. They expected that he would be interested in hearing about the splendours, pomp and parade of the Persian monarchy. They had stories to tell him about the famous hanging gardens, which were artificially constructed in the most magnificent manner, on arches raised high in the air; and about a vine made of gold, with all sorts of precious stones upon it instead of fruit, which was wrought as an ornament over the throne on which the King of Persia often gave audience; of the splendid palaces and vast cities of the Persians; and the banquets, and fêtes, and magnificent entertainments and celebrations which they used to have there. They found, however, to their surprise, that Alexander was not interested in hearing about any of these things. He would always turn the conversation from them to inquire about the geographical position of the different Persian countries, the various routes leading into the interior, the organization of the Asiatic armies, their system of military tactics and, especially, the character and habits of Artaxerxes, the Persian king.

Maturity of Alexander's Mind

The ambassadors were very much surprised at such evidences of maturity of mind, and of far-seeing and reflective powers on the part of the young prince. They could not help comparing him with Artaxerxes. 'Alexander,' said they, 'is *great*, while our king is only *rich*.' The truth of the judgment which these ambassadors thus formed in respect to the qualities of the young Macedonian, compared with those held in highest estimation on the Asiatic side, was fully confirmed in the subsequent stages of Alexander's career.

Secret of Alexander's Success – The Story of Bucephalus

In fact, this combination of a calm and calculating thoughtfulness, with the ardour and energy which formed the basis of his character, was one great secret of Alexander's success. The story of Bucephalus, his famous horse, illustrates this in a very striking manner. This animal was a war-horse of very spirited character, which had been sent as a present to Philip while Alexander was young. They took the horse out into one of the parks connected with the palace, and the king, together with many of his courtiers, went out to view him. The horse pranced about in a very furious manner, and seemed entirely unmanageable. No one dared to mount him. Philip, instead of being gratified at the present, was rather disposed to be displeased that they had sent him an animal of so fiery and apparently vicious a nature that nobody dared to attempt to subdue him.

In the meantime, while all the other bystanders were joining in the general condemnation of the horse, Alexander stood quietly by, watching his motions, and attentively studying his character. He perceived that a part of the difficulty was caused by the agitations which the horse experienced in so strange and new a scene, and that he appeared, also, to be somewhat frightened by his own shadow, which happened at that time to be thrown very strongly and distinctly upon the ground. He saw other indications, also, that the high excitement which the horse felt was not viciousness, but the excess of noble and generous impulses. It was courage, ardour and the consciousness of great nervous and muscular power.

Philip Condemns the Horse – Alexander Desires to Mount Him

Philip had decided that the horse was useless, and had given orders to have him sent back to Thessaly, whence he came. Alexander was very much concerned at the prospect of losing so fine an animal. He begged his father to allow him to make the experiment of mounting him. Philip at first refused, thinking it very presumptuous for such a youth to attempt to subdue an animal so vicious that all his experienced horsemen and grooms condemned him; however, he at length consented. Alexander went up to the horse and took hold of his bridle. He patted him upon the neck, and soothed him with his voice, showing, at the same time, by his easy and unconcerned manner, that he was not in the least afraid of him. A spirited horse knows immediately when anyone approaches him in a timid or cautious manner. He appears to look with contempt on such a master, and to determine not to submit to him. On the contrary, horses seem to love to yield obedience to man, when the individual who exacts the obedience possesses those qualities of coolness and courage which their instincts enable them to appreciate.

Bucephalus Calmed – An Exciting Ride

At any rate, Bucephalus was calmed and subdued by the presence of Alexander. He allowed himself to be caressed. Alexander turned his head in such a direction as to prevent his seeing his shadow. He quietly and gently laid off a sort of cloak which he wore, and sprang upon the horse's back. Then, instead of attempting to restrain him, and worrying and checking him by useless efforts to hold him in, he gave him the rein freely, and animated and encouraged him with his voice, so that the horse flew across the plains at the top of his speed, the king and the courtiers looking on, at first with fear and trembling, but soon afterward with feelings of the greatest admiration and pleasure. After the horse had satisfied himself with his run it was easy to rein him in, and Alexander returned with him in safety to the king. The courtiers overwhelmed him with their praises and congratulations. Philip commended him very highly: he told him that he deserved a larger kingdom than Macedon to govern.

Sagacity of Bucephalus – Becomes Alexander's Favourite

Alexander's judgment of the true character of the horse proved to be correct. He became very tractable and docile, yielding a ready submission to his master in everything. He would kneel upon his fore legs at Alexander's command, in order that he might mount more easily. Alexander retained him for a long time, and made him his favourite war horse. A great many stories are related by the historians of those days of his sagacity and his feats of war. Whenever he was equipped for the field with his military trappings, he seemed to be highly elated with pride and pleasure, and at such times he would not allow anyone but Alexander to mount him.

Fate of Bucephalus

What became of him at last is not certainly known. There are two accounts of his end. One is, that on a certain occasion Alexander got carried too far into the midst of his enemies on a battlefield and that, after fighting desperately for some time, Bucephalus made the most extreme exertions to carry him away. He was severely wounded again and again, and though his strength was nearly gone, he would not stop, but pressed forward till he had carried his master away to a place of safety, and that then he dropped down exhausted, and died. It may be, however, that he did not actually die at this time, but slowly recovered; for some historians relate that he lived to be thirty years old – which is quite an old age for a horse – and that he then died. Alexander caused him to be buried with great ceremony, and built a small city upon the spot in honour of his memory. The name of this city was Bucephalia.

Alexander Made Regent

Alexander's character matured rapidly, and he began very early to act the part of a man. When he was only sixteen years of age, his father, Philip, made him regent of Macedon while he was absent on a great military campaign among the other states of Greece. Without doubt Alexander had, in this regency, the counsel and aid of high officers of state of great experience and ability. He acted, however, himself, in this high position, with great energy and with complete success; and, at the same time, with all that modesty of deportment, and that delicate consideration for the officers under him – who, though inferior in rank, were yet his superiors in age and experience – which his position rendered proper, but which few persons so young as he would have manifested in circumstances so well calculated to awaken the feelings of vanity and elation.

Alexander's First Battle – Chaeronea

Afterward, when Alexander was about eighteen years old, his father took him with him on a campaign toward the south, during which Philip fought one of his great battles at Chaeronea, in Boeotia. In the arrangements for this battle, Philip gave the command of one of the wings of the army to Alexander, while he reserved the other for himself. He felt some solicitude in giving his young son so important a charge, but he endeavoured to guard against the danger of an unfortunate result by putting the ablest generals on Alexander's side, while he reserved those on whom he could place less reliance for his own. Thus organized, the army went into battle.

Philip soon ceased to feel any solicitude for Alexander's part of the duty. Boy as he was, the young prince acted with the utmost bravery, coolness and discretion. The wing which he commanded was victorious, and Philip was obliged to urge himself and the officers with him to greater exertions, to avoid being outdone by his son. In the end Philip was completely victorious, and the result of this great battle was to make his power paramount and supreme over all the states of Greece.

Alexander's Impetuosity – Philip Repudiates Olympias

Notwithstanding, however, the extraordinary discretion and wisdom which characterized the mind of Alexander in his early years, he was often haughty and headstrong, and in cases where his pride or his resentment were aroused, he was sometimes found very impetuous and uncontrollable. His mother Olympias was of a haughty and imperious temper, and she quarrelled with her husband, King Philip; or, perhaps, it ought rather to be said that he quarrelled with her. Each is said to have been unfaithful to the other, and, after a bitter contention, Philip repudiated his wife and married another lady, named Cleopatra Eurydice. Among the festivities held on the occasion of this marriage, there was a great banquet, at which Alexander was present, and an incident occurred which strikingly illustrates the impetuosity of his character.

Alexander's Violent Temper

One of the guests at this banquet, in saying something complimentary to the new queen, made use of expressions which Alexander considered as in disparagement of the character of his mother and of his own birth. His anger was immediately aroused. He threw the cup from which he had been drinking at the offender's head. Attalus, for this was his name, threw his cup at Alexander in return; the guests at the table where they were sitting rose, and a scene of uproar and confusion ensued.

Philip's Attempt on His Son

Philip, incensed at such an interruption of the order and harmony of the wedding feast, drew his sword and rushed toward Alexander but by some accident he stumbled and fell upon the floor. Alexander looked upon his fallen father with contempt and scorn, and exclaimed, 'What a fine hero the states of Greece have to lead their armies – a man that cannot get across the floor without tumbling down.' He then turned away and left the palace. Immediately afterward he joined his mother Olympias, and went away with her to her native country, Epirus, where the mother and son remained for a time in a state of open quarrel with the husband and father.

Philip's Power – His Plans of Conquest

In the meantime Philip had been planning a great expedition into Asia. He had arranged the affairs of his own kingdom, and had formed a strong combination among the states of Greece, by which powerful armies had been raised, and he had been designated to command them. His mind was very intently engaged in this vast enterprise. He was in the flower of his years, and at the height of his power. His own kingdom was in a very prosperous and thriving condition, and his ascendency over the other kingdoms and states on the European side had been fully established. He was excited with ambition, and full of hope. He was proud of his son Alexander, and was relying upon his efficient aid in his schemes of conquest and aggrandizement. He had married a youthful and beautiful bride, and was surrounded by scenes of festivity, congratulation and rejoicing. He was looking forward to a very brilliant career considering all the deeds that he had done and all the glory which he had acquired as only the introduction and prelude to the far more distinguished and conspicuous part which he was intending to perform.

Alexander's Impatience to Reign

Alexander, in the meantime, ardent and impetuous, and eager for glory as he was, looked upon the position and prospects of his father with some envy and jealousy. He was impatient to be monarch himself. His taking sides so promptly with his mother in the domestic quarrel was partly owing to the feeling that his father was a hindrance and an obstacle in the way of his own greatness and fame. He felt within himself powers and capacities qualifying him to take his father's place, and reap for himself the harvest of glory and power which seemed to await the Grecian armies in the coming campaign. While his father lived, however, he could be only a prince; influential, accomplished and popular, it is true, but still without any substantial and independent power. He was restless and uneasy at the thought that, as his father was in the prime and vigour of manhood, many long years must elapse before he could emerge from this confined and subordinate condition. His restlessness and uneasiness were, however, suddenly ended by a very extraordinary occurrence, which called him, with scarcely an hour's notice, to take his father's place upon the throne.

Chapter II
Beginning of His Reign, BCE 336

❋

ALEXANDER WAS SUDDENLY called upon to succeed his father on the Macedonian throne, in the most unexpected manner, and in the midst of scenes of the greatest excitement and agitation. The circumstances were these:

Philip is Reconciled to Olympias and Alexander

Philip had felt very desirous, before setting out upon his great expedition into Asia, to become reconciled to Alexander and Olympias. He wished for Alexander's co-operation in his plans; and then, besides, it would be dangerous to go away from his own dominions with such a son left behind, in a state of resentment and hostility.

Olympias and Alexander Returned

So Philip sent kind and conciliatory messages to Olympias and Alexander, who had gone, it will be recollected, to Epirus, where her friends resided. The brother of Olympias was King of Epirus. He had been at first incensed at the indignity which had been put upon his sister by Philip's treatment of her; but Philip now tried to appease his anger, also, by friendly negotiations and messages. At last he arranged a marriage between this King of Epirus and one of his own daughters (Cleopatra, the sister of Alexander the Great, and niece of King Alexander I of Epirus), and this completed the reconciliation. Olympias and Alexander returned to Macedon, and great preparations were made for a very splendid wedding.

The Great Wedding

Philip wished to make this wedding not merely the means of confirming his reconciliation with his former wife and son, and establishing friendly relations with the King of Epirus: he also prized it as an occasion for paying marked and honourable attention to the princes and great generals of the other states of Greece. He consequently made his preparations on a very extended and sumptuous scale, and sent invitations to the influential and prominent men far and near.

These great men, on the other hand, and all the other public authorities in the various Grecian states, sent compliments, congratulations and presents to Philip, each seeming ambitious to contribute his share to the splendour of the celebration. They were not wholly disinterested in this, it is true. As Philip had been made commander-in-chief of the Grecian armies which were about to undertake the conquest of Asia, and as, of course, his influence and power in all that related to that vast enterprise would be paramount and supreme; and as all were ambitious to have a large share in the glory of that expedition, and to participate, as much as possible, in the power and in the renown which seemed to be at Philip's disposal, all were, of course, very anxious to secure his favour. A short time before, they were contending against him; but now, since he had established his ascendency, they all eagerly joined in the work of magnifying it and making it illustrious.

Preparations for the Wedding – Costly Presents

Nor could Philip justly complain of the hollowness and falseness of these professions of friendship. The compliments and favours which he offered to them were equally hollow and heartless. He wished to secure *their* favour as a means of aiding him up the steep path to fame and power which he was attempting to climb. They wished for his, in order that he might, as he ascended himself, help them up with him. There was, however, the greatest appearance of cordial and devoted friendship. Some cities sent him presents of golden crowns, beautifully wrought, and of high cost. Others dispatched embassies, expressing their good wishes for him, and their confidence in the success of his plans. Athens, the city which was the great seat of literature and science in Greece sent a *poem*, in which the history of the expedition into Persia was given by anticipation. In this poem Philip was, of course, triumphantly successful in his enterprise. He conducted his armies in safety through the most dangerous passes and defiles; he fought glorious battles, gained magnificent victories and possessed himself of all the treasures of Asiatic wealth and power. It ought to be stated, however, in justice to the poet, that, in narrating these imaginary exploits, he had sufficient delicacy to represent Philip and the Persian monarch by fictitious names.

Celebration of the Wedding – Games and Spectacles

The wedding was at length celebrated, in one of the cities of Macedon, with great pomp and splendour. There were games, shows and military and civic spectacles of all kinds to amuse the thousands of spectators that assembled to witness them. In one of these spectacles they had a procession of statues of the gods. There were twelve of these statues, sculptured with great art, and they were borne along on elevated pedestals, with censers, incense and various ceremonies of homage, while vast multitudes of spectators lined the way. There was a thirteenth statue, more magnificent than the other twelve, which represented Philip himself in the character of a god.

Statues of the Gods

This was not, however, so impious as it would at first view seem, for the gods whom the ancients worshiped were, in fact, only deifications of old heroes and kings who had lived in early times, and had acquired a reputation for supernatural powers by the fame of their exploits, exaggerated in descending by tradition in superstitious times. The ignorant multitude accordingly, in those days, looked up to a living king with almost the same reverence and homage which they felt for their deified heroes; and these deified heroes furnished them with all the ideas they had of God. Making a monarch a god, therefore, was no very extravagant flattery.

Military Procession

After the procession of the statues passed along, there came bodies of troops, with trumpets sounding and banners flying. The officers rode on horses elegantly ornamented and prancing proudly. These troops escorted princes, ambassadors, generals and great officers of state, all gorgeously decked in their robes, and wearing their badges and insignia.

Appearance of Philip

At length King Philip himself appeared in the procession. He had arranged to have a large space left, in the middle of which he was to walk. This was done in order to make his position the more conspicuous, and to mark more strongly his own high distinction above all the other potentates present on the occasion. Guards preceded and followed him, though at considerable distance, as has been already said. He was himself clothed with white robes, and his head was adorned with a splendid crown.

The Scene Changed – Assassination of Philip

The procession was moving toward a great theatre, where certain games and spectacles were to be exhibited. The statues of the gods were to be taken into the theatre, and placed in conspicuous positions there, in the view of the assembly, and then the procession itself was to follow. All the statues had entered except that of Philip, which was just at the door, and Philip himself was advancing in the midst of the space left for him, up the avenue by which the theatre was approached, when an occurrence took place by which the whole character of the scene, the destiny of Alexander, and the fate of fifty nations, was suddenly and totally changed. It was this. An officer of the guards, who had his position in the procession near the king, was seen advancing impetuously toward him, through the space which separated him from the rest, and, before the spectators had time even to wonder what he was going to do, he stabbed him to the heart. Philip fell down in the street and died.

A scene of indescribable tumult and confusion ensued. The murderer was immediately cut to pieces by the other guards. They found, however, before he was dead, that it was Pausanias, a man of high standing and influence, a general officer of the guards. He had had horses provided, and other assistance ready, to enable him to make his escape, but he was cut down by the guards before he could avail himself of them.

Alexander Proclaimed King – Alexander's Speech

An officer of state immediately hastened to Alexander, and announced to him his father's death and his own accession to the throne. An assembly of the leading counsellors and statesmen was called, in a hasty and tumultuous manner, and Alexander was proclaimed king with prolonged and general acclamations. Alexander made a speech in reply. The great assembly looked upon his youthful form and face as he arose, and listened with intense interest to hear what he had to say. He was between nineteen and twenty years of age; but, though thus really a boy, he spoke with all the decision and confidence of an energetic man. He said that he should at once assume his father's position, and carry forward his plans. He hoped to do this so efficiently that everything would go directly onward, just as if his father had continued to live, and that the nation would find that the only change which had taken place was in the *name* of the king.

Demosthenes' Philippics

The motive which induced Pausanias to murder Philip in this manner was never fully ascertained. There were various opinions about it. One was, that it was an act of private revenge, occasioned by some neglect or injury which Pausanias had received from Philip. Others thought that the murder was instigated by a party in the states of Greece, who were hostile to Philip, and unwilling that he should command the allied armies that were about to penetrate into Asia. Demosthenes, the celebrated orator, was Philip's great enemy among the Greeks. Many of his most powerful orations were made for the purpose of arousing his countrymen to resist his ambitious plans and to curtail his power. These orations were called his Philippics, and from this origin has arisen the practice, which has prevailed ever since that day, of applying the term philippics to denote, in general, any strongly denunciatory harangues.

The Greeks Suspected of the Murder

Now Demosthenes, it is said, who was at this time in Athens, announced the death of Philip in an Athenian assembly before it was possible that the news could have been conveyed there. He accounted for his early possession of the intelligence by saying it was communicated to him by some of the gods. Many persons have accordingly supposed that the plan of assassinating Philip was devised in Greece; that Demosthenes was a party to it; that Pausanias was the agent for carrying it into execution; and that Demosthenes was so confident of the success of the plot, and exulted so much in this certainty, that he could not resist the temptation of thus anticipating its announcement.

The Persians Also

There were other persons who thought that the *Persians* had plotted and accomplished this murder, having induced Pausanias to execute the deed by the promise of great rewards. As Pausanias himself, however, had been instantly killed, there was no opportunity of gaining any information from him on the motives of his conduct, even if he would have been disposed to impart any.

Alexander's New Position

At all events, Alexander found himself suddenly elevated to one of the most conspicuous positions in the whole political world. It was not simply that he succeeded to the throne of Macedon; even this would have been a lofty position for so young a man; but Macedon was a very small part of the realm over which Philip had extended his power. The ascendency which he had acquired over the whole Grecian empire, and the vast arrangements he had made for an incursion into Asia, made Alexander the object of universal interest and attention. The question was, whether Alexander should attempt to take his father's place in respect to all this general power, and undertake to sustain and carry on his vast projects, or whether he should content himself with ruling, in quiet, over his native country of Macedon.

His Designs

Most prudent persons would have advised a young prince, under such circumstances, to have decided upon the latter course. But Alexander had no idea of bounding his ambition by any such limits. He resolved to spring at once completely into his father's seat, and not only to possess himself of the whole of the power which his father had acquired, but to commence, immediately, the most energetic and vigorous efforts for a great extension of it.

Murderers of Philip Punished

His first plan was to punish his father's murderers. He caused the circumstances of the case to be investigated, and the persons suspected of having been connected with Pausanias in the plot to be tried. Although the designs and motives of the murderers could never be fully ascertained, still several persons were found guilty of participating in it, and were condemned to death and publicly executed.

Alexander's First Acts

Alexander next decided not to make any change in his father's appointments to the great offices of state, but to let all the departments of public affairs go on in the same hands as before. How sagacious a line of conduct was this! Most ardent and enthusiastic young men, in the circumstances in which he was placed, would have been elated and vain at their elevation, and would have replaced the old and well-tried servants of the father with personal favourites of their own age, inexperienced and incompetent, and as conceited as themselves. Alexander, however, made no such changes. He continued the old officers in command, endeavouring to have everything go on just as if his father had not died.

Parmenio

There were two officers in particular who were the ministers on whom Philip had mainly relied. Their names were Antipater and Parmenio. Antipater had charge of the civil, and Parmenio of military affairs. Parmenio was a very distinguished general. He was at this time nearly sixty years of age. Alexander had great confidence in his military powers, and felt a strong personal attachment for him. Parmenio entered into the young king's service with great readiness, and accompanied him through almost the whole of his career. It seemed strange to see men of such age, standing and experience, obeying the orders of such a boy; but there was something in the genius, the power and the enthusiasm of Alexander's character which inspired ardour in all around him, and made everyone eager to join his standard and to aid in the execution of his plans.

Cities of Southern Greece – Athens and Corinth

Macedon, as will be seen on the following map, was in the northern part of the country occupied by the Greeks, and the most powerful states of the confederacy and all the great and influential cities were south of it. There was Athens, which was magnificently built, its splendid citadel crowning a rocky hill in the centre of it. It was the great seat of literature, philosophy and the arts, and was thus a centre of attraction for all the civilized world. There was Corinth, which was distinguished for the merriment and pleasure which reigned there. All possible means of luxury and amusement were concentrated within its walls. The lovers of knowledge and of art, from all parts of the earth, flocked to Athens, while those in pursuit of pleasure, dissipation and indulgence chose Corinth for their home. Corinth was beautifully situated on the isthmus, with prospects of the sea on either hand. It had been a famous city for a thousand years in Alexander's day.

Map of Macedon and Greece – Thebes

There was also Thebes. Thebes was farther north than Athens and Corinth. It was situated on an elevated plain, and had, like other ancient cities, a strong citadel, where there was at this time a Macedonian garrison, which Philip had placed there. Thebes was very wealthy and powerful. It had also been celebrated as the birthplace of many poets and philosophers, and other eminent men. Among these was Pindar, a very celebrated poet who had flourished one or two centuries before the time of Alexander. His descendants still lived in Thebes, and Alexander, sometime after this, had occasion to confer upon them a very distinguished honour.

Sparta

There was Sparta also, called sometimes Lacedaemon. The inhabitants of this city were famed for their courage, hardihood and physical strength, and for the energy with which they devoted themselves to the work of war. They were nearly all soldiers, and all the arrangements of the state and of society, and all the plans of education, were designed to promote military ambition and pride among the officers and fierce and indomitable courage and endurance in the men.

Conquests of Philip

These cities and many others, with the states which were attached to them, formed a large, and flourishing, and very powerful community, extending over all that part of Greece which lay south of Macedon. Philip, as has been already said, had established his own ascendency over all this region, though it had cost him many perplexing negotiations and some hard-fought battles to do it. Alexander considered it somewhat uncertain whether the people of all these states and cities would be disposed to transfer readily, to so youthful a prince as he, the high commission which his father, a very powerful monarch and soldier, had extorted from them with so much difficulty. What should he do in the case? Should he give up the expectation of it? Should he send ambassadors to them, presenting his claims to occupy his father's place? Or should he not act at all, but wait quietly at home in Macedon until they should decide the question?

Alexander Marches Southward

Instead of doing either of these things, Alexander decided on the very bold step of setting out himself, at the head of an army, to march into southern Greece, for the purpose of presenting in person, and, if necessary, of enforcing his claim to the same post of honour and power which had been conferred upon his father. Considering all the circumstances of the case, this was perhaps one of the boldest and most decided steps of Alexander's whole career. Many of his Macedonian advisers counselled him not to make such an attempt; but Alexander would not listen to any such cautions. He collected his forces, and set forth at the head of them.

Pass of Thermopylae

Between Macedon and the southern states of Greece was a range of lofty and almost impassable mountains. These mountains extended through the whole interior of the country, and the main route leading into southern Greece passed around to the eastward of them, where they terminated in cliffs, leaving a narrow passage between the cliffs and the sea. This pass was called the Pass of Thermopylae, and it was considered the key to Greece. There was a town named Anthela near the pass, on the outward side.

The Amphictyonic Council

There was in those days a sort of general congress or assembly of the states of Greece, which was held from time to time, to decide questions and disputes in which the different states were continually getting involved with each other. This assembly was called the Amphictyonic Council, on account, as is said, of its having been established by a certain king named Amphictyon. A meeting of this council was appointed to receive Alexander. It was to be held at Thermopylae, or, rather, at Anthela, which was just without the pass, and was the usual place at which the council assembled. This was because the pass was in an intermediate position between the northern and southern portions of Greece, and thus equally accessible from either.

March Through Thessaly – Alexander's Traits of Character

In proceeding to the southward, Alexander had first to pass through Thessaly, which was a very powerful state immediately south of Macedon. He met with some show of resistance at first, but not much. The country was impressed with the boldness and decision of character manifested in the taking of such a course by so young a man. Then, too, Alexander, so far as he became personally known, made a very favourable impression upon everyone. His manly and athletic form, his frank and open manners, his spirit, his generosity, and a certain air of confidence, independence and conscious superiority, which were combined, as they always are in the case of true greatness, with an unaffected and unassuming modesty – these and other traits, which were obvious to all who saw him, in the person and character of Alexander, made everyone his friend. Common men take pleasure in yielding to the influence and ascendency of one whose spirit they see and feel stands on a higher eminence and wields higher powers than their own. They like a leader. It is true, they must feel confident of his superiority; but when this superiority stands out so clearly and distinctly marked, combined, too, with all the graces and attractions of youth and manly beauty, as it was in the case of Alexander, the minds of men are brought very easily and rapidly under its sway.

The Thessalians Join Alexander

The Thessalians gave Alexander a very favourable reception. They expressed a cordial readiness to instate him in the position which his father had occupied. They joined their forces to his, and proceeded southward toward the Pass of Thermopylae.

He Sits In the Amphictyonic Council

Here the great council was held. Alexander took his place in it as a member. Of course, he must have been an object of universal interest and attention. The impression which he made here seems to have been very favourable. After this assembly separated, Alexander proceeded southward, accompanied by his own forces, and tended by the various princes and potentates of Greece, with their attendants and followers. The feelings of exultation and pleasure with which the young king marched through the Pass of Thermopylae, thus attended, must have been exciting in the extreme.

Thermopylae – Leonidas and His Spartans

The Pass of Thermopylae was a scene strongly associated with ideas of military glory and renown. It was here that, about a hundred and fifty years before, Leonidas, a Spartan general, with only three hundred soldiers, had attempted to withstand the pressure of an immense Persian force which was at that time invading Greece. He was one of the kings of Sparta, and he had the command, not only of his three hundred Spartans, but also of all the allied forces of the Greeks that had been assembled to repel the Persian invasion. With the help of these allies he withstood the Persian forces for some time, and as the pass was so narrow between the cliffs and the sea, he was enabled to resist them successfully. At length, however, a strong detachment from the immense Persian army contrived to find their way over the mountains and around the pass, so as to establish themselves in a position from which they could come down upon the small Greek army in their rear. Leonidas, perceiving this, ordered all his allies from the other states of Greece to withdraw, leaving himself and his three hundred countrymen alone in the defile.

Death of Leonidas – Spartan Valor

He did not expect to repel his enemies or to defend the pass. He knew that he must die, and all his brave followers with him, and that the torrent of invaders would pour down through the pass over their bodies. But he considered himself stationed there to defend the passage, and he would not desert his post. When the battle came on he was the first to fall. The soldiers gathered around him and defended his dead body as long as they could. At length, overpowered by the immense numbers of their foes, they were all killed but one man. He made his escape and returned to Sparta. A monument was erected on the spot with this inscription: 'Go, traveller, to Sparta, and say that we lie here, on the spot at which we were stationed to defend our country.'

Alexander Made Commander-in-Chief – He Returns to Macedon

Alexander passed through the steep narrow corridor. He advanced to the great cities south of it – to Athens, to Thebes and to Corinth. Another great assembly of all the monarchs and potentates of Greece was convened in Corinth; and here Alexander attained the object of his ambition, in having the command of the great expedition into Asia conferred upon him. The impression which he made upon those with whom he came into connection by his personal qualities must have been favourable in the extreme. That such a youthful prince should be selected by so powerful a confederation of nations as their leader in such an enterprise as they were about to engage in, indicates a most extraordinary power on his part of acquiring an ascendency over the minds of men, and of impressing all with a sense of his commanding superiority. Alexander returned to Macedon from his expedition to the southward in triumph, and began at once to arrange the affairs of his kingdom, so as to be ready to enter, unembarrassed, upon the great career of conquest which he imagined was before him.

Chapter III
The Reaction, BCE 335

Mount Haemus

THE COUNTRY WHICH was formerly occupied by Macedon and the other states of Greece is now Turkey in Europe. In the northern part of it is a vast chain of mountains called now the Balkan. In Alexander's day it was Mount Haemus. This chain forms a broad belt of lofty and uninhabitable land, and extends from the Black Sea to the Adriatic.

Thrace – The Hebrus

A branch of this mountain range, called Rhodope, extends southwardly from about the middle of its length. Rhodope separated Macedonia from a large and powerful country, which was occupied by a somewhat rude but warlike race of men. This country was Thrace. Thrace was one great fertile basin or valley, sloping toward the centre in every direction, so that all the streams from the mountains, increased by the rains which fell over the whole surface of the ground, flowed together into one river, which meandered through the centre of the valley, and flowed out at last into the Aegean Sea. The name of this river was the Hebrus.

Valley of the Danube – Thrace

The Balkan, or Mount Haemus, as it was then called, formed the great northern frontier of Macedon and Thrace. From the summits of the range, looking northward, the eye surveyed a vast extent of land, constituting one of the most extensive and fertile valleys on the globe. It was the valley of the Danube. It was inhabited, in those days, by rude tribes whom the Greeks and Romans always designated as barbarians. They were, at any rate, wild and warlike, and, as they had not the art of writing, they have left us no records of their institutions or their history. We know nothing of them, or of the other half-civilized nations that occupied the central parts of Europe in those days, except what their inveterate and perpetual enemies have thought fit to tell us. According to their story, these countries were filled with nations and tribes of a wild and half-savage character, who could be kept in check only by the most vigorous exertion of military power.

Revolt Among the Northern Nations

Soon after Alexander's return into Macedon, he learned that there were symptoms of revolt among these nations. Philip had subdued them, and established the kind of peace which the Greeks and Romans were accustomed to enforce upon their neighbours. But now, as they had heard that Philip, who had been so terrible a warrior, was no more, and that his son, scarcely out of his teens, had succeeded to the throne, they thought a suitable occasion had arrived to try their strength. Alexander made immediate arrangements for moving northward with his army to settle this question.

Alexander Marches North – Old Boreas

He conducted his forces through a part of Thrace without meeting with any serious resistance, and approached the mountains. The soldiers looked upon the rugged precipices and lofty summits before them with awe. These northern mountains were the seat and throne, in the imaginations of the Greeks and Romans, of old Boreas, the hoary god of the north wind. They conceived of him as dwelling among those cold and stormy summits, and making excursions in winter, carrying with him his vast stores of frost and snow, over the southern valleys and plains. He had wings, a long beard and white locks, all powdered with flakes of snow. Instead of feet, his body terminated in tails of serpents, which, as he flew along, lashed the air, writhing from under his robes. He was violent and impetuous in temper, rejoicing in the devastation of winter, and in all the sublime phenomena of tempests, cold and snow. The Greek conception of Boreas made an impression upon the human mind that twenty centuries have not been able to efface. The north wind of winter is personified as Boreas to the present day in the literature of every nation of the Western world.

Contest Among the Mountains – The Loaded Wagons

The Thracian forces had assembled in the steep narrow pass, with other troops from the northern countries, to arrest Alexander's march, and he had some difficulty in repelling them. They had got, it is said, some sort of loaded wagons upon the summit of an ascent, in the pass of the mountains, up which Alexander's forces would have to march. These wagons were to be run down upon them as they ascended. Alexander ordered his men to advance, notwithstanding this danger. He directed them, where it was practicable, to open to one side and the other, and allow the descending wagon to pass through. When this could not be done, they were to fall down upon the ground when they saw this strange military engine coming, and locking their shields together over their heads, allow the wagon to roll on over them, bracing up energetically against its weight. Notwithstanding these precautions, and the prodigious muscular power with which they were carried into effect, some of the men were crushed. The great body of the army was, however, unharmed; as soon as the force of the wagons was spent, they rushed up the ascent, and attacked their enemies with their pikes. The barbarians fled in all directions, terrified at the force and invulnerability of men whom loaded wagons, rolling over their bodies down a steep descent, could not kill.

Alexander's Victorious March – Mouths of the Danube

Alexander advanced from one conquest like this to another, moving toward the northward and eastward after he had crossed the mountains, until at length he approached the mouths of the Danube. Here one of the great chieftains of the barbarian tribes had taken up his position, with his family and court, and a principal part of his army, upon an island called Peucé. This island divided the current of the stream, and Alexander, in attempting to attack it, found that it would be best to endeavour to effect a landing upon the upper point of it.

Alexander Resolves to Cross the Danube

To make this attempt, he collected all the boats and vessels which he could obtain, and embarked his troops in them above, directing them to fall down with the current, and to land upon the island. This plan, however, did not succeed very well; the current was too rapid for the proper management of the boats. The shores, too, were lined with the forces of the enemy, who discharged showers of spears and arrows at the men, and pushed off the boats when they attempted to land. Alexander at length gave up the attempt, and concluded to leave the island, and to cross the river itself further above, and thus carry the war into the very heart of the country.

It is a serious undertaking to get a great body of men and horses across a broad and rapid river, when the people of the country have done all in their power to remove or destroy all possible means of transit, and when hostile bands are on the opposite bank, to embarrass and impede the operations by every mode in their power. Alexander, however, advanced to the undertaking with great resolution. To cross the Danube especially, with a military force, was, in those days, in the estimation of the Greeks and Romans, a very great exploit. The river was so distant, so broad and rapid, and its banks were bordered and defended by such ferocious foes, that to cross its eddying tide, and penetrate into the unknown and unexplored regions beyond, leaving the broad, deep and rapid stream to cut off the hopes of retreat, implied the possession of extreme self-reliance, courage and decision.

Preparations – The River Crossed

Alexander collected all the canoes and boats which he could obtain up and down the river. He built large rafts, attaching to them the skins of beasts sewed together and inflated, to give them buoyancy. When all was ready, they began the transportation of the army in the night, in a place where the enemy had not expected that the attempt would have been made. There were a thousand horses, with their riders, and four thousand foot soldiers, to be conveyed across. It is customary, in such cases, to swim the horses over, leading them by lines, the ends of which are held by men in boats. The men themselves, with all the arms, ammunition, and baggage, had to be carried over in the boats or upon the rafts. Before morning the whole was accomplished.

The Landing

The army landed in a field of grain. This circumstance, which is casually mentioned by historians, and also the story of the wagons in the passes of Mount Haemus, proves that these northern nations were not absolute barbarians in the sense in which that term is used at the present day. The arts of cultivation and of construction must have made some progress among them, at any rate; and they proved, by some of their conflicts with Alexander, that they were well-trained and well-disciplined soldiers.

Northern Nations Subdued

The Macedonians swept down the waving grain with their pikes, to open a way for the advance of the cavalry, and early in the morning Alexander found and attacked the army of his enemies, who were utterly astonished at finding him on their side of the river. As may be easily anticipated, the barbarian army was beaten in the battle that ensued. Their city was taken. The booty was taken back across the Danube to be distributed among the soldiers of the army. The neighbouring nations and tribes were overawed and subdued by this exhibition of Alexander's courage and energy. He made satisfactory treaties with them all; took hostages, where necessary, to secure the observance of the treaties, and then recrossed the Danube and set out on his return to Macedon.

Alexander Returns to Macedon

He found that it was *time* for him to return. The southern cities and states of Greece had not been unanimous in raising him to the office which his father had held. The Spartans and some others were opposed to him. The party thus opposed were inactive and silent while Alexander was in their country, on his first visit to southern Greece; but after his return they began to contemplate more decisive action, and afterward, when they heard of his having undertaken so desperate an enterprise as going northward with his forces, and actually crossing the Danube, they considered him as so completely out of the way that they grew very courageous, and meditated open rebellion.

Rebellion of Thebes – Siege of the Citadel

The city of Thebes did at length rebel. Philip had conquered this city in former struggles, and had left a Macedonian garrison there in the citadel. The name of the citadel was Cadmeia. The officers of the garrison, supposing that all was secure, left the soldiers in the citadel, and came, themselves, down to the city to reside. Things were in this condition when the rebellion against Alexander's authority broke out. They killed the officers who were in the city, and summoned the garrison to surrender. The garrison refused, and the Thebans besieged it.

This outbreak against Alexander's authority was in a great measure the work of the great orator Demosthenes, who spared no exertions to arouse the southern states of Greece to resist Alexander's dominion. He especially exerted all the powers of his eloquence in Athens in the endeavour to bring over the Athenians to take sides against Alexander.

Sudden Appearance of Alexander

While things were in this state – the Thebans having understood that Alexander had been killed at the north, and supposing that, at all events, if this report should not be true, he was, without doubt, still far away, involved in contentions with the barbarian nations, from which it was not to be expected that he could be very speedily extricated – the whole city was suddenly thrown into consternation by the report that a large Macedonian army was approaching from the north, with Alexander at its head, and that it was, in fact, close upon them.

It was now, however, too late for the Thebans to repent of what they had done. They were far too deeply impressed with a conviction of the decision and energy of Alexander's character, as manifested in the whole course of his proceedings since he began to reign, and especially by his sudden reappearance among them so soon after this outbreak against his authority, to imagine that there was now any hope for them except in determined and successful resistance. They shut themselves up, therefore, in their city, and prepared to defend themselves to the last extremity.

He Invests Thebes – The Thebans Refuse to Surrender

Alexander advanced, and, passing round the city toward the southern side, established his headquarters there, so as to cut off effectually all communication with Athens and the southern cities. He then extended his posts all around the place so as to invest it entirely. These preparations made, he paused before he commenced the work of subduing the city, to give the inhabitants an opportunity to submit, if they would, without compelling him to resort to force. The conditions, however, which he imposed were such that the Thebans thought it best to take their chance of resistance. They refused to surrender, and Alexander began to prepare for the onset.

Storming a City

He was very soon ready, and with his characteristic ardour and energy he determined on attempting to carry the city at once by assault. Fortified cities generally require a siege, and sometimes a very long siege, before they can be subdued. The army within, sheltered behind the parapets of the walls, and standing there in a position above that of their assailants, have such great advantages in the contest that a long time often elapses before they can be compelled to surrender. The besiegers have to invest the city on all sides to cut off all supplies of provisions, and then, in those days, they had to construct engines to make a breach somewhere in the walls, through which an assaulting party could attempt to force their way in.

Making a Breach – Surrender

The time for making an assault upon a besieged city depends upon the comparative strength of those within and without, and also, still more, on the ardour and resolution of the besiegers. In warfare, an army, in investing a fortified place, spends ordinarily a considerable time in burrowing their way along in trenches, half underground, until they get near enough to plant their cannon where the balls can take effect upon some part of the wall. Or in Alexander's case, his siege engines and catapults. Then some time usually elapses before a breach is made, and the garrison is sufficiently weakened to render an assault advisable. When, however, the time at length arrives, the most bold and desperate portion of the army are designated to lead the attack. Alexander himself lead his elite troops on the attack, often being first up the scaling ladders. Bundles of small branches of trees are provided to fill up ditches with, and ladders for mounting embankments and walls. The city, sometimes, seeing these preparations going on, and convinced that the assault will be successful, surrenders before it is made. When the besieged do thus surrender, they save themselves a vast amount of suffering, for the carrying of a city by assault is perhaps the most horrible scene which the passions and crimes of men ever offer to the view of heaven.

Carrying a City By Assault – Scenes of Horror

It is horrible, because the soldiers, exasperated to fury by the resistance which they meet with, and by the awful malignity of the passions always excited in the hour of battle, if they succeed, burst suddenly into the precincts of domestic life, and find sometimes thousands of families – mothers, children and defenceless maidens – at the mercy of passions excited to frenzy. Alexander often gave orders that the women were not to be violated and tried to control the savagery of his men. Soldiers, under such circumstances, cannot be restrained, and no imagination can conceive the horrors of the sacking of a city, carried by assault, after a protracted siege. Tigers do not spring upon their prey with greater ferocity than man springs, under such circumstances, to the perpetration of every possible cruelty upon his fellow man. After an ordinary battle upon an open field, the conquerors have only men, armed like themselves, to wreak their vengeance upon. The scene is awful enough, however, here. But in carrying a city by storm, which takes place usually at an unexpected time, and often in the night, the maddened and victorious assaulter suddenly bursts into the sacred scenes of domestic peace, seclusion and love – the very worst of men, filled with the worst of passions, stimulated by the resistance they have encountered, and licensed by their victory to give all these passions the fullest and most unrestricted gratification. To plunder, burn, destroy and kill, are the lighter and more harmless of the crimes they perpetrate. Thebes was a special case and one of the only cities Alexander razed.

Thebes Carried by Assault – Great Loss of Life

Thebes was carried by assault. Alexander did not wait for the slow operations of a siege. He watched a favourable opportunity, and burst over and through the outer line of fortifications which defended the city. The attempt to do this was very desperate, and the loss of life great; but it was triumphantly successful. The Thebans were driven back toward the inner wall, and began to crowd in, through the gates, into the city, in terrible confusion. The Macedonians were close upon them, and pursuers and pursued, struggling together, and trampling upon and killing each other as they went, flowed in, like a boiling and raging torrent which nothing could resist, through the open arch-way.

It was impossible to close the gates. The whole Macedonian force were soon in full possession of the now defenceless houses, and for many hours screams, wailings and cries of horror and despair testified to the awful atrocity of the crimes attendant on the sacking of a city. At length the soldiery were restrained. Order was restored. The army retired to the posts assigned them, and Alexander began to deliberate what he should do with the conquered town.

He determined to destroy it – to offer, once for all, a terrible example of the consequences of rebellion against him. The case was not one, he considered, of the ordinary conquest of a *foe*. The states of Greece – Thebes with the rest – had once solemnly conferred upon him the authority against which the Thebans had now rebelled. They were *traitors*, therefore, in his judgment, not mere enemies, and he determined that the penalty should be utter destruction.

Thebes Destroyed

But, in carrying this terrible decision into effect, he acted in a manner so deliberate, discriminating and cautious, as to diminish very much the irritation and resentment which it would otherwise have caused, and to give it its full moral effect as a measure, not of angry resentment, but of calm and deliberate retribution – just and proper, according to the ideas of the time. In the first place, he released all the priests. Then, in respect to the rest of the population, he discriminated carefully between those who had favoured the rebellion and those who had been true to their allegiance to him. The latter were allowed to depart in safety. And if, in the case of any family, it could be shown that one individual had been on the Macedonian side, the single instance of fidelity outweighed the treason of the other members, and the whole family was saved.

Alexander's Moderation and Forbearance – Family of Pindar Spared

And the officers appointed to carry out these provisions were liberal in the interpretation and application of them, so as to save as many as there could be any possible pretext for saving. The descendants and family connections of Pindar, the celebrated poet, who has been already mentioned as having been born in Thebes, were all pardoned also, whichever side they may have taken in the contest. The truth was, that Alexander, though he had the sagacity to see that he was placed in circumstances where prodigious moral effect in strengthening his position would be produced by an act of great severity, was swayed by so many generous impulses, which raised him above the ordinary excitements of irritation and revenge, that he had every desire to make the suffering as light, and to limit it by as narrow bounds, as the nature of the case would allow. He doubtless also had an instinctive feeling that the moral effect itself of so dreadful a retribution as he was about to inflict upon the devoted city would be very much increased by forbearance and generosity, and by extreme regard for the security and protection of those who had shown themselves his friends.

The Number Saved

After all these exceptions had been made, and the persons to whom they applied had been dismissed, the rest of the population were sold into slavery, and then the city was utterly and entirely destroyed. The number thus sold was about thirty thousand, and six thousand had been killed in the assault and storming of the city. Thus Thebes was made a ruin and a desolation, and it remained so, a monument of Alexander's terrible energy and decision, for twenty years.

Efforts of Demosthenes

The effect of the destruction of Thebes upon the other cities and states of Greece was what might have been expected. It came upon them like a thunderbolt. Although Thebes was the only city which had openly revolted, there had been strong symptoms of disaffection in many other places. Demosthenes, who had been silent while Alexander was present in Greece, during his first visit there, had again been endeavouring to arouse opposition to Macedonian ascendency, and to concentrate and bring out into action the influences which were hostile to Alexander. He said in his speeches that Alexander was a mere boy, and that it was disgraceful for such cities as Athens, Sparta and Thebes to submit to his sway. Alexander had heard of these things, and, as he was coming down into Greece, through the Straits of Thermopylae, before the destruction of Thebes, he said, 'They say I am a boy. I am coming to teach them that I am a man.'

The Boy Proves to be a Man – All Disaffection Subdued

He did teach them that he was a man. His unexpected appearance, when they imagined him entangled among the mountains and wilds of unknown regions in the north; his sudden investiture of Thebes; the assault; the calm deliberations in respect to the destiny of the city, and the slow, cautious, discriminating, but inexorable energy with which the decision was carried into effect, all coming in such rapid succession, impressed the Grecian commonwealth with the conviction that the personage they had to deal with was no boy in character, whatever might be his years. All symptoms of disaffection against the rule of Alexander instantly disappeared, and did not soon revive again.

Moral Effect of the Destruction of Thebes

Nor was this effect due entirely to the terror inspired by the retribution which had been visited upon Thebes. All Greece was impressed with a new admiration for Alexander's character as they witnessed these events, in which his impetuous energy, his cool and calm decision, his forbearance, his magnanimity and his faithfulness to his friends, were all so conspicuous. His pardoning the priests, whether they had been for him or against him, made every friend of religion incline to his favour. The same interposition in behalf of the poet's family and descendants spoke directly to the heart of every poet, orator, historian, and philosopher throughout the country, and tended to make all the lovers of literature his friends. His magnanimity, also, in deciding that one single friend of his in a family should save that family, instead of ordaining, as a more short-sighted conqueror would have done, that a single enemy should condemn it, must have awakened a strong feeling of gratitude and regard in the hearts of all who could appreciate fidelity to friends and generosity of spirit. Thus, as the news of the destruction of Thebes, and the selling of so large a portion of the inhabitants into slavery, spread over the land, its effect was to turn over so great a part of the population to a feeling of admiration of Alexander's character, and confidence in his extraordinary powers, as to leave only a small minority disposed to take sides with the punished rebels, or resent the destruction of the city.

Alexander Returns to Macedon – Celebrates his Victories

From Thebes Alexander proceeded to the southward. Deputations from the cities were sent to him, congratulating him on his victories, and offering their adhesion to his cause. His influence and ascendency seemed firmly established now in the country of the Greeks, and in due time he returned to Macedon, and celebrated at Aegae, which was at this time his capital, the establishment and confirmation of his power, by games, shows, spectacles, illuminations and sacrifices to the gods, offered on a scale of the greatest pomp and magnificence. He was now ready to turn his thoughts toward the long-projected plan of the expedition into Asia.

Chapter IV
Crossing the Hellespont, BCE 334

The Expedition into Asia

ON ALEXANDER'S ARRIVAL in Macedon, he immediately began to turn his attention to the subject of the invasion of Asia. He was full of ardour and enthusiasm to carry this project into effect. Considering his extreme youth, and the captivating character of the enterprise, it is strange that he should have exercised so much deliberation and caution as his conduct did really evince. He had now settled everything in the most thorough manner, both within his dominions and among the nations on his borders, and, as it seemed to him, the time had come when he was to commence active preparations for the great Asiatic campaign.

Debates Upon It

He brought the subject before his ministers and counselors. They, in general, concurred with him in opinion. There were, however, two who were in doubt, or rather who were, in fact, opposed to the plan, though they expressed their non-concurrence in the form of doubts. These two persons were Antipater and Parmenio, the venerable officers who have been already mentioned as having served Philip so faithfully, and as transferring, on the death of the father, their attachment and allegiance at once to the son.

Objections of Antipater and Parmenio

Antipater and Parmenio represented to Alexander that if he were to go to Asia at that time, he would put to extreme hazard all the interests of Macedon. As he had no family, there was, of course, no direct heir to the crown, and, in case of any misfortune happening by which his life should be lost, Macedon would become at once the prey of contending factions, which would immediately arise, each presenting its own candidate for the vacant throne. The sagacity and foresight which these statesmen evinced in these suggestions were abundantly confirmed in the end. Alexander did die in Asia, his vast kingdom at once fell into pieces and it was desolated with internal commotions and civil wars for a long period after his death.

Parmenio and Antipater accordingly advised the king to postpone his expedition. They advised him to seek a wife among the princesses of Greece, and then to settle down quietly to the duties of domestic life, and to the government of his kingdom for a few years; then, when everything should have become settled and consolidated in Greece, and his family was established in the hearts of his countrymen, he could leave Macedon more safely. Public affairs would go on more steadily while he lived, and, in case of his death, the crown would descend, with comparatively little danger of civil commotion, to his heir.

Alexander Decides To Go

But Alexander was fully decided against any such policy as this. He resolved to embark in the great expedition at once. He concluded to make Antipater his vicegerent in Macedon during his absence, and to take Parmenio with him into Asia. It will be remembered that Antipater was the statesman and Parmenio the general; that is, Antipater had been employed more by Philip in civil, and Parmenio in military affairs, though in those days everybody who was in public life was more or less a soldier.

Preparations

Alexander left an army of ten or twelve thousand men with Antipater for the protection of Macedon. He organized another army of about thirty-five thousand to go with him. This was considered a very small army for such a vast undertaking. One or two hundred years before this time, Darius, a king of Persia, had invaded Greece with an army of five hundred thousand men, and yet he had been defeated and driven back, and now Alexander was undertaking to retaliate with a great deal less than one tenth part of the force.

Description of Thessaly – Vale of Tempe – Olympus – Pelion and Ossa

Of Alexander's army of thirty-five thousand, thirty thousand were foot soldiers, and about five thousand were horse. More than half the whole army was from Macedon. The remainder was from the southern states of Greece. A large body of the horse was from Thessaly, which was a country south of Macedon. It was, in fact, one broad expanded valley, with mountains all around. Torrents descended from these mountains, forming streams which flowed in currents more and more deep and slow as they descended into the plains, and combining at last into one central river, which flowed to the eastward, and escaped from the circle of mountains through a most celebrated dell called the Vale of Tempe. On the north of this valley is Olympus, and on the south the two twin mountains Pelion and Ossa. There was an ancient story of a war in Thessaly between the giants who were imagined to have lived there in very early days, and the gods. The giants piled Pelion upon Ossa to enable them to get up to heaven in their assault upon their celestial enemies. The fable has led to a proverb which prevails in every language in Europe, by which all extravagant and unheard-of exertions to accomplish an end is said to be a piling of Pelion upon Ossa.

Thessaly was famous for its horses and its horsemen. The slopes of the mountains furnished the best of pasturage for the rearing of the animals, and the plains below afforded broad and open fields for training and exercising the bodies of cavalry formed by means of them. The Thessalian horses were famous throughout all Greece. Bucephalus was reared in Thessaly.

Alexander's Generosity

Alexander, as king of Macedon, possessed extensive estates and revenues, which were his own personal property, and were independent of the revenues of the state. Before setting out on his expedition, he apportioned these among his great officers and generals, both those who were to go and those who were to remain. He evinced great generosity in this, but it was, after all, the spirit of ambition, more than that of generosity, which led him to do it. The two great impulses which animated him were the pleasure of doing great deeds, and the fame and glory of having done them. These two principles are very distinct in their nature, though often conjoined. They were paramount and supreme in Alexander's character, and every other human principle was subordinate to them. Money was to him, accordingly, only a means to enable him to accomplish these ends. His distributing his estates and revenues in the manner above described was only a judicious appropriation of the money to the promotion of the great ends he wished to attain; it was expenditure, not gift. It answered admirably the end he had in view. His friends all looked upon him as extremely generous and self-sacrificing. They asked him what he had reserved for himself. 'Hope,' said Alexander.

Religious Sacrifices and Spectacles

At length all things were ready, and Alexander began to celebrate the religious sacrifices, spectacles and shows which, in those days, always preceded great undertakings of this kind. There was a great ceremony in honour of Jupiter and the nine Muses, which had long been celebrated in Macedon as a sort of annual national festival. Alexander now caused great preparations for this festival.

Ancient Forms of Worship

In the days of the Greeks, public worship and public amusement were combined in one and the same series of spectacles and ceremonies. All worship was a theatrical show, and almost all shows were forms of worship. The religious instincts of the human heart demand some sort of sympathy and aid, real or imaginary, from the invisible world, in great and solemn undertakings, and in every momentous crisis in its history. It is true that Alexander's soldiers, about to leave their homes to go to another quarter of the globe, and into scenes of danger and death from which it was very improbable that many of them would ever return, had no other celestial protection to look up to than the spirits of ancient heroes, who, they imagined, had, somehow or other, found their final home in a sort of heaven among the summits of the mountains, where they reigned, in some sense, over human affairs; but this, small as it seems to us, was a great deal to them. They felt, when sacrificing to these gods, that they were invoking their presence and sympathy. These deities having been engaged in the same enterprises themselves, and animated with the same hopes and fears, the soldiers imagined that the semi-human divinities invoked by them would take an interest in their dangers, and rejoice is their success.

The Nine Muses

The Muses, in honour of whom, as well as Jupiter, this great Macedonian festival was held, were nine singing and dancing maidens, beautiful in countenance and form, and enchantingly graceful in all their movements. They came, the ancients imagined, from Thrace, in the north, and went first to Jupiter upon Mount Olympus, who made them goddesses. Afterward they went southward, and spread over Greece, making their residence, at last, in a palace upon Mount Parnassus, which is just north of the Gulf of Corinth and west of Boeotia. They were worshiped all over Greece and Italy as the goddesses of music and dancing. In later times particular sciences and arts were assigned to them respectively, as history, astronomy, tragedy, etc., though there was no distinction of this kind in early days.

Festivities in Honour of Jupiter

The festivities in honour of Jupiter and the Muses were continued in Macedon nine days, a number corresponding with that of the dancing goddesses. Alexander made very magnificent preparations for the celebration on this occasion. He had a tent made, under which, it is said, a hundred tables could be spread; and here he entertained, day after day, an enormous company of princes, potentates and generals. He offered sacrifices to such of the gods as he supposed it would please the soldiers to imagine that they had propitiated. Connected with these sacrifices and feastings, there were athletic and military spectacles and shows – races and wrestlings – and mock contests, with blunted spears. All these things encouraged and quickened the ardour and animation of the soldiers. It aroused their ambition to distinguish themselves by their exploits, and gave them an increased and stimulated desire for honour and fame. Thus inspirited by new desires for human praise, and trusting in the sympathy and protection of powers which were all that they conceived of as divine, the army prepared to set forth from their native land, bidding it a long, and, as it proved to most of them, a final farewell.

Alexander Begins his March

Alexander's route lay first along the northern coasts of the Aegean Sea. He was to pass from Europe into Asia by crossing the Hellespont between Sestos and Abydos. He sent a fleet of one-hundred-and-fifty galleys, of three banks of oars each, over the Aegean Sea, to land at Sestos, and be ready to transport his army across the straits. The army, in the meantime, marched by land. They had to cross the rivers which flow into the Aegean Sea on the northern side; but as these rivers were in Macedon, and no opposition was encountered upon the banks of them, there was no serious difficulty in effecting the passage. When they reached Sestos, they found the fleet ready there, awaiting their arrival.

Romantic Adventure

It is very strikingly characteristic of the mingling of poetic sentiment and enthusiasm with calm and calculating business efficiency, which shone conspicuously so often in Alexander's career, that when he arrived at Sestos, and found that the ships were there, and the army safe, and that there was no enemy to oppose his landing on the Asiatic shore, he left Parmenio to conduct the transportation of the troops across the water, while he himself went away in a single galley on an excursion of sentiment and romantic adventure. A little south of the place where his army was to cross, there lay, on the Asiatic shore, an extended plain, on which were the ruins of Troy. Now Troy was the city which was the scene of Homer's poems – those poems which had excited so much interest in the mind of Alexander in his early years; and he determined, instead of crossing the Hellespont with the main body of his army, to proceed southward in a single galley, and land, himself, on the Asiatic shore, on the very spot which the romantic imagination of his youth had dwelt upon so often and so long.

The Plain of Troy – Tenedos – Mount Ida – The Scamander

Troy was situated upon a plain. Homer describes an island off the coast, named Tenedos, and a mountain near called Mount Ida. There was also a river called the Scamander. The island, the mountain, and the river remain, preserving their original names to the present day, except that the river is now called the Mender. The site of Troy is now believed to have been first discovered by Henrich Schliemann, and has continued to be excavated and studied by various others, as recently as 2014. It is located in Hisarlik in present day Turkey. In Homer's story he states there was a great and powerful city there, with a kingdom attached to it, and that this city was besieged by the Greeks for ten years, at the end of which time it was taken and destroyed.

The Trojan War – Dream of Priam's wife – Exposure of Paris

The story of the origin of this war is substantially this. Priam was king of Troy. His wife, a short time before her son was born, dreamed that at his birth the child turned into a torch and set the palace on fire. She told this dream to the soothsayers, and asked them what it meant. They said it must mean that her son would be the means of bringing some terrible calamities and disasters upon the family. The mother was terrified, and, to avert these calamities, gave the child to a slave as soon as it was born, and ordered him to destroy it. The slave pitied the helpless babe, and, not liking to destroy it with his own hand, carried it to Mount Ida, and left it there in the forests to die.

A she bear, roaming through the woods, found the child, and, experiencing a feeling of maternal tenderness for it, she took care of it, and reared it as if it had been her own offspring. The child was found, at last, by some shepherds who lived upon the mountain, and they adopted it as their own, robbing the brute mother of her charge. They named the boy Paris. He grew in strength and beauty, and gave early and extraordinary proofs of courage and energy, as if he had imbibed some of the qualities of his fierce foster mother with the milk she gave him. He was so remarkable for athletic beauty and manly courage, that he not only easily won the heart of a nymph of Mount Ida, named Oenone, whom he married, but he also attracted the attention of the goddesses in the heavens.

The Apple of Discord

At length these goddesses had a dispute which they agreed to refer to him. The origin of the dispute was this. There was a wedding among them, and one of them, irritated at not having been invited, had a golden apple made, on which were engraved the words, 'To be given to the most beautiful.' She threw this apple into the assembly: her object was to make them quarrel for it. In fact, she was herself the goddess of discord, and, independently of her cause of pique in this case, she loved to promote disputes. It is in allusion to this ancient tale that any subject of dispute, brought up unnecessarily among friends, is called to this day an *apple* of discord.

The Dispute About the Apple

Three of the goddesses claimed the apple, each insisting that she was more beautiful than the others, and this was the dispute which they agreed to refer to Paris. They accordingly exhibited themselves before him in the mountains, that he might look at them and decide. They did not, however, seem willing, either of them, to trust to an impartial decision of the question, but each offered the judge a bribe to induce him to decide in her favour. One promised him a kingdom, another great fame, and the third, Venus, promised him the most beautiful woman in the world for his wife. He decided in favour of Venus; whether because she was justly entitled to the decision, or through the influence of the bribe, the story does not say.

The Story of the Bull

All this time Paris remained on the mountain, a simple shepherd and herdsman, not knowing his relationship to the monarch who reigned over the city and kingdom on the plain below. King Priam, however, about this time, in some games which he was celebrating, offered, as a prize to the victor, the finest bull which could be obtained on Mount Ida. On making examination, Paris was found to have the finest bull and the king, exercising the despotic power which kings in those days made no scruple of assuming in respect to helpless peasants, took it away. Paris was very indignant. It happened, however, that a short time afterward there was another opportunity to contend for the same bull, and Paris, disguising himself as a prince, appeared in the lists, conquered every competitor and bore away the bull again to his home in the fastnesses of the mountain.

Paris Restored to His Parents

In consequence of this his appearance at court, the daughter of Priam, whose name was Cassandra, became acquainted with him, and, inquiring into his story, succeeded in ascertaining that he was her brother, the long-lost child, that had been supposed to be put to death. King Priam was convinced by the evidence which she brought forward, and Paris was brought home to his father's house. After becoming established in his new position, he remembered the promise of Venus that he should have the most beautiful woman in the world for his wife, and he began, accordingly, to inquire where he could find her.

Abduction of Helen

There was in Sparta, one of the cities of Southern Greece, a certain king Menelaus, who had a youthful bride named Helen, who was famed far and near for her beauty. Paris came to the conclusion that she was the most lovely woman in the world, and that he was entitled, in virtue of Venus's promise, to obtain possession of her, if he could do so by any means whatever. He accordingly made a journey into Greece, visited Sparta, formed an acquaintance with Helen, persuaded her to abandon her husband and her duty, and elope with him to Troy.

Destruction of Troy

Menelaus was indignant at this outrage. He called on all Greece to take up arms and join him in the attempt to recover his bride. They responded to this demand. They first sent to Priam, demanding that he should restore Helen to her husband. Priam refused to do so, taking part with his son. The Greeks then raised a fleet and an army, and came to the plains of Troy, encamped before the city, and persevered for ten long years in besieging it, when at length it was taken and destroyed.

Homer's Writings

These stories relating to the origin of the war, however, marvellous and entertaining as they are, were not the points which chiefly interested the mind of Alexander. The portions of Homer's narratives which most excited his enthusiasm were those relating to the characters of the heroes who fought, on one side and on the other, at the siege, their various adventures, and the delineations of their motives and principles of conduct, and the emotions and excitements they experienced in the various circumstances in which they were placed. Homer described with great beauty and force the workings of ambition, of resentment, of pride, of rivalry and all those other impulses of the human heart which would excite and control the action of impetuous men in the circumstances in which his heroes were placed.

Achilles – The Styx

Each one of the heroes whose history and adventures he gives, possessed a well-marked and striking character, and differed in temperament and action from the rest. Achilles was one. He was fiery, impetuous and implacable in character, fierce and merciless; and, though perfectly undaunted and fearless, entirely destitute of magnanimity. There was a river called the Styx, the waters of which were said to have the property of making anyone invulnerable. The mother of Achilles dipped him into it in his infancy, holding him by the heel. The heel, not having been immersed, was the only part which could be wounded. Thus he was safe in battle, and was a terrible warrior. He, however, quarreled with his comrades and withdrew from their cause on slight pretexts, and then became reconciled again, influenced by equally frivolous reasons.

Agamemnon

Agamemnon was the commander-in-chief of the Greek army. After a certain victory, by which some captives were taken, and were to be divided among the victors, Agamemnon was obliged to restore one, a noble lady, who had fallen to his share, and he took away the one that had been assigned to Achilles to replace her. This incensed Achilles, and he withdrew for a long time from the contest; and, in consequence of his absence, the Trojans gained great and continued victories against the Greeks. For a long time, nothing could induce Achilles to return.

Death of Patroclus – Hector Slain by Achilles

At length, however, though he would not go himself, he allowed his intimate friend, whose name was Patroclus, to take his armour and go into battle. Patroclus was at first successful, but was soon killed by Hector, the brother of Paris. This aroused anger and a spirit of revenge in the mind of Achilles. He gave up his quarrel with Agamemnon and returned to the combat. He did not remit his exertions till he had slain Hector, and then he expressed his brutal exultation, and satisfied his revenge, by dragging the dead body at the wheels of his chariot around the walls of the city. He then sold the body to the distracted father for a ransom.

It was such stories as these, which are related in the poems of Homer with great beauty and power, that had chiefly interested the mind of Alexander. The subjects interested him; the accounts of the contentions, the rivalries, the exploits of these warriors, the delineations of their character and springs of action and the narrations of the various incidents and events to which such a war gave rise, were all calculated to captivate the imagination of a young martial hero.

Alexander Proceeds to Troy

Alexander accordingly resolved that his first landing in Asia should be at Troy. He left his army under the charge of Parmenio, to cross from Sestos to Abydos, while he himself set forth in a single galley to proceed to the southward. There was a port on the Trojan shore where the Greeks had been accustomed to disembark, and he steered his course for it. He had a bull on board his galley which he was going to offer as a sacrifice to Neptune when half way from shore to shore.

Neptune

Neptune was the god of the sea. It is true that the Hellespont is not the open ocean, but it is an arm of the sea, and thus belonged properly to the dominions which the ancients assigned to the divinity of the waters. Neptune was conceived of by the ancients as a monarch dwelling on the seas or upon the coasts, and riding over the waves seated in a great shell, or sometimes in a chariot, drawn by dolphins or sea-horses. In these excursions he was attended by a train of sea-gods and nymphs, who, half floating, half swimming, followed him over the billows. Instead of a sceptre Neptune carried a trident. A trident was a sort of three-pronged harpoon, such as was used in those days by the fishermen of the Mediterranean. It was from this circumstance, probably, that it was chosen as the badge of authority for the god of the sea.

Landing of Alexander – Sacrifices to the Gods

Alexander took the helm, and steered the galley with his own hands toward the Asiatic shore. Just before he reached the land, he took his place upon the prow, and threw a javelin at the shore as he approached it, a symbol of the spirit of defiance and hostility with which he advanced to the frontiers of the eastern world. He was also the first to land. After disembarking his company, he offered sacrifices to the gods, and then proceeded to visit the places which had been the scenes of the events which Homer had described.

Homer had written five hundred years before the time of Alexander, and there is some doubt whether the ruins and the remains of cities which our hero found there were really the scenes of the narratives which had interested him so deeply. He, however, at any rate, believed them to be so, and he was filled with enthusiasm and pride as he wandered among them. He seems to have been most interested in the character of Achilles, and he said that he envied him his happy lot in having such a friend as Patroclus to help him perform his exploits, and such a poet as Homer to celebrate them.

Alexander Proceeds on His March

After completing his visit upon the plain of Troy, Alexander moved toward the northeast with the few men who had accompanied him in his single galley. In the meantime, Parmenio had crossed safely, with the main body of the army, from Sestos to Abydos. Alexander overtook them on their march, not far from the place of their landing. To the northward of this place, on the left of the line of march which Alexander was taking, was the city of Lampsacus.

Alexander Spares Lampsacus

Now a large portion of Asia Minor, although for the most part under the dominion of Persia, had been in a great measure settled by Greeks, and, in previous wars between the two nations, the various cities had been in possession, sometimes of one power and sometimes of the other. In these contests the city of Lampsacus had incurred the high displeasure of the Greeks by rebelling, as they said, on one occasion, against them. Alexander determined to destroy it as he passed. The inhabitants were aware of this intention, and sent an ambassadors to Alexander to implore his mercy. When the ambassadors approached, Alexander, knowing his errand, uttered a declaration in which he bound himself by a solemn oath not to grant the request he was about to make. 'I have come,' said the ambassadors, 'to implore you to *destroy* Lampsacus.' Alexander, pleased with the readiness of the ambassadors in giving his language such a sudden turn, and perhaps influenced by his oath, spared the city.

Arrival at the Granicus

He was now fairly in Asia. The Persian forces were gathering to attack him, but so unexpected and sudden had been his invasion that they were not prepared to meet him at his arrival, and he advanced without opposition till he reached the banks of the little river Granicus.

Chapter V
Campaign in Asia Minor, BCE 334–333

Alexander Hemmed in by Mount Ida and the Granicus

ALTHOUGH ALEXANDER HAD LANDED SAFELY on the Asiatic shore, the way was not yet fairly open for him to advance into the interior of the country. He was upon a sort of plain, which was separated from the territory beyond by natural barriers. On the south was the range of lofty land called Mount Ida. From the north-eastern slopes of this mountain there descended a stream which flowed north into the sea, thus hemming Alexander's army in. He must either scale the mountain or cross the river before he could penetrate into the interior.

The Granicus

He thought it would be easiest to cross the river. It is very difficult to get a large body of horsemen and of heavy-armed soldiers, with all their attendants and baggage, over high elevations of land. This was the reason why the army turned to the northward after landing upon the Asiatic shore. Alexander thought the Granicus less of an obstacle than Mount Ida. It was not a large stream, and was easily fordable.

Prodromi

It was the custom in those days, as it is now when armies are marching, to send forward small bodies of men in every direction to explore the roads, remove obstacles and discover sources of danger. These men are called, in modern times, *scouts*; in Alexander's day, and in the Greek language, they were called *prodromi*, which means forerunners. It is the duty of these pioneers to send messengers back continually to the main body of the army, informing the officers of everything important which comes under their observation.

Alexander Stopped at the Granicus

In this case, when the army was gradually drawing near to the river, the *prodromi* came in with the news that they had been to the river, and found the whole opposite shore, at the place of crossing, lined with Persian troops, collected there to dispute the passage. The army continued their advance, while Alexander called the leading generals around him, to consider what was to be done.

Parmenio recommended that they should not attempt to pass the river immediately. The Persian army consisted chiefly of cavalry. Now cavalry, though very terrible as an enemy on the field of battle by day, are peculiarly exposed and defenceless in an encampment by night. The horses are scattered, feeding or at rest. The arms of the men are light, and they are not accustomed to fighting on foot; and on a sudden incursion of an enemy at midnight into their camp, their horses and their horsemanship are alike useless, and they fall an easy prey to resolute invaders. Parmenio thought, therefore, that the Persians would not dare to remain and encamp many days in the vicinity of Alexander's army, and that, accordingly, if they waited a little, the enemy would retreat, and Alexander could then cross the river without incurring the danger of a battle.

Alexander Resolves to Advance

But Alexander was unwilling to adopt any such policy. He felt confident that his army was courageous and strong enough to march on, directly through the river, ascend the bank upon the other side, and force their way through all the opposition which the Persians could make. He knew, too, that if this were done it would create a strong sensation throughout the whole country, impressing everyone with a sense of the energy and power of the army which he was conducting, and would thus tend to intimidate the enemy, and facilitate all future operations. But this was not all; he had a more powerful motive still for wishing to march right on, across the river, and force his way through the vast bodies of cavalry on the opposite shore, and this was the pleasure of performing the exploit.

The Macedonian Phalanx

Accordingly, as the army advanced to the banks, they manoeuvred to form in order of battle, and prepared to continue their march as if there were no obstacle to oppose them. The general order of battle of the Macedonian army was this. There was a certain body of troops, armed and organized in a peculiar manner, called the Phalanx. This body was placed in the centre. The men composing it were very heavily armed. They had shields upon the left arm, and they carried spears sixteen feet long, and pointed with iron, which they held firmly in their two hands, with the points projecting far before them. The men were arranged in lines, one behind the other, and all facing the enemy – sixteen lines, and a thousand in each line, or, as it is expressed in military phrase, a thousand in rank and sixteen in file, so that the phalanx contained sixteen thousand men.

Formidable Character of the Phalanx

The spears were so long that when the men stood in close order, the rear ranks being brought up near to those before them, the points of the spears of eight or ten of the ranks projected in front, forming a bristling wall of points of steel, each one of which was held in its place by the strong arms of an athletic and well-trained soldier. This wall no force which could in those days be brought against it could penetrate. Men, horses, elephants, everything that attempted to rush upon it, rushed only to their own destruction. Every spear, feeling the impulse of the vigorous arms which held it, seemed to be alive, and darted into its enemy, when an enemy was at hand, as if it felt itself the fierce hostility which directed it. If the enemy remained at a distance, and threw javelins or darts at the phalanx, they fell harmless, stopped by the shields which the soldiers wore upon the left arm, and which were held in such a manner as to form a system of scales, which covered and protected the whole mass, and made the men almost invulnerable. The phalanx was thus, when only defending itself and in a state of rest, an army and a fortification all in one, and it was almost impregnable. But when it took an aggressive form, put itself in motion, and advanced to an attack, it was infinitely more formidable. It became then a terrible monster, covered with scales of brass, from beneath which there projected forward ten thousand living, darting points of iron. It advanced deliberately and calmly, but with a prodigious momentum and force. There was nothing human in its appearance at all. It was a huge animal, ferocious, dogged, stubborn, insensible to pain, knowing no fear and bearing down with resistless and merciless destruction upon everything that came in its way. The phalanx was the centre and soul of Alexander's army. Powerful and impregnable as it was, however, in ancient days, it would be helpless and defenceless on a modern battlefield. Modern weapons would tear their way through the pikes and the shields, and the bodies of the men who bore them, without even feeling the obstruction.

Divisions of the Phalanx

The phalanx was subdivided into brigades, regiments and battalions, and regularly officered. In marching, it was separated into these its constituent parts, and sometimes in battle it acted in divisions. It was stationed in the centre of the army on the field, and on the two sides of it were bodies of cavalry and foot soldiers, more lightly armed than the soldiers of the phalanx, who could accordingly move with more alertness and speed, and carry their action readily wherever it might be called for. Those troops on the sides were called the wings. Alexander himself was accustomed to command one wing and Parmenio the other, while the phalanx crept along slowly but terribly between.

Battle of the Granicus

The army, thus arranged and organized, advanced to the river. It was a broad and shallow stream. The Persians had assembled in vast numbers on the opposite shore. Some historians say there were one hundred thousand men, others say two hundred thousand, and others six hundred thousand. However this may be, there is no doubt their numbers were vastly superior to those of Alexander's army, which it will be recollected was less than forty thousand. There was a narrow plain on the opposite side of the river, next to the shore, and a range of hills beyond. The Persian cavalry covered the plain, and were ready to dash upon the Macedonian troops the moment they should emerge from the water and attempt to ascend the bank.

Defeat of the Persians

The army, led by Alexander, descended into the stream, and moved on through the water. They encountered the onset of their enemies on the opposite shore. A terrible and a protracted struggle ensued, but the coolness, courage and strength of Alexander's army carried the day. The Persians were driven back, the Greeks effected their landing, reorganized and formed on the shore, and the Persians, finding that all was lost, fled in all directions.

Alexander's Prowess

Alexander himself took a conspicuous and a very active part in the contest. He was easily recognized on the field of battle by his dress, and by a white plume which he wore in his helmet. He exposed himself to the most imminent danger. At one time, when desperately engaged with a troop of horse, which had galloped down upon him, a Persian horseman aimed a blow at his head with a sword. Alexander saved his head from the blow, but it took off his plume and a part of his helmet. Alexander immediately thrust his antagonist through the body. At the same moment, another horseman, on another side, had his sword raised, and would have killed Alexander before he could have turned to defend himself, had no help intervened; but just at this instant a third combatant, one of Alexander's friends, seeing the danger, brought down so terrible a blow upon the shoulder of this second assailant as to separate his arm from his body.

Such are the stories that are told. They may have been literally and fully true, or they may have been exaggerations of circumstances somewhat resembling them which really occurred, or they may have been fictitious altogether. Great generals, like other great men, have often the credit of many exploits which they never perform. It is the special business of poets and historians to magnify and embellish the actions of the great, and this art was understood as well in ancient days as it is now.

We must remember, too, in reading the accounts of these transactions, that it is only the Greek side of the story that we hear. The Persian narratives have not come down to us. At any rate, the Persian army was defeated, and that, too, without the assistance of the phalanx. The horsemen and the light troops were alone engaged. The phalanx could not be formed, nor could it act in such a position. The men, on emerging from the water, had to climb up the banks, and rush on to the attack of an enemy consisting of squadrons of horse ready to dash at once upon them.

Results of the Battle

The Persian army was defeated and driven away. Alexander did not pursue them. He felt that he had struck a very heavy blow. The news of this defeat of the Persians would go with the speed of the wind all over Asia Minor, and operate most powerfully in his favour. He sent home to Greece an account of the victory, and with the account he forwarded three hundred suits of armour, taken from the Persian horsemen killed on the field. These suits of armour were to be hung up in the Parthenon, a great temple at Athens; the most conspicuous position for them, perhaps, which all Europe could afford.

Memnon Overruled

The name of the Persian general who commanded at the battle of the Granicus was Memnon. He had been opposed to the plan of hazarding a battle. Alexander had come to Asia with no provisions and no money. He had relied on being able to sustain his army by his victories. Memnon, therefore, strongly urged that the Persians should retreat slowly, carrying off all the valuable property, and destroying all that could not be removed, taking especial care to leave no provisions behind them. In this way he thought that the army of Alexander would be reduced by privation and want, and would, in the end, fall an easy prey. His opinion was, however, overruled by the views of the other commanders, and the battle of the Granicus was the consequence.

Alexander Visits the Wounded

Alexander encamped to refresh his army and to take care of the wounded. He went to see the wounded men one by one, inquired into the circumstances of each case, and listened to each one who was able to talk, while he gave an account of his adventures in the battle, and the manner in which he received his wound. To be able thus to tell their story to their general, and to see him listening to it with interest and pleasure, filled their hearts with pride and joy; and the whole army was inspired with the highest spirit of enthusiasm, and with eager desires to have another opportunity occur in which they could encounter danger and death in the service of such a leader. It is in such traits as these that the true greatness of the soul of Alexander shines. It must be remembered that all this time he was but little more than twenty-one. He was but just of age.

Alexander Resumes His March – The Country Surrenders

From his encampment on the Granicus Alexander turned to the southward, and moved along on the eastern shores of the Aegean Sea. The country generally surrendered to him without opposition. In fact, it was hardly Persian territory at all. The inhabitants were mainly of Greek extraction, and had been sometimes under Greek and sometimes under Persian rule. The conquest of the country resulted simply in a change of the executive officer of each province. Alexander took special pains to lead the people to feel that they had nothing to fear from him. He would not allow the soldiers to do any injury. He protected all private property. He took possession only of the citadels, and of such governmental property as he found there, and he continued the same taxes, the same laws, and the same tribunals as had existed before his invasion. The cities and the provinces accordingly surrendered to him as he passed along, and in a very short time all the western part of Asia Minor submitted peacefully to his sway.

Incidents – Alexander's Generosity

The narrative of this progress, as given by the ancient historians, is diversified by a great variety of adventures and incidents, which give great interest to the story, and strikingly illustrate the character of Alexander and the spirit of the times. In some places there would be a contest between the Greek and the Persian parties before Alexander's arrival. At Ephesus, the animosity had been so great that a sort of civil war had broken out. The Greek party had gained the ascendency, and were threatening a general massacre of the Persian inhabitants. Alexander promptly interposed to protect them, though they were his enemies. The intelligence of this act of forbearance and generosity spread all over the land, and added greatly to the influence of Alexander's name, and to the estimation in which he was held.

Omens – The Eagle on the Mast – Interpretations

It was the custom in those days for the mass of the common soldiers to be greatly influenced by what they called *omens*, that is, signs and tokens which they observed in the flight or the actions of birds, and other similar appearances. In one case, the fleet, which had come along the sea, accompanying the march of the army on land, was pent up in a harbour by a stronger Persian fleet outside. One of the vessels of the Macedonian fleet was aground. An eagle lighted upon the mast, and stood perched there for a long time, looking toward the sea. Parmenio said that, as the eagle looked toward the sea, it indicated that victory lay in that quarter, and he recommended that they should arm their ships and push boldly out to attack the Persians. But Alexander maintained that, as the eagle alighted on a ship which was aground, it indicated that they were to look for their success on the shore. The omens could thus almost always be interpreted any way, and sagacious generals only sought in them the means of confirming the courage and confidence of their soldiers, in respect to the plans which they adopted under the influence of other considerations altogether. Alexander knew very well that he was not a sailor, and had no desire to embark in contests from which, however they might end, he would himself personally obtain no glory.

Approach of Winter – The Newly Married Permitted to go Home

When the winter came on, Alexander and his army were about three or four hundred miles from home; and, as he did not intend to advance much farther until the spring should open, he announced to the army that all those persons, both officers and soldiers who had been married within the year, might go home if they chose, and spend the winter with their brides, and return to the army in the spring. No doubt this was an admirable stroke of policy; for, as the number could not be large, their absence could not materially weaken his force, and they would, of course, fill all Greece with tales of Alexander's energy and courage, and of the nobleness and generosity of his character. It was the most effectual way possible of disseminating through Europe the most brilliant accounts of what he had already done.

A Detachment of Bridegrooms

Besides, it must have awakened a new bond of sympathy and fellow-feeling between himself and his soldiers, and greatly increased the attachment to him felt both by those who went and those who remained. And though Alexander must have been aware of all these advantages of the act, still no one could have thought of or adopted such a plan unless he was accustomed to consider and regard, in his dealings with others, the feelings and affections of the heart, and to cherish a warm sympathy for them. The bridegroom soldiers, full of exultation and pleasure, set forth on their return to Greece, in a detachment under the charge of three generals, themselves bridegrooms too.

Taurus – Passage Through the Sea

Alexander, however, had no idea of remaining idle during the winter. He marched on from province to province, and from city to city, meeting with every variety of adventures. He went first along the southern coast, until at length he came to a place where a mountain chain, called Taurus, comes down to the seacoast, where it terminates abruptly in cliffs and precipices, leaving only a narrow beach between them and the water below. This beach was sometimes covered and sometimes bare. It is true, there is very little tide in the Mediterranean, but the level of the water along the shores is altered considerably by the long-continued pressure exerted in one direction or another by winds and storms. The water was *up* when Alexander reached this pass; still he determined to march his army through it. There was another way, back among the mountains, but Alexander seemed disposed to gratify the love of adventure which his army felt, by introducing them to a novel scene of danger. They accordingly traversed along a steep narrow pass under these cliffs, marching, as they say, sometimes up to the waist in water, the swell rolling in upon them all the time from the offing.

Hardships – The Meander

Having at length succeeded in passing safely round this frowning buttress of the mountains, Alexander turned northward, and advanced into the very heart of Asia Minor. In doing this he had to pass *over* the range which he had come *round* before; and, as it was winter, his army were, for a time, enveloped in snows and storms among the wild and frightful defiles. They had here, in addition to the dangers and hardships of the way and of the season, to encounter the hostility of their foes, as the tribes who inhabited these mountains assembled to dispute the passage. Alexander was victorious, and reached a valley through which there flows a river which has handed down its name to the English language and literature. This river was the Meander. Its beautiful windings through verdant and fertile valleys were so renowned, that every stream which imitates its example is said to *meander* to the present day.

Gordium

During all this time Parmenio had remained in the western part of Asia Minor with a considerable body of the army. As the spring approached, Alexander sent him orders to go to Gordium, whither he was himself proceeding, and meet him there. He also directed that the detachment which had gone home should, on recrossing the Hellespont, on their return, proceed eastward to Gordium, thus making that city the general rendezvous for the commencement of his next campaign.

Story of the Gordian knot

One reason why Alexander desired to go to Gordium was that he wished to untie the famous Gordian knot. The story of the Gordian knot was this. Gordius was a sort of mountain farmer. One day he was plowing, and an eagle came down and alighted upon his yoke, and remained there until he had finished his plowing. This was an omen, but what was the signification of it? Gordius did not know, and he accordingly went to a neighbouring town in order to consult the prophets and soothsayers. On his way he met a damsel, who, like Rebecca in the days of Abraham, was going forth to draw water. Gordius fell into conversation with her, and related to her the occurrence which had interested him so strongly. The maiden advised him to go back and offer a sacrifice to Jupiter. Finally, she consented to go back with him and aid him. The affair ended in her becoming his wife, and they lived together in peace for many years upon their farm.

Midas – Gordius Made King

They had a son named Midas. The father and mother were accustomed to go out sometimes in their cart or wagon, drawn by the oxen, Midas driving. One day they were going into the town in this way, at a time when it happened that there was an assembly convened, which was in a state of great perplexity on account of the civil dissensions and contests which prevailed in the country. They had just inquired of an oracle what they should do. The oracle said that 'a cart would bring them a king, who would terminate their eternal broils.' Just then Midas came up, driving the cart in which his father and mother were seated. The assembly thought at once that this must be the cart meant by the oracle, and they made Gordius king by acclamation. They took the cart and the yoke to preserve as sacred relics, consecrating them to Jupiter; and Gordius tied the yoke to the pole of the cart by a thong of leather, making a knot so close and complicated that nobody could untie it again. It was called the Gordian knot. The oracle afterward said that whoever should untie this knot should become monarch of all Asia. Thus far, nobody had succeeded.

Alexander Cuts the Knot

Alexander felt a great desire to see this knot and try what he could do. He went, accordingly, into the temple where the sacred cart had been deposited, and, after looking at the knot, and satisfying himself that the task of untying it was hopeless, he cut it to pieces with his sword. How far the circumstances of this whole story are true, and how far fictitious, no one can tell; the story itself, however, as thus related, has come down from generation to generation, in every country of Europe, for two thousand years, and any extrication of one's self from a difficulty by violent means has been called cutting the Gordian knot to the present day.

He Resumes His March

At length the whole army was assembled, and the king recommenced his progress. He went on successfully for some weeks, moving in a south-easterly direction, and bringing the whole country under his dominion, until, at length, when he reached Tarsus, an event occurred which nearly terminated his career. There were some circumstances which caused him to press forward with the utmost effort in approaching Tarsus, and, as the day was warm, he got very much overcome with heat and fatigue. In this state, he went and plunged suddenly into the River Cydnus to bathe.

Alexander's Bath in the Cydnus

Now the Cydnus is a small stream, flowing by Tarsus, and it comes down from Mount Taurus at a short distance back from the city. Such streams are always very cold. Alexander was immediately seized with a very violent chill, and was taken out of the water shivering excessively, and, at length, fainted away. They thought he was dying. They bore him to his tent, and, as tidings of their leader's danger spread through the camp, the whole army, officers and soldiers, were thrown into the greatest consternation and grief.

His sickness – Suspicions of poison

A violent and protracted fever came on. In the course of it, an incident occurred which strikingly illustrates the boldness and originality of Alexander's character. The name of his physician was Philip. Philip had been preparing a particular medicine for him, which, it seems, required some days to make ready. Just before it was presented, Alexander received a letter from Parmenio, informing him that he had good reason to believe that Philip had been bribed by the Persians to murder him, during his sickness, by administering poison in the name of medicine. He wrote, he said, to put him on his guard against any medicine which Philip might offer him.

Alexander put the letter under his pillow, and communicated its contents to no one. At length, when the medicine was ready, Philip brought it in. Alexander took the cup containing it with one hand, and with the other he handed Philip the communication which he had received from Parmenio, saying, 'Read that letter.' As soon as Philip had finished reading it, and was ready to look up, Alexander drank off the draught in full, and laid down the cup with an air of perfect confidence that he had nothing to fear.

Some persons think that Alexander watched the countenance of his physician while he was reading the letter, and that he was led to take the medicine by his confidence in his power to determine the guilt or the innocence of a person thus accused by his looks. Others suppose that the act was an expression of his implicit faith in the integrity and fidelity of his servant, and that he intended it as testimony, given in a very pointed and decisive, and, at the same time, delicate manner, that he was not suspicious of his friends, or easily led to distrust their faithfulness. Philip was, at any rate, extremely gratified at the procedure, and Alexander recovered.

Asia Subdued – The Plain of Issus

Alexander had now traversed the whole extent of Asia Minor, and had subdued the entire country to his sway. He was now advancing to another district, that of Syria and Palestine, which lies on the eastern shores of the Mediterranean Sea. To enter this new territory, he had to pass over a narrow plain which lay between the mountains and the sea, at a place called Issus. Here he was met by the main body of the Persian army, and the great battle of Issus was fought. This battle will be the subject of the next chapter.

Chapter VI
Defeat of Darius, BCE 333

Darius's Opinion of Alexander

THUS FAR ALEXANDER had had only the lieutenants and generals of the Persian monarch to contend with. Darius had at first looked upon the invasion of his vast dominions by such a mere boy, as he called him, and by so small an army, with contempt. He sent word to his generals in Asia Minor to seize the young fool, and send him to Persia bound hand and foot. By the time, however, that Alexander had possessed himself of all Asia Minor, Darius began to find that, though young, he was no fool, and that it was not likely to be very easy to seize him.

He Prepares to Meet Him – Greek Mercenaries

Accordingly, Darius collected an immense army himself, and advanced to meet the Macedonians in person. Nothing could exceed the pomp and magnificence of his preparations. There were immense numbers of troops, and they were of all nations. There were even a great many Greeks among his forces, many of them enlisted from the Greeks of Asia Minor. There were some from Greece itself – mercenaries, as they were called; that is, soldiers who fought for pay, and who were willing to enter into any service which would pay them best.

Counsel of Charidemus

There were even some Greek officers and counsellors in the family and court of Darius. One of them, named Charidemus, offended the king very much by the free opinion which he expressed of the uselessness of all his pomp and parade in preparing for an encounter with such an enemy as Alexander. 'Perhaps,' said Charidemus, 'you may not be pleased with my speaking to you plainly, but if I do not do it now, it will be too late hereafter. This great parade and pomp, and this enormous multitude of men, might be formidable to your Asiatic neighbours; but such sort of preparation will be of little avail against Alexander and his Greeks. Your army is resplendent with purple and gold. No one who had not seen it could conceive of its magnificence; but it will not be of any avail against the terrible energy of the Greeks. Their minds are bent on something very different from idle show. They are intent on securing the substantial excellence of their weapons, and on acquiring the discipline and the hardihood essential for the most efficient use of them. They will despise all your parade of purple and gold. They will not even value it as plunder. They glory in their ability to dispense with all the luxuries and conveniences of life. They live upon the coarsest food. At night they sleep upon the bare ground. By day they are always on the march. They brave hunger, cold and every species of exposure with pride and pleasure, having the greatest contempt for anything like softness and gentleness of character. All this pomp and pageantry, with inefficient weapons, and inefficient men to wield them, will be of no avail against their invincible courage and energy; and the best disposition that you can make of all your gold, silver and other treasures, is to send it away and procure good soldiers with it, if indeed gold and silver will procure them.'

Darius's Displeasure at Charidemus

The Greeks were habituated to energetic speaking as well as acting, but Charidemus did not sufficiently consider that the Persians were not accustomed to hear such plain language as this. Darius was very much displeased. In his anger he condemned him to death. 'Very well,' said Charidemus, 'I can die. But my avenger is at hand. My advice is good, and Alexander will soon punish you for not regarding it.'

Magnificence of Darius's Army – Worship of the Sun

Very gorgeous descriptions are given of the pomp and magnificence of the army of Darius, as he commenced his march from the Euphrates to the Mediterranean. The Persians worship the sun and fire. Over the king's tent there was an image of the sun in crystal, and supported in such a manner as to be in the view of the whole army. They had also silver altars, on which they kept constantly burning what they called the sacred fire. These altars were borne by persons appointed for the purpose, who were clothed in magnificent costumes. Then came a long procession of priests and magi, who were dressed also in very splendid robes. They performed the services of public worship. Following them came a chariot consecrated to the sun. It was drawn by white horses, and was followed by a single white horse of large size and noble form, which was a sacred animal, being called the horse of the sun. The equerries, that is, the attendants who had charge of this horse, were also all dressed in white, and each carried a golden rod in his hand.

The Kinsmen – The Immortals

There were bodies of troops distinguished from the rest, and occupying positions of high honour, but these were selected and advanced above the others, not on account of their courage, strength or superior martial efficiency, but from considerations connected with their birth, rank and other aristocratic qualities. There was one body called the Kinsmen, who were the relatives of the king, or, at least, so considered, though, as there were fifteen thousand of them, it would seem that the relationship could not have been, in all cases, very near. They were dressed with great magnificence, and prided themselves on their rank, wealth and the splendour of their armour. There was also a corps called the Immortals. They were ten thousand in number. They wore a dress of gold tissue, which glittered with spangles and precious stones.

Appearance of Darius

These bodies of men, thus dressed, made an appearance more like that of a civic procession, on an occasion of ceremony and rejoicing, than like the march of an army. The appearance of the king in his chariot was still more like an exhibition of pomp and parade. The carriage was very large, elaborately carved and gilded, and ornamented with statues and sculptures. Here the king sat on a very elevated seat, in sight of all. He was clothed in a vest of purple, striped with silver, and over his vest he wore a robe glittering with gold and precious stones. Around his waist was a golden girdle, from which was suspended his scimitar – a species of sword – the scabbard of which was resplendent with gems. He wore a tiara upon his head of very costly and elegant workmanship, and enriched, like the rest of his dress, with brilliant ornaments. The guards who preceded and followed him had pikes of silver, mounted and tipped with gold.

His Family

It is very extraordinary that King Darius took his wife and all his family with him, and a large portion of his treasures, on this expedition against Alexander. His mother, whose name was Sisygambis, was in his family, and she and his wife came, each in her own chariot, immediately after the king. Then there were fifteen carriages filled with the children and their attendants, and three or four hundred ladies of the court, all dressed like queens. After the family there came a train of many hundreds of camels and mules, carrying the royal treasures.

Darius Advances to Meet Alexander

It was in this style that Darius set out upon his expedition, and he advanced by a slow progress toward the westward, until at length he approached the shores of the Mediterranean Sea. He left his treasures in the city of Damascus, where they were deposited under the charge of a sufficient force to protect them, as he supposed. He then advanced to meet Alexander, going himself from Syria toward Asia Minor just at the time that Alexander was coming from Asia Minor into Syria.

Map of the Plain of Issus – Mount Taurus – Route of Darius

The chain of mountains called Mount Taurus extends down near to the coast, at the north-eastern corner of the Mediterranean. Among these mountains there are various tracts of open country, through which an army may march to and fro, between Syria and Asia Minor. Now it happened that Darius, in going toward the west, took a more inland route than Alexander, who, on coming eastward, kept nearer to the sea. Alexander did not know that Darius was so near; and as for Darius, he was confident that Alexander was retreating before him; for, as the Macedonian army was so small, and his own forces constituted such an innumerable host, the idea that Alexander would remain to brave a battle was, in his opinion, entirely out of the question. He had, therefore, no doubt that Alexander was retreating. It is, of course, always difficult for two armies, fifty miles apart, to obtain correct ideas of each other's movements. All the ordinary intercommunications of the country are of course stopped, and each general has his scouts out, with orders to intercept all travellers, and to interrupt the communication of intelligence by every means in their power.

Situation of Issus – The Armies Pass Each Other

In consequence of these and other circumstances of a similar nature, it happened that Alexander and Darius actually passed each other, without either of them being aware of it. Alexander advanced into Syria by the plains of Issus, and a narrow pass beyond, called the Gates of Syria, while Darius went farther to the north, and arrived at Issus after Alexander had left it. Here each army learned to their astonishment that their enemy was in their rear. Alexander could not credit this report when he first heard it. He dispatched a galley with thirty oars along the shore, up the Gulf of Issus, to ascertain the truth. The galley soon came back and reported that, beyond the Gates of Syria, they saw the whole country, which was nearly level land, though gently rising from the sea, covered with the vast encampments of the Persian army.

The king then called his generals and counselors together, informed them of the facts, and made known to them his determination to return immediately through the Gates of Syria and attack the Persian army. The officers received the intelligence with enthusiastic expressions of joy.

Reconnoitering Parties

It was now near the evening. Alexander sent forward a strong reconnoitering party, ordering them to proceed cautiously, to ascend eminences and look far before them, to guard carefully against surprise, and to send back word immediately if they came upon any traces of the enemy. At the present day the operations of such a reconnoitering party are very much aided by the use of spyglasses, which are made now with great care expressly for military purposes. The instrument, however, was not known in Alexander's day.

The Night Before the Battle – Sublime and Solemn Scenes

When the evening came on, Alexander followed the reconnoitering party with the main body of the army. At midnight they reached the pass. When they were secure in the possession of it, they halted. Strong watches were stationed on all the surrounding heights to guard against any possible surprise. Alexander himself ascended one of the eminences, from whence he could look down upon the great plain beyond, which was dimly illuminated in every part by the smouldering fires of the Persian encampment. An encampment at night is a spectacle which is always grand, and often sublime. It must have appeared sublime to Alexander in the highest degree, on this occasion. To stand stealthily among these dark and somber mountains, with the gorges and passes below filled with the columns of his small but undaunted army, and to look onward, a few miles beyond, and see the countless fires of the vast hosts which had got between him and all hope of retreat to his native land; to feel, as he must have done, that his fate, and that of all who were with him, depended upon the events of the day that was soon to dawn – to see and feel these things must have made this night one of the most exciting and solemn scenes in the conqueror's life. He had a soul to enjoy its excitement and sublimity. He gloried in it; and, as if he wished to add to the solemnity of the scene, he caused an altar to be erected, and offered a sacrifice, by torchlight, to the deities on whose aid his soldiers imagined themselves most dependent for success on the morrow. Of course, a place was selected where the lights of the torches would not attract the attention of the enemy, and sentinels were stationed at every advantageous point to watch the Persian camp for the slightest indications of movement or alarm.

Defeat of the Persians – Flight of Darius

In the morning, at break of day, Alexander commenced his march down to the plain. In the evening, at sunset, all the valleys and gorges among the mountains around the plain of Issus were thronged with vast masses of the Persian army, broken, disordered and in confusion, all pressing forward to escape from the victorious Macedonians. They crowded all the roads, they choked up the mountain passes, they trampled upon one another, they fell, exhausted with fatigue and mental agitation. Darius was among them, though his flight had been so sudden that he had left his mother, his wife and all his family behind. He pressed on in his chariot as far as the road allowed his chariot to go, and then, leaving everything behind, he mounted a horse and rode on for his life.

Alexander and his army soon abandoned the pursuit, and returned to take possession of the Persian camp. The tents of King Darius and his household were inconceivably splendid, and were filled with gold and silver vessels, caskets, vases, boxes of perfumes and every imaginable article of luxury and show. The mother and wife of Darius bewailed their hard fate with cries and tears, and continued all the evening in an agony of consternation and despair.

The Mother and Wife of Darius Taken Captive

Alexander, hearing of this, sent Leonnatus, his former teacher, a man of years and gravity, to quiet their fears and comfort them, so far as it was possible to comfort them. In addition to their own captivity, they supposed that Darius was killed, and the mother was mourning bitterly for her son, and the wife for her husband. Leonnatus, attended by some soldiers, advanced toward the tent where these mourners were dwelling. The attendants at the door ran in and informed them that a body of Greeks were coming. This threw them into the greatest consternation. They anticipated violence and death, and threw themselves upon the ground in agony. Leonnatus waited sometime at the door for the attendants to return. At length he entered the tent. This renewed the terrors of the women. They began to entreat him to spare their lives, at least until there should be time for them to see the remains of the son and husband whom they mourned, and to pay the last sad tribute to his memory.

Alexander's Kindness to the Captives

Leonnatus soon relieved their fears. He told them that he was charged by Alexander to say to them that Darius was alive, having made his escape in safety. As to themselves, Alexander assured them, he said, that they should not be injured; that not only were their persons and lives to be protected, but no change was to be made in their condition or mode of life; they should continue to be treated like queens. He added, moreover, that Alexander wished him to say that he felt no animosity or ill will whatever against Darius. He was but technically his enemy, being only engaged in a generous and honourable contest with him for the empire of Asia. Saying these things, Leonnatus raised the disconsolate ladies from the ground, and they gradually regained some degree of composure.

Hephaestion

Alexander himself went to pay a visit to the captive princesses the next day. He took with him Hephaestion. Hephaestion was Alexander's personal friend. The two young men were of the same age, and, though Alexander had the good sense to retain in power all the old and experienced officers which his father had employed, both in the court and army, he showed that, after all, ambition had not overwhelmed and stifled all the kindlier feelings of the heart, by his strong attachment to this young companion. Hephaestion was his confidant, his associate, his personal friend. He did what very few monarchs have done, either before or since; in securing for himself the pleasures of friendship, and of intimate social communion with a heart kindred to his own, without ruining himself by committing to a favourite powers which he was not qualified to wield. Alexander left the wise and experienced Parmenio to manage the camp, while he took the young and handsome Hephaestion to accompany him on his visit to the captive queens.

Alexander's Interview With the Queens

When the two friends entered the tent, the ladies were, from some cause, deceived, and mistook Hephaestion for Alexander, and addressed him, accordingly, with tokens of high respect and homage. One of their attendants immediately rectified the mistake, telling them that the other was Alexander. The ladies were at first overwhelmed with confusion, and attempted to apologize; but the king reassured them at once by the easy and good-natured manner with which he passed over the mistake, saying it was no mistake at all. 'It is true,' said he, 'that I am Alexander, but then he is Alexander too.'

Boldness of Alexander's Policy

The wife of Darius was young and very beautiful, and they had a little son who was with them in the camp. It seems almost unaccountable that Darius should have brought such a helpless and defenceless charge with him into camps and fields of battle. But the truth was that he had no idea of even a battle with Alexander, and as to defeat, he did not contemplate the remotest possibility of it. He regarded Alexander as a mere boy – energetic and daring it is true, and at the head of a desperate band of adventurers; but he considered his whole force as altogether too insignificant to make any stand against such a vast military power as he was bringing against him. He presumed that he would retreat as fast as possible before the Persian army came near him. The idea of such a boy coming down at break of day, from narrow passes of the mountains, upon his vast encampment covering all the plains, and in twelve hours putting the whole mighty mass to flight, was what never entered his imagination at all. The exploit was, indeed, a very extraordinary one. Alexander's forces may have consisted of forty or fifty thousand men, and, if we may believe their story, there were over a hundred thousand Persians left dead upon the field. Many of these were, however, killed by the dreadful confusion and violence of the retreat as vast bodies of horsemen, pressing through the pass, rode over and trampled down the foot soldiers who were toiling in awful confusion along the way, having fled before the horsemen left the field.

Capture Of Immense Treasure

Alexander had heard that Darius had left the greater part of his royal treasures in Damascus, and he sent Parmenio there to seize them. This expedition was successful. An enormous amount of gold and silver fell into Alexander's hands. The plate was coined into money, and many of the treasures were sent to Greece.

Negotiations

Darius got together a small remnant of his army and continued his flight. He did not stop until he had crossed the Euphrates. He then sent an ambassador to Alexander to make propositions for peace. He remonstrated with him, in the communication which he made, for coming thus to invade his dominions, and urged him to withdraw and be satisfied with his own kingdom. He offered him any sum he might name as a ransom for his mother, wife and child, and agreed that if he would deliver them up to him on the payment of the ransom, and depart from his dominions, he would thenceforth regard him as an ally and a friend.

Alexander's Message to Darius

Alexander replied by a letter, expressed in brief but very decided language. He said that the Persians had, under the ancestors of Darius, crossed the Hellespont, invaded Greece, laid waste the country and destroyed cities and towns, and had thus done them incalculable injury; and that Darius himself had been plotting against his (Alexander's) life, and offering rewards to anyone who would kill him. 'I am acting, then,' continued Alexander, 'only on the defensive. The gods, who always favour the right, have given me the victory. I am now monarch of a large part of Asia, and your sovereign king. If you will admit this, and come to me as my subject, I will restore to you your mother, your wife and your child, without any ransom. And, at any rate, whatever you decide in respect to these proposals, if you wish to communicate with me on any subject hereafter, I shall pay no attention to what you send unless you address it to me as your king.'

Grecian Captives – The Theban Envoys

One circumstance occurred at the close of this great victory which illustrates the magnanimity of Alexander's character, and helps to explain the very strong personal attachment which everybody within the circle of his influence so obviously felt for him. He found a great number of envoys and ambassadors from the various states of Greece at the Persian court, and these persons fell into his hands among the other captives. Now the states and cities of Greece, all except

Sparta and Thebes, which last city he had destroyed, were combined ostensibly in the confederation by which Alexander was sustained. It seems, however, that there was a secret enmity against him in Greece, and various parties had sent messengers and agents to the Persian court to aid in plots and schemes to interfere with and defeat Alexander's plans. The Thebans, scattered and disorganized as they were, had sent envoys in this way. Now Alexander, in considering what disposition he should make of these emissaries from his own land, decided to regard them all as traitors except the Thebans. All except the Thebans were *traitors*, he maintained, for acting secretly against him, while ostensibly, and by solemn covenants, they were his friends. 'The case of the Thebans is very different,' said he. 'I have destroyed their city, and they have a right to consider me their enemy, and to do all they can to oppose my progress, and to regain their own lost existence and their former power.' So he gave them their liberty and sent them away with marks of consideration and honour.

Alexander's Victorious Progress

As the vast army of the Persian monarch had now been defeated, of course none of the smaller kingdoms or provinces thought of resisting. They yielded one after another, and Alexander appointed governors of his own to rule over them. He advanced in this manner along the eastern shores of the Mediterranean Sea, meeting with no obstruction until he reached the great and powerful city of Tyre.

Chapter VII
The Siege of Tyre, BCE 333

The City of Tyre

THE CITY OF TYRE stood on a small island, three or four miles in diameter, on the eastern shores of the Mediterranean Sea. It was, in those days, the greatest commercial city in the world, and it

exercised a great maritime power by means of its fleets and ships, which traversed every part of the Mediterranean.

Its Situation and Extent

Tyre had been built originally on the mainland; but in some of the wars which it had to encounter with the kings of Babylon in the East, this old city had been abandoned by the inhabitants, and a new one built upon an island not far from the shore, which could be more easily defended from an enemy. The old city had gone to ruin, and its place was occupied by old walls, fallen towers, stones, columns, arches and other remains of the ancient magnificence of the place.

Pursuits of the Tyrians

The island on which the Tyre of Alexander's day had been built was about half-mile from the shore. The water between was about eighteen feet deep, and formed a harbour for the vessels. The great business of the Tyrians was commerce. They bought and sold merchandise in all the ports of the Mediterranean Sea, and transported it by their merchant vessels to and fro. They had also fleets of war galleys, which they used to protect their interests on the high seas, and in the various ports which their merchant vessels visited. They were thus wealthy and powerful, and yet they lived shut up upon their little island, and were almost entirely independent of the main-land.

Their Great Wealth and Resources – The Walls of Tyre

The city itself, however, though contracted in extent on account of the small dimensions of the island, was very compactly built and strongly fortified, and it contained a vast number of stately and magnificent edifices, which were filled with stores of wealth that had been accumulated by the mercantile enterprise and thrift of many generations. Extravagant stories are told by the historians and geographers of those days, in respect to the scale on which the structures of Tyre were built. It was said, for instance, that the walls were one hundred and fifty feet high. It is true that the walls rose directly from the surface of the water, and of course a considerable part of their elevation was required to bring them up to the level of the surface of the land; and then, in addition to this, they had to be carried up the whole ordinary height of a city wall to afford the usual protection to the edifices and dwellings within. There might have been some places where the walls themselves, or structures connected with them, were carried up to the elevation above named, though it is scarcely to be supposed that such could have been their ordinary dimensions.

Influence and Power of Tyre

At any rate, Tyre was a very wealthy, magnificent, and powerful city, intent on its commercial operations, and well furnished with means of protecting them at sea, but feeling little interest, and taking little part, in the contentions continually arising among the rival powers which had possession of the land. Their policy was to retain their independence, and yet to keep on good terms with all other powers, so that their commercial intercourse with the ports of all nations might go on undisturbed.

Alexander Hesitates

It was, of course, a very serious question with Alexander, as his route lay now through Phoenicia and in the neighbourhood of Tyre, what he should do in respect to such a port. He did not like to leave it behind him and proceed to the eastward; for, in case of any reverses happening to him, the Tyrians would be very likely to act decidedly against him, and their power on the Mediterranean would enable them to act very efficiently against him on all the coasts of Greece and Asia Minor. On the other hand, it seemed a desperate undertaking to attack the city. He had none but land forces, and the island was half a mile from the shore. Besides its enormous walls, rising perpendicularly out of the water, it was defended by ships well armed and manned. It was not possible to surround the city and starve it into submission, as the inhabitants had wealth to buy, and ships to bring in, any quantity of provisions and stores by sea. Alexander, however, determined not to follow Darius toward the east, and leave such a stronghold as this behind him.

Presents from the Tyrians

The Tyrians wished to avoid a quarrel if it were possible. They sent complimentary messages to Alexander, congratulating him on his conquests, and disavowing all feelings of hostility to him. They also sent him a golden crown, as many of the other states of Asia had done, in token of their yielding a general submission to his authority. Alexander returned very gracious replies, and expressed to them his intention of coming to Tyre for the purpose of offering sacrifices, as he said, to Hercules, a god whom the Tyrians worshiped.

Alexander Refused Admittance into Tyre

The Tyrians knew that wherever Alexander went he went at the head of his army, and his coming into Tyre at all implied necessarily his taking military possession of it. They thought it might, perhaps, be somewhat difficult to dispossess such a visitor after he should once get installed in their castles and palaces. So they sent him word that it would not be in their power to receive him in the city itself, but that he could offer the sacrifice which he intended on the mainland, as there was a temple sacred to Hercules among the ruins there.

He Resolves to Attack It

Alexander then called a council of his officers, and stated to them his views. He said that, on reflecting fully upon the subject, he had come to the conclusion that it was best to postpone pushing his expedition forward into the heart of Persia until he should have subdued Tyre completely, and made himself master of the Mediterranean Sea. He said, also, that he should take possession of Egypt before turning his arms toward the forces that Darius was gathering against him in the East. The generals of the army concurred in this opinion, and Alexander advanced toward Tyre. The Tyrians prepared for their defence.

Alexander's Plan

After examining carefully all the circumstances of the case, Alexander conceived the very bold plan of building a broad causeway from the mainland to the island on which the city was founded, out of the ruins of old Tyre, and then marching his army over upon it to the walls of the city, where he could then plant his engines and make a breach. This would seem to be a very desperate undertaking. It is true the stones remaining on the site of the old city afforded sufficient materials for the construction of the pier, but then the work must go on against a tremendous opposition, both from the walls of the city itself and from the Tyrian ships in the harbour. It would seem to be almost impossible to protect the men from these attacks so as to allow the operations to proceed at all, and the difficulty and danger must increase very rapidly as the work should approach the walls of the city. But, notwithstanding these objections, Alexander determined to proceed. Tyre must be taken, and this was obviously the only possible mode of taking it.

Enthusiasm of the Army

The soldiers advanced to undertake the work with great readiness. Their strong personal attachment to Alexander; their confidence that whatever he should plan and attempt would succeed; the novelty and boldness of this design of reaching an island by building an isthmus to it from the mainland – these and other similar considerations excited the ardour and enthusiasm of the troops to the highest degree.

Construction of the Pier

In constructing works of this kind in the water, the material used is sometimes stone and sometimes earth. So far as earth is employed, it is necessary to resort to some means to prevent its spreading under the water, or being washed away by the dash of the waves at its sides. This is usually effected by driving what are called *piles*, which are long beams of wood, pointed at the end, and driven into the earth by means of powerful engines. Alexander sent parties of men into the mountains of Lebanon, where were vast forests of cedars, which were very celebrated in ancient times, and which are often alluded to in the sacred scriptures. They cut down these trees, and brought the stems of them to the shore, where they sharpened them at one end and drove them into the sand, in order to protect the sides of their embankment. Others brought stones from the ruins and tumbled them into the sea in the direction where the pier was to be built. It was some time before the work made such progress as to attract much attention from Tyre. At length, however, when the people of the city saw it gradually increasing in size and advancing toward them, they concluded that they must engage in earnest in the work of arresting its progress.

Counter Operations of the Tyrians

They accordingly constructed engines on the walls to throw heavy darts and stones over the water to the men upon the pier. They sent secretly to the tribes that inhabited the valleys and ravines among the mountains, to attack the parties at work there, and they landed forces from the city at some distance from the pier, and then marched along the shore, and attempted to drive away the men that were engaged in carrying stones from the ruins. They also fitted up and manned some galleys of large size, and brought them up near to the pier itself, and attacked the men who were at work upon it with stones, darts, arrows, and missiles of every description.

Structures Erected on the Pier

But all was of no avail. The work, though impeded, still went on. Alexander built large screens of wood upon the pier, covering them with hides, which protected his soldiers from the weapons of the enemy, so that they could carry on their operations safely behind them. By these means the work advanced for some distance further. As it advanced, various structures were erected upon it, especially along the sides and at the end toward the city. These structures consisted of great engines for driving piles, and machines for throwing stones and darts, and towers carried up to a great height, to enable the men to throw stones and heavy weapons down upon the galleys which might attempt to approach them.

The Tyrians Fit Up a Fire Ship – The Ship Fired and Set Adrift

At length the Tyrians determined on attempting to destroy all these wooden works by means of what is called in modern times a *fire ship*. They took a large galley, and filled it with combustibles of every kind. They loaded it first with light dry wood, and they poured pitch, tar and oil over all this wood to make it burn with fiercer flames. They saturated the sails and the cordage in the same manner, and laid trains of combustible materials through all parts of the vessel, so that when fire should be set in one part it would immediately spread everywhere, and set the whole mass in flames at once. They towed this ship, on a windy day, near to the enemy's works, and on the side from which the wind was blowing. They then put it in motion toward the pier at a point where there was the greatest collection of engines and machines, and when they had got as near as they dared to go themselves, the men who were on board set the trains on fire, and made their escape in boats. The flames ran all over the vessel with inconceivable rapidity. The vessel itself drifted down upon Alexander's works, notwithstanding the most strenuous exertions of his soldiers to keep it away. The frames and engines, and the enormous and complicated machines which had been erected, took fire, and the whole mass was soon enveloped in a general conflagration.

The men made desperate attempts to defend their works, but all in vain. Some were killed by arrows and darts, some were burned to death, and others, in the confusion, fell into the sea. Finally, the army was obliged to draw back, and to abandon all that was combustible in the vast construction they had reared, to the devouring flames.

Effects of the Storm

Not long after this the sea itself came to the aid of the Tyrians. There was a storm; and, as a consequence of it, a heavy swell rolled in from the offing, which soon undermined and washed away a large part of the pier. The effects of a heavy sea on the most massive and substantial structures, when they are fairly exposed to its impulse, are far greater than would be conceived possible by those who had not witnessed them. The most ponderous stones are removed, the strongest fastenings are torn asunder, and embankments the most compact and solid are undermined and washed away. The storm, in this case, destroyed in a few hours the work of many months, while the army of Alexander looked on from the shore witnessing its ravages in dismay.

The Work Began Anew – Alexander Collects a Fleet – Warlike Engines

When the storm was over, and the first shock of chagrin and disappointment had passed from the minds of the men, Alexander prepared to resume the work with fresh vigour and energy. The men commenced repairing the pier and widening it, so as to increase its strength and capacity. They dragged whole trees to the edges of it, and sunk them, branches and all, to the bottom, to form a sort of platform there, to prevent the stones from sinking into the slime. They built new towers and engines, covering them with green hides to make them fireproof; and thus they were soon advancing again, and gradually drawing nearer to the city, and in a more threatening and formidable manner than ever.

Alexander, finding that his efforts were impeded very much by the ships of the Tyrians, determined on collecting and equipping a fleet of his own. This he did at Sidon, which was a town a short distance north of Tyre. He embarked on board this fleet himself, and came down with it into the Tyrian seas. With this fleet he had various success. He chained many of the ships together, two and two, at a little distance apart, covering the enclosed space with a platform, on which the soldiers could stand to fight. The men also erected engines on these platforms to attack the city. These engines were of various kinds. There was what they called the battering ram, which was a long and very heavy beam of wood, headed with iron or brass. This beam was suspended by a chain in the middle, so that it could be swung back and forth by the soldiers, its head striking against the wall each time, by which means the wall would sometimes be soon battered down. They had also machines for throwing great stones, or beams of wood, by means of the elastic force of strong bars of wood, or of steel, or that of twisted ropes. The part of the machine upon which the stone was placed would be drawn back by the united strength of many of the soldiers, and then, as it recovered itself when released, the stone would be thrown off into the air with prodigious velocity and force.

Double Galleys – The Women Removed from Tyre

Alexander's double galleys answered very well as long as the water was smooth; but sometimes, when they were caught out in a swell, the rolling of the waves would rack and twist them so as to tear the platforms asunder, and sink the men in the sea. Thus difficulties unexpected and formidable were continually arising. Alexander, however, persevered through them all. The Tyrians, finding themselves pressed more and more, and seeing that the dangers impending became more and more formidable every day, at length concluded to send a great number of the women and children away to Carthage, which was a great commercial city in Africa. They were determined not to submit to Alexander, but to carry their resistance to the very last extremity. And as the closing scenes of a siege, especially if the place is at last taken by storm, are awful beyond description, they wished to save their wives, daughters and helpless babes from having to witness them.

The Siege Advances

In the meantime, as the siege advanced, the parties became more and more incensed against each other. They treated the captives which they took on either side with greater and greater cruelty, each thinking that they were only retaliating worse injuries from the other. The Macedonians approached nearer and nearer. The resources of the unhappy city were gradually cut off and its strength worn away. The engines approached nearer and nearer to the walls, until the battering rams bore directly upon them, and breaches began to be made. At length one great breach on the southern side was found to be 'practicable,' as they call it. Alexander began to prepare for the final assault, and the Tyrians saw before them the horrible prospect of being taken by storm.

Undaunted Courage of the Tyrians

Still they would not submit. Submission would now have done but little good, though it might have saved some of the final horrors of the scene. Alexander had become greatly exasperated by the long resistance which the Tyrians had made. They probably could not now have averted destruction, but they might, perhaps, have prevented its coming upon them in so terrible a shape as the irruption of thirty thousand frantic and infuriated soldiers through the breaches in their walls to take their city by storm.

A Breach Made

The breach by which Alexander proposed to force his entrance was on the southern side. He prepared a number of ships, with platforms raised upon them in such a manner that, on getting near the walls, they could be let down, and form a sort of bridge, over which the men could pass to the broken fragments of the wall, and thence ascend through the breach above.

The Assault

The plan succeeded. The ships advanced to the proposed place of landing. The bridges were let down. The men crowded over them to the foot of the wall. They clambered up through the breach to the battlements above, although the Tyrians thronged the passage and made the most desperate resistance. Hundreds were killed by darts, and arrows, and falling stones, and their bodies tumbled into the sea. The others, paying no attention to their falling comrades, and drowning the horrid screams of the crushed and the dying with their own frantic shouts of rage and fury, pressed on up the broken wall till they reached the battlements above. The vast throng then rolled along upon the top of the wall till they came to stairways and slopes by which they could descend into the city, and, pouring down through all these avenues, they spread over the streets, and satiated the hatred and rage, which had been gathering strength for seven long months, in bursting into houses, and killing and destroying all that came in their way. Thus the city was stormed.

Changes in Alexander's Character

After the soldiers were weary with the work of slaughtering the wretched inhabitants of the city, they found that many still remained alive, and Alexander tarnished the character for generosity and forbearance for which he had thus far been distinguished by the cruelty with which he treated them. Some were executed, some thrown into the sea; and it is even said that two thousand were *crucified* along the seashore. This may mean that their bodies were placed upon crosses after life had been destroyed by some more humane method than crucifixion. At any rate, we find frequent indications from this time that prosperity and power were beginning to exert their usual unfavourable influence upon Alexander's character. He became haughty, imperious and cruel. He lost the modesty and gentleness which seemed to characterize him in the earlier part of his life, and began to assume the moral character, as well as perform the exploits, of a military hero.

A good illustration of this is afforded by the answer that he sent to Darius, about the time of the storming of Tyre, in reply to a second communication which he had received from him proposing terms of peace. Darius offered him a very large sum of money for the ransom of his mother, wife and child, and agreed to give up to him all the country he had conquered, including the whole territory west of the Euphrates. He also offered him his daughter Stateira in marriage. He recommended to him to accept these terms, and be content with the possessions he had already acquired; that he could not expect to succeed, if he should try, in crossing the mighty rivers of the East, which were in the way of his march toward the Persian dominions.

His Harsh Message to Darius

Alexander replied, that if he wished to marry his daughter he could do it without his consent; as to the ransom, he was not in want of money; in respect to Darius's offering to give him up all west of the Euphrates, it was absurd for a man to speak of giving what was no longer his own; that he had crossed too many seas in his military expeditions, since he left Macedon, to feel any concern about the *rivers* that he might find in his way; and that he should continue to pursue Darius wherever he might retreat in search of safety and protection, and he had no fear but that he should find and conquer him at last.

Alexander's Reply to Parmenio

It was a harsh and cruel message to send to the unhappy monarch whom he had already so greatly injured. Parmenio advised him to accept Darius's offers. 'I would,' said he, 'if I were Alexander.' 'Yes,' said Alexander, 'and so would I if I were Parmenio.' What a reply from a youth of twenty-two to a venerable general of sixty, who had been so tried and faithful a friend, and so efficient a lieutenant both to his father and to himself, for so many years.

The Hero Rises, but the Man Sinks

The siege and storming of Tyre has always been considered one of the greatest of Alexander's exploits. The boldness, the perseverance, the indomitable energy which he himself and all his army manifested, during the seven months of their Herculean toil, attracted the admiration of the world. And yet we find our feelings of sympathy for his character, and interest in his fate, somewhat alienated by the indications of pride, imperiousness and cruelty which begin to appear. While he rises in our estimation as a military hero, he begins to sink somewhat as a man.

Lysimachus – Alexander's Adventure in the Mountains

And yet the change was not sudden. He bore during the siege his part in the privations and difficulties which the soldiers had to endure; and the dangers to which they had to be exposed, he was always willing to share. One night he was out with a party upon the mountains. Among his few immediate attendants was Lysimachus, one of his former teachers, who always loved to accompany him at such times. Lysimachus was advanced in life, and somewhat infirm, and consequently could not keep up with the rest in the march. Alexander remained with Lysimachus, and ordered the rest to go on. The road at length became so rugged that they had to dismount from their horses and walk. Finally they lost their way, and found themselves obliged to stop for the night. They had no fire. They saw, however, at a distance, some camp fires blazing which belonged to the barbarian tribes against whom the expedition was directed. Alexander went to the nearest one. There were two men lying by it, who had been stationed to take care of it. He advanced stealthily to them and killed them both, probably while they were asleep. He then took a brand from their fire, carried it back to his own encampment, where he made a blazing fire for himself and Lysimachus, and they passed the night in comfort and safety. This is the story. How far we are to give credit to it, each reader must judge for himself. One thing is certain, however, that there are many military heroes of whom such stories would not be even fabricated.

Chapter VIII
Alexander in Egypt, BCE 332

Alexander in Judea

AFTER COMPLETING THE SUBJUGATION of Tyre, Alexander commenced his march for Egypt. His route led him through Judea. The time was about three hundred years before the birth of Christ, and, of course, this passage of the great conqueror through the land of Israel took place between the historical periods of the Old Testament and of the New, so that no account of it is given in the sacred volume.

Josephus, and the Character of His Writings

There was a Jewish writer named Josephus, who lived and wrote a few years after Christ, and, of course, more than three hundred years after Alexander. He wrote a history of the Jews, which is a very entertaining book to read; but he liked so much to magnify the importance of the events in the history of his country, and to embellish them with marvelous and supernatural incidents, that his narratives have not always been received with implicit faith. Josephus says that, as Alexander passed through Palestine, he went to pay a visit to Jerusalem. The circumstances of this visit, according to his account, were these.

Josephus's Account of Alexander's Visit
to Jerusalem

The city of Tyre, before Alexander besieged it, as it lived entirely by commerce, and was surrounded by the sea, had to depend on the neighbouring countries for a supply of food. The people were accordingly accustomed to purchase grain in Phoenicia, Judea and Egypt, and transport it by their ships to the island. Alexander, in the same manner, when besieging the city, found that he must depend upon the neighbouring countries for supplies of food; and he accordingly sent requisitions for such supplies to several places, and, among others, to Judea. The Jews, as Josephus says, refused to send any such supplies, saying that it would be inconsistent with fidelity to Darius, under whose government they were.

Alexander took no notice of this reply at the time, being occupied with the siege of Tyre; but, as soon as that city was taken, and he was ready to pass through Judea, he directed his march toward Jerusalem with the intention of destroying the city.

The High Priest Jaddus

Now the chief magistrate at Jerusalem at this time, the one who had the command of the city, ruling it, of course, under a general responsibility to the Persian government, was the high priest. His name was Jaddus. In the time of Christ, about three hundred years after this, the name of the high priest, as the reader will recollect, was Caiaphas. Jaddus and all the inhabitants of Jerusalem were very much alarmed. They knew not what to do. The siege and capture of Tyre had impressed them all with a strong sense of Alexander's terrible energy and martial power, and they began to anticipate certain destruction.

His Dreams

Jaddus caused great sacrifices to be offered to Almighty God, and public and solemn prayers were made, to implore his guidance and protection. The next day after these services, he told the people that they had nothing to fear. God had appeared to him in a dream, and directed him what to do. 'We are not to resist the conqueror,' said he, 'but to go forth to meet him and welcome him. We are to strew the city with flowers, and adorn it as for a festive celebration. The priests are to be dressed in their pontifical robes and go forth, and the inhabitants are to follow them in a civic procession. In this way we are to go out to meet Alexander as he advances – and all will be well.'

The Procession of Priests

These directions were followed. Alexander was coming on with a full determination to destroy the city. When, however, he saw the procession, and came near enough to distinguish the appearance and dress of the high priest, he stopped, seemed surprised and pleased, and advanced toward him with an air of the profoundest deference and respect. He seemed to pay him almost religious homage and adoration. Everyone was astonished. Parmenio asked him for an explanation. Alexander made the following extraordinary statement:

Alexander's Account of His Dream

'When I was in Macedon, before setting out on this expedition, while I was revolving the subject in my mind, musing day after day on the means of conquering Asia, one night I had a remarkable dream. In my dream this very priest appeared before me, dressed just as he is now. He exhorted me to banish every fear, to cross the Hellespont boldly, and to push forward into the heart of Asia. He said that God would march at the head of my army, and give me the victory over all the Persians. I recognize this priest as the same person that appeared to me then. He has the same countenance, the same dress, the same stature, the same air. It is through his encouragement and aid that I am here, and I am ready to worship and adore the God whose service he administers.'

Alexander Joins in the Jewish Ceremonies – Prophecies of Daniel

Alexander joined the high priest in the procession, and they returned to Jerusalem together. There Alexander united with them and with the Jews of the city in the celebration of religious rites, by offering sacrifices and oblations in the Jewish manner. The writings which are now printed together in our Bibles, as the Old Testament, were, in those days, written separately on parchment rolls, and kept in the temple. The priests produced from the rolls the one containing the prophecies of Daniel, and they read and interpreted some of these prophecies to Alexander, which they considered to have reference to him, though written many hundred years before. Alexander was, as Josephus relates, very much pleased at the sight of these ancient predictions, and the interpretation put upon them by the priests. He assured the Jews that they should be protected in the exercise of all their rights, and especially in their religious worship, and he also promised them that he would take their brethren who resided in Media and Babylon under his special charge when he should come into possession of those places. These Jews of Media and Babylon were the descendants of captives which had been carried away from their native land in former wars.

Doubts About Alexander's Visit

Such is the story which Josephus relates. The Greek historians, on the other hand, make no mention of this visit to Jerusalem; and some persons think that it was never made, but that the story arose and was propagated from generation to generation among the Jews, through the influence of their desire to magnify the importance and influence of their worship, and that Josephus incorporated the account into his history without sufficiently verifying the facts.

Siege

However it may be in regard to Jerusalem, Alexander was delayed at Gaza, which is on the shore of the Mediterranean Sea. It was a place of considerable commerce and wealth, and was, at this time, under the command of a governor whom Darius had stationed there. His name was Betis. Betis refused to surrender the place. Alexander stopped to besiege it, and the siege delayed him two months. He was very much exasperated at this, both against Betis and against the city.

Alexander Receives a Wound

His unreasonable anger was very much increased by a wound which he received. He was near a mound which his soldiers had been constructing near the city, to place engines upon for an attack upon the walls, when an arrow shot from one of the engines upon the walls struck him in the breast. It penetrated his armour, and wounded him deeply in the shoulder. The wound was very painful for some time, and the suffering which he endured from it only added fuel to the flame of his anger against the city.

Gaza Taken by Storm – Alexander's Brutality to the Brave Betis

At last breaches were made in the walls, and the place was taken by storm. Alexander treated the wretched captives with extreme cruelty. He cut the garrison to pieces, and sold the inhabitants to slavery. As for Betis, he dealt with him in a manner almost too horrible to be described. The reader will recollect that Achilles, at the siege of Troy, after killing Hector, dragged his dead body around the walls of the city. Alexander, growing more cruel as he became more accustomed to war and bloodshed, had been intending to imitate this example so soon as he could find an enemy worthy of such a fate. He now determined to carry his plan into execution with Betis. He ordered him into his presence. A few years before, he would have rewarded him for his fidelity in his master's service; but now, grown selfish, hard hearted and revengeful, he looked upon him with a countenance full of vindictive exultation, and said, 'You are not going to die the simple death that you desire. You have got the worst torments that revenge can invent to suffer.'

Betis did not reply, but looked upon Alexander with a calm, composed and unsubdued air, which incensed the conqueror more and more.

'Observe his dumb arrogance,' said Alexander; 'but I will conquer him. I will show him that I can draw groans from him, if nothing else.'

He then ordered holes to be made through the heels of his unhappy captive, and, passing a rope through them, had the body fastened to a chariot, and dragged about the city till no life remained.

Rich Treasures

Alexander found many rich treasures in Gaza. He sent a large part of them to his mother Olympias, whom he had left in Macedon. Alexander's affection for his mother seems to have been more permanent than almost any other good trait in his character. He found, in addition to other stores of valuable merchandise, a large quantity of frankincense and myrrh. These are gums which were brought from Arabia, and were very costly. They were used chiefly in making offerings and in burning incense to the gods.

Story of Alexander's Youth

When Alexander was a young man in Macedon, before his father's death, he was one day present at the offering of sacrifices, and one of his teachers and guardians, named Leonnatus, who was standing by, thought he was rather profuse in his consumption of frankincense and myrrh. He was taking it up by handfuls and throwing it upon the fire. Leonnatus reproved him for this extravagance, and told him that when he became master of the countries where these costly gums were procured, he might be as prodigal of them as he pleased, but that in the meantime it would be proper for him to be more prudent and economical. Alexander remembered this reproof, and, finding vast stores of these expensive gums in Gaza, he sent the whole quantity to Leonnatus, telling him that he sent him this abundant supply that he might not have occasion to be so reserved and sparing for the future in his sacrifices to the gods.

Pelusium

After this conquest and destruction of Gaza, Alexander continued his march southward to the frontiers of Egypt. He reached these frontiers at the city of Pelusium. The Egyptians had been under the Persian dominion, but they abhorred it, and were very ready to submit to Alexander's sway. They sent ambassadors to meet him upon the frontiers. The governors of the cities, as he advanced into the country, finding that it would be useless to resist, and warned by the terrible example of Thebes, Tyre and Gaza, surrendered to him as fast as he summoned them.

Memphis – Fertility of Egypt

He went to Memphis. Memphis was a great and powerful city, situated in what was called Lower Egypt, on the Nile, just above where the branches which form the mouths of the Nile separate from the main stream. All that part of Egypt is flat country, having been formed by the deposits brought down by the Nile. Such land is called *alluvial*; it is always level, and, as it consists of successive deposits from the turbid waters of the river, made in the successive inundations, it forms always a very rich soil, deep and inexhaustible, and is, of course, extremely fertile. Egypt has been celebrated for its unexampled fertility from the earliest times. It waves with fields of corn and grain, and is adorned with groves of the most luxuriant growth and richest verdure.

Deserts of Egypt – Cause of Their Sterility

It is only, however, so far as the land is formed by the deposits of the Nile, that this scene of verdure and beauty extends. On the east it is bounded by ranges of barren and rocky hills, and on the west by vast deserts, consisting of moving sands, from which no animal or vegetable life can derive the means of existence. The reason of this sterility seems to be the absence of water. The geological formation of the land is such that it furnishes few springs of water, and no streams, and in that climate it seldom or never rains. If there is water, the most barren sands will clothe themselves with some species of vegetation, which, in its decay, will form a soil that will nourish more and more fully each succeeding generation of plants. But in the absence of water, any surface of earth will soon become a barren sand. The wind will drive away everything imponderable, leaving only the heavy sands, to drift in storms, like fields of snow.

Among these African deserts, however, there are some fertile spots. They are occasioned by springs which arise in little dells, and which saturate the ground with moisture for some distance around them. The water from these springs flows for some distance, in many cases, in a little stream, before it is finally lost and absorbed in the sands. The whole tract under the influence of this irrigation clothes itself with verdure. Trees grow up to shade it. It forms a spot whose beauty, absolutely great, is heightened by the contrast which it presents to the gloomy and desolate desert by which it is surrounded. Such a green spot in the desert is called an Oasis. They are the resort and the refuge of the traveler and the pilgrim, who seek shelter and repose upon them in their weary journeys over the trackless wilds.

The Great Oasis – Oasis of Siwa

Nor must it be supposed that these islands of fertility and verdure are always *small*. Some of them are very extensive, and contain a considerable population. There is one called the Great Oasis, which consists of a chain of fertile tracts of about a hundred miles in length. Another, called the Oasis of Siwa, has, in modern times, a population of eight thousand souls. This last is situated not far from the shores of the Mediterranean Sea – at least not very far: perhaps two or three hundred miles – and it was a very celebrated spot in Alexander's day.

Jupiter Ammon and His Temple

The cause of its celebrity was that it was the seat and centre of the worship of a famous deity called Jupiter Ammon. This god was said to be the son of Jupiter, though there were all sorts of stories about his origin and early history. He had the form of a ram, and was worshiped by the people of Egypt, and also by the Carthaginians, and by the people of Northern Africa generally. His temple was in this Oasis, and it was surrounded by a considerable population, which was supported, in a great degree, by the expenditures of the worshipers who came as pilgrims, or otherwise, to sacrifice at his shrine.

Alexander Aspires to Divine Honours

It is said that Alexander, finding that the various objects of human ambition which he had been so rapidly attaining by his victories and conquests for the past few years were insufficient to satisfy him, began now to aspire for some supernatural honours, and he accordingly conceived the design of having himself declared to be the son of a god. The heroes of Homer were sons of the gods. Alexander envied them the fame and honour which this distinction gave them in the opinion of mankind. He determined to visit the temple of Jupiter Ammon in the Oasis of Siwa, and to have the declaration of his divine origin made by the priests there.

He proceeded, accordingly, to the mouth of the Nile, where he found a very eligible place, as he believed, for the foundation of a commercial city, and he determined to build it on his return. Thence he marched along the shores of the Mediterranean, toward the west, until he reached a place called Paraetonium. He then left the seashore and marched south, striking at once into the desert when he left the sea. He was accompanied by a small detachment of his army as an escort, and they journeyed eleven days before they reached the Oasis.

Alexander Crosses the Desert

They had a variety of perilous adventures in crossing the desert. For the first two days the soldiers were excited and pleased with the novelty and romantic grandeur of the scene. The desert has, in some degree, the sublimity of the ocean. There is the same boundless expanse, the same vast, unbroken curve of the horizon, the same tracklessness, the same solitude. There is, in addition, a certain profound and awful stillness and repose, which imparts to it a new element of impressiveness and grandeur. Its dread and solemn silence is far more imposing and sublime than the loudest thunders of the seas.

The Camel

The third day the soldiers began to be weary of such a march. They seemed afraid to penetrate any further into such boundless and terrible solitudes. They had been obliged to bring water with them in goat skins, which were carried by camels. The camel is the only beast of burden which can be employed upon the deserts. There is a peculiarity in the anatomical structure of this animal by which he can take in, at one time, a supply of water for many days. He is formed, in fact, for the desert. In his native state he lives in the oases and in the valleys. He eats the herbage which grows among the rocks and hills that alternate with the great sandy plains in all these countries. In passing from one of his scanty pasturages to another, he has long journeys to make across the sands, where, though he can find food here and there, there is no water. Providence has formed him with a structure adapted to this exigency, and by means of it he becomes extremely useful to man.

Scarcity of Water

The soldiers of Alexander did not take a sufficient supply of water, and were reduced, at one time, to great distress. They were relieved, the story says, by a rain, though rain is extremely unusual in the deserts. Alexander attributed this supply to the miraculous interposition of Heaven. They catch the rain, in such cases, with cloths, and afterward wring out the water; though in this instance, as the historians of that day say, the soldiers did not wait for this tardy method of supply, but the whole detachment held back their heads and opened their mouths, to catch the drops of rain as they fell.

Sandstorms in the Desert

There was another danger to which they were exposed in their march, more terrible even than the scarcity of water. It was that of being overwhelmed in the clouds of sand and dust which sometimes swept over the desert in gales of wind. These were called sandstorms. The fine sand flew, in such cases, in driving clouds, which filled the eyes and stopped the breath of the traveller, and finally buried his body under its drifts when he laid down to die. A large army of fifty thousand men, under a former Persian king, had been overwhelmed and destroyed in this way, some years before, in some of the Egyptian deserts. Alexander's soldiers had heard of this calamity, and they were threatened sometimes with the same fate. They, however, at length escaped all the dangers of the desert, and began to approach the green and fertile land of the Oasis.

Arrival at the Oasis – Magnificent Ceremonies – Return to Memphis

The change from the barren and dismal loneliness of the sandy plains to the groves and the villages, the beauty and the verdure of the Oasis, was delightful both to Alexander himself and to all his men. The priests at the great temple of Jupiter Ammon received them all with marks of great distinction and honour. The most solemn and magnificent ceremonies were performed, with offerings, oblations, and sacrifices. The priests, after conferring in secret with the god in the temple, came out with the annunciation that Alexander was indeed his son, and they paid him, accordingly, almost divine honours. He is supposed to have bribed them to do this by presents and pay. Alexander returned at length to Memphis, and in all his subsequent orders and decrees he styled himself Alexander king, son of Jupiter Ammon.

Alexander Jokes About His Divinity

But, though Alexander was thus willing to impress his ignorant soldiers with a mysterious veneration for his fictitious divinity, he was not deceived himself on the subject; he sometimes even made his pretensions to the divine character a subject of joke. For instance, they one day brought him in too little fire in the *focus*. The focus, or fireplace, used in Alexander's day was a small metallic stand, on which the fire was built. It was placed wherever convenient in the tent, and the smoke escaped above. They had put upon the focus too little fuel one day when they brought it in. Alexander asked the officer to let him have either some wood or some frankincense; they might consider him, he said, as a god or as a man, whichever they pleased, but he wished to be treated either like one or the other.

Founding of Alexandria

On his return from the Oasis Alexander carried forward his plan of building a city at the mouth of the Nile. He drew the plan, it is said, with his own hands. He superintended the constructions, and invited artisans and mechanics from all nations to come and reside in it. They accepted the invitation in great numbers, and the city soon became large, and wealthy, and powerful. It was intended as a commercial post, and the wisdom and sagacity which Alexander manifested in the selection of the site, is shown by the fact that the city rose immediately to the rank of the great seat of trade and commerce for all those shores, and has continued to hold that rank now for twenty centuries.

Island of Pharos – The Lighthouse

There was an island near the coast, opposite the city, called the island of Pharos. They built a most magnificent lighthouse upon one extremity of this island, which was considered, in those days, one of the wonders of the world. It was said to be five hundred feet high. This may have been an exaggeration. At any rate, it was celebrated throughout the world in its day, and its existence and its greatness made an impression on the human mind which has not yet been effaced. Pharos is the name for lighthouse, in many languages, to the present day.

Alexandria the Only Remaining Monument of Alexander's Greatness

In building the city of Alexandria, Alexander laid aside, for a time, his natural and proper character, and assumed a mode of action in strong contrast with the ordinary course of his life. He was, throughout most of his career, a destroyer. He roamed over the world to interrupt commerce, to break in upon and disturb the peaceful pursuits of industry, to batter down city walls, and burn dwellings, and kill men. This is the true vocation of a hero and a conqueror; but at the mouth of the Nile Alexander laid aside this character. He turned his energies to the work of planning means to do good. He constructed a port; he built warehouses; he provided accommodations and protection for merchants and artisans. The nations exchanged their commodities far more easily and extensively in consequence of these facilities, and the means of comfort and enjoyment were multiplied and increased in thousands and thousands of huts in the great cities of Egypt, and in the rural districts along the banks of the Nile. The good, too, which he thus commenced, has perpetuated itself. Alexandria has continued to fulfil its beneficent function for two thousand years. It is the only monument of his greatness which remains. Everything else which he accomplished perished when he died. How much better would it have been for the happiness of mankind, as well as for his own true fame and glory, if doing good had been the rule of his life instead of the exception.

Chapter IX
The Great Victory, BCE **331**

Alexander Makes Tyre His Rendezvous – Festivities

ALL THE WESTERN PART OF ASIA was now in Alexander's power. He was undisputed master of Asia Minor, Phoenicia, Judea and Egypt. He returned from Egypt to Tyre, leaving governors to rule in his name in all the conquered provinces. The injuries which had been done to Tyre, during the siege and at the assault, were repaired, and it was again a wealthy, powerful and prosperous city. Alexander rested and refreshed his army there, and spent some weeks in most splendid festivities and rejoicings. The princes and potentates of all the neighbouring countries assembled to partake of his hospitality, to be entertained by the games, plays, spectacles and feastings, and to unite in swelling his court and doing him honour. In a word, he was the general centre of attraction for all eyes, and the object of universal homage.

Alexander Prepares to March East

All this time, however, he was very far from being satisfied, or feeling that his work was done. Darius, whom he considered his great enemy, was still in the field unsubdued. He had retreated across the Euphrates, and was employed in assembling a vast collection of forces from all the Eastern nations which were under his sway, to meet Alexander in the final contest. Alexander therefore made arrangements at Tyre for the proper government of the various kingdoms and provinces which he had already conquered, and then began to prepare for marching eastward with the main body of his army.

The Captive Queens and Their Treatment

During all this time the ladies of Darius's family, who had been taken captive at Issus, had been retained in captivity, and made to accompany Alexander's army in its marches. Alexander refused to accede to any of the plans and propositions which Darius made and offered for the redemption of his wife and mother, but insisted on retaining them as his prisoners. He, however, treated them with respect and high consideration. He provided them with royal tents of great magnificence, and had them conveyed from place to place, when his army moved, with all the royal state to which they had been accustomed when in the court of Darius.

It has been generally thought a proof of nobleness of spirit and generosity in Alexander that he treated his captives in this manner. It would seem, however, that true generosity would have prompted the restoration of these unhappy and harmless prisoners to the husband and father who mourned their separation from him, and their cruel sufferings, with bitter grief. It is more probable, therefore, that policy, and a regard for his own aggrandizement, rather than compassion for the suffering, led him to honour his captive queens. It was a great glory to him, in a martial point of view, to have such trophies of his victory in his train; and, of course, the more highly he honoured the personages, the more glorious the trophy appeared. Accordingly, Alexander did everything in his power to magnify the importance of his royal captives, by the splendour of their retinue, and the pomp and pageantry with which he invested their movements.

Death of Stateira – Agony of Sisygambis

A short time after leaving Tyre, on the march eastward, Stateira, the wife of Darius, was taken suddenly ill and died during childbirth. The tidings were immediately brought to Alexander, and he repaired without delay to Sisygambis's tent. Sisygambis was the mother of Darius. She was in the greatest agony of grief. She was lying upon the floor of her tent, surrounded by the ladies of her court, and entirely overwhelmed with sorrow. Alexander did all in his power to calm and comfort her.

Grief of Darius

One of the officers of Queen Stateira's household made his escape from the camp immediately after his mistress's death, and fled across the country to Darius, to carry him the heavy tidings. Darius was overwhelmed with affliction. The officer, however, in farther interviews, gave him such an account of the kind and respectful treatment which the ladies had received from Alexander, during all the time of their captivity, as greatly to relieve his mind, and to afford him a high degree of comfort and consolation. He expressed a very strong sense of gratitude to Alexander for his generosity and kindness, and said that if his kingdom of Persia *must* be conquered, he sincerely wished that it might fall into the hands of such a conqueror as Alexander.

Alexander Crosses the Euphrates

The Tigris and the Euphrates are parallel streams, flowing through the heart of the western part of Asia toward the southeast, and emptying into the Persian Gulf. The country between these two rivers, which was extremely populous and fertile, was called Mesopotamia. Darius had collected an immense army here. The various detachments filled all the plains of Mesopotamia. Alexander turned his course a little northward, intending to pass the River Euphrates at a famous ancient crossing at Thapsacus. When he arrived at this place he found a small Persian army there. They, however, retired as he approached. Alexander built two bridges across the river, and passed his army safely over.

Darius Crosses the Tigris

In the meantime, Darius, with his enormous host, passed across the Tigris, and moved toward the northward, along the eastern side of the river. He had to cross the various branches of the Tigris as he advanced. At one of them, called the Lycus, there was a bridge. It took the vast host which Darius had collected *five days* to pass this bridge.

Alexander Crosses the Tigris

While Darius had been thus advancing to the northward into the latitude where he knew that Alexander must cross the rivers, Alexander himself, and his small but compact and fearless body of Grecian troops, were moving eastward, toward the same region to which Darius's line of march was tending. Alexander at length reached the Tigris. He was obliged to ford this stream. The banks were steep and the current was rapid, and the men were in great danger of being swept away. To prevent this danger, the ranks, as they advanced, linked their arms together, so that each man might be sustained by his comrades. They held their shields above their heads to keep them from the water. Alexander waded like the rest, though he kept in front, and reached the bank before the others. Standing there, he indicated to the advancing column, by gesticulation, where to land, the noise of the water being too great to allow his voice to be heard. To see him standing there, safely landed, and with an expression of confidence and triumph in his attitude and air, awakened fresh energy in the heart of every soldier in the columns which were crossing the stream.

Fording the River – The Passage Effected

Notwithstanding this encouragement, however, the passage of the troops and the landing on the bank produced a scene of great confusion. Many of the soldiers had tied up a portion of their clothes in bundles, which they held above their heads, together with their arms, as they waded along through the swift current of the stream. They, however, found it impossible to carry these bundles, but had to abandon them at last in order to save themselves, as they staggered along through deep and rapid water, and over a concealed bottom of slippery stones. Thousands of these bundles, mingled with spears, darts, and every other sort of weapon that would float, were swept down by the current, to impede and embarrass the men who were passing below.

At length, however, the men themselves succeeded in getting over in safety, though a large quantity of arms and of clothing was lost. There was no enemy upon the bank to oppose them. Darius could not, in fact, well meet and oppose Alexander in his attempt to cross the river, because he could not determine at what point he would probably make the attempt, in season to concentrate so large an army to oppose him. Alexander's troops, being a comparatively small and compact body, and being accustomed to move with great promptness and celerity, could easily evade any attempt of such an unwieldy mass of forces to oppose his crossing at any particular point upon the stream. At any rate, Darius did not make any such attempt, and Alexander had no difficulties to encounter in crossing the Tigris other than the physical obstacles presented by the current of the stream.

Plan of Darius – The Plain of Arbela

Darius's plan was, therefore, not to intercept Alexander on his march, but to choose some great and convenient battle-field, where he could collect his forces, and marshal them advantageously, and so await an attack there. He knew very well that his enemy would seek him out, wherever he was, and, consequently, that he might choose his position. He found such a field in an extensive plain at Gaugamela, not far from the city of Arbela. The spot has received historical immortality under the name of the plain of Arbela.

The Caltrop – Its Use in War

Darius was several days in concentrating his vast armies upon this plain. He constructed encampments; he leveled the inequalities which would interfere with the movements of his great bodies of cavalry; he guarded the approaches, too, as much as possible. There is a little instrument used in war called a *caltrop*. It consists of a small ball of iron, with several sharp points projecting from it one or two inches each way. If these instruments are thrown upon the ground at random, one of the points must necessarily be upward, and the horses that tread upon them are lamed and disabled at once. Darius caused caltrops to be scattered in the grass and along the roads, wherever the army of Alexander would be likely to approach his troops on the field of battle.

Eclipse of the Moon – Consternation of Alexander's Army

Alexander, having crossed the river, encamped for a day or two on the banks, to rest and refresh, and to rearrange his army. While here, the soldiers were one night thrown into consternation by an eclipse of the moon. Whenever an eclipse of the moon takes place, it is, of course, when the moon is full, so that the eclipse is always a sudden, and, among an ignorant people, an unexpected waning of the orb in the height of its splendour; and as such people know not the cause of the phenomenon, they are often extremely terrified. Alexander's soldiers were thrown into consternation by the eclipse. They considered it the manifestation of the displeasure of Heaven at their presumptuous daring in crossing such rivers, and penetrating to such a distance to invade the territories of another king.

Emotions Produced by An Eclipse – Its Sublimity

In fact, the men were predisposed to fear. Having wandered to a vast distance from home, having passed over such mountains and deserts, and now, at last, having crossed a deep and dangerous river, and thrown themselves into the immediate vicinity of a foe ten times as numerous as themselves, it was natural that they should feel some misgivings. And when, at night, impressed with the sense of solemnity which night always imparts to strange and novel scenes, they looked up to the bright round moon, pleased with the expression of cheerfulness and companionship which beams always in her light, to find her suddenly waning, changing her form, withdrawing her bright beams, and looking down upon them with a lurid and murky light, it was not surprising that they felt an emotion of terror. In fact, there is always an element of terror in the emotion excited by looking upon an eclipse, which an instinctive feeling of the heart inspires. It invests the spectacle with a solemn grandeur. It holds the spectator, however cultivated and refined, in silence while he gazes at it. It mingles with a scientific appreciation of the vastness of the movements and magnitudes by which the effect is produced, and while the one occupies the intellect, the other impresses the soul. The mind that has lost, through its philosophy, the power of feeling this emotion of awe in such scenes, has sunk, not risen. Its possessor has made himself inferior, not superior, to the rest of his species, by having paralysed one of his susceptibilities of pleasure. To him an eclipse is only curious and wonderful; to others it is sublime.

Measures Taken by Alexander to Allay the Fears of the Soldiers

The soldiers of Alexander were extremely terrified. A great panic spread throughout the encampment. Alexander himself, instead of attempting to allay their fears by reasoning, or treating them as of no importance, immediately gave the subject his most serious attention. He called together the soothsayers, and directed them to consult together, and let him know what this great phenomenon portended. This mere committing of the subject to the attention of the soothsayers had a great effect among all the soldiers of the army. It calmed them. It changed their agitation and terror into a feeling of suspense, in awaiting the answer of the soothsayers, which was far less painful and dangerous; and at length, when the answer came, it allayed their anxiety and fear altogether. The soothsayers said that the sun was on Alexander's side, and the moon on that of the Persians, and that this sudden waning of her light foreshadowed the defeat and destruction which the Persians were about to undergo. The army were satisfied with this decision, and were inspired with new confidence and ardour. It is often idle to attempt to oppose ignorance and absurdity by such feeble instruments as truth and reason, and the wisest managers of mankind have generally been most successful when their plan has been to counteract one folly by means of the influence of another.

Alexander Approaches the Persian Army

Alexander's army consisted of about fifty thousand men, with the phalanx in the centre. This army moved along down the eastern bank of the Tigris, the scouts pressing forward as far as possible in every direction in front of the main army, in order to get intelligence of the foe. It is in this way that two great armies *feel* after each other, as it were, like insects creeping over the ground, exploring the way before them with their *antennae*. At length, after three days' advance, the scouts came in with intelligence of the enemy. Alexander pressed forward with a detachment of his army to meet them. They proved to be, however, not the main body of Darius's army, but only a single corps of a thousand men, in advance of the rest. They retreated as Alexander approached. He, however, succeeded in capturing some horsemen, who gave the information that Darius had assembled his vast forces on the plain of Arbela, and was waiting there in readiness to give his advancing enemy battle.

Preparations For the Battle

Alexander halted his troops. He formed an encampment, and made arrangements for depositing his baggage there. He refreshed the men, examined and repaired their arms, and made the arrangements for battle. These operations consumed several days. At the end of that time, early one morning, long before day, the camp was in motion, and the columns, armed and equipped for immediate contest, moved forward.

Alexander Surveys the Persian Army

They expected to have reached the camp of Darius at daybreak, but the distance was greater than they had supposed. At length, however, the Macedonians, in their march, came upon the brow of a range of hills, from which they looked down upon numberless and endless lines of infantry and cavalry, and ranges after ranges of tents, which filled the plain. Here the army paused while Alexander examined the field, studying for a long time, and with great attention, the numbers and disposition of the enemy. They were four miles distant still, but the murmuring sounds of their voices and movements came to the ears of the Macedonians through the calm autumnal air.

Council of Officers – Number of the Armies

Alexander called the leading officers together, and held a consultation on the question whether to march down and attack the Persians on the plain that night, or to wait till the next day. Parmenio was in favour of a night attack, in order to surprise the enemy by coming upon them at an unexpected time. But Alexander said no. He was sure of victory. He had got his enemies all before him; they were fully in his power. He would, therefore, take no advantage, but would attack them fairly and in open day. Alexander had fifty thousand men; the Persians were variously estimated between five hundred thousand and a million. There is something sublime in the idea of such a pause, made by the Macedonian phalanx and its wings, on the slopes of the hills, suspending its attack upon ten times its number, to give the mighty mass of their enemies the chances of a fair and equal contest.

Alexander's Address

Alexander made congratulatory addresses to his soldiers on the occasion of their having now at last before them, what they had so long toiled and laboured to attain, the whole concentrated force of the Persian empire. They were now going to contend, not for single provinces and kingdoms, as heretofore, but for general empire; and the victory which they were about to achieve would place them on the summit of human glory. In all that he said on the subject, the unquestionable certainty of victory was assumed.

Parmenio and Alexander

Alexander completed his arrangements, and then retired to rest. He went to sleep – at least he appeared to do so. Early in the morning Parmenio arose, summoned the men to their posts and arranged everything for the march. He then went to Alexander's tent. Alexander was still asleep. He awoke him, and told him that all was ready. Parmenio expressed surprise at his sleeping so quietly at a time when such vast issues were at stake. 'You seem as calm,' said he, 'as if you had had the battle and gained the victory.' 'I have done so,' said Alexander. 'I consider the whole work done when we have gained access to Darius and his forces, and find him ready to give us battle.'

Alexander's Dress

Alexander soon appeared at the head of his troops. Of course, this day was one of the most important ones of his life, and one of the historians of the time has preserved an account of his dress as he went into battle. He wore a short tunic, girt close around him, and over it a linen breast-plate, strongly quilted. The belt by which the tunic was held was embossed with figures of beautiful workmanship. This belt was a present to him from some of the people of the conquered countries through which he had passed, and it was very much admired. He had a helmet upon his head, of polished steel, with a neck piece, also of steel, ornamented with precious stones. His helmet was surmounted with a white plume. His sword, which was a present to him from the King of Cyprus, was very light and slender, and of the most perfect temper. He carried, also, a shield and a lance, made in the best possible manner for use, not for display. Thus his dress corresponded with the character of his action. It was simple, compact, and whatever of value it possessed consisted in those substantial excellencies which would give the bearer the greatest efficiency on the field of battle.

War Elephants – The Phalanx

The Persians were accustomed to make use of elephants in their wars. They also had chariots, with scythes placed at the axles, which they were accustomed to drive among their enemies and mow them down. Alexander resorted to none of these contrivances. There was the phalanx – the terrible phalanx – advancing irresistibly either in one body or in detachments, with columns of infantry and flying troops of horsemen on the wings. Alexander relied simply on the strength, the courage, the energy and the calm and steady but resistless ardour of his men, arranging them in simple combinations, and leading them forward directly to their work.

Defeat of the Persians – Flight of Darius

The Macedonians cut their way through the mighty mass of their enemies with irresistible force. The elephants turned and fled. The foot soldiers seized the horses of some of the scythe-armed chariots and cut the traces. In respect to others, they opened to the right and left and let them pass through, when they were easily captured by the men in the rear. In the meantime, the phalanx pressed on, enjoying a great advantage in the level nature of the ground. The Persian troops were broken in upon and driven away wherever they were attacked. In a word, before night the whole mighty mass was scattering everywhere in confusion, except some hundreds of thousands left trampled upon and dead, or else writhing upon the ground, and groaning in their dying agonies. Darius himself fled. Alexander pursued him with a troop of horse as far as Arbela, which had been Darius's headquarters, and where he had deposited immense treasures. Darius had gone through and escaped when Alexander arrived at Arbela, but the city and the treasures fell into Alexander's hands.

Alexander Driven From the Field

Although Alexander had been so completely victorious over his enemies on the day of battle, and had maintained his ground against them with such invincible power, he was, nevertheless, a few days afterward, driven entirely off the field, and completely away from the region where the battle had been fought. What the living men, standing erect in arms, and full of martial vigour, could not do, was easily and effectually accomplished by their dead bodies corrupting on the plain. The corpses of three hundred thousand men, and an equal bulk of the bodies of elephants and horses, was too enormous a mass to be buried. It had to be abandoned; and the horrible effluvia and pestilence which it emitted drove all the inhabitants of the country away. Alexander marched his troops rapidly off the ground, leaving, as the direct result of the battle, a wide extent of country depopulated and desolate, with this vast mass of putrefaction and pestilence reigning in awful silence and solitude in the midst of it.

March to Babylon

Alexander went to Babylon. The governor of the city prepared to receive him as a conqueror. The people came out in throngs to meet him, and all the avenues of approach were crowded with spectators. All the city walls, too, were covered with men and women, assembled to witness the scene. As for Alexander himself, he was filled with pride and pleasure at thus arriving at the full accomplishment of his earliest and long-cherished dreams of glory.

Surrender of Susa – Plunder of the Palace

The great storehouse of the royal treasures of Persia was at Susa, a strong city east of Babylon. Susa was the winter residence of the Persian kings, as Ecbatana, further north, among the mountains, was their summer residence. There was a magnificent palace and a very strong citadel at Susa, and the treasures were kept in the citadel. It is said that in times of peace the Persian monarchs had been accustomed to collect coin, melt it down and cast the gold in earthen jars. The jars were afterward broken off from the gold, leaving the bullion in the form of the interior of the jars. An enormous amount of gold and silver, and of other treasures, had been thus collected. Alexander was aware of this depository before he advanced to meet Darius, and, on the day of the battle of Arbela, as soon as the victory was decided, he sent an officer from the very field to summon Susa to surrender. They obeyed the summons, and Alexander, soon after his great public entrance into Babylon, marched to Susa, and took possession of the vast stores of wealth accumulated there. The amount was enormous, both in quantity and value, and the seizing of it was a very magnificent act of plunder. In fact, it is probable that Alexander's slaughter of the Persian army at Arbela, and subsequent spoliation of Susa, constitute, taken together, the most gigantic case of murder and robbery which was ever committed by man; so that, in performing these deeds, the great hero attained at last to the glory of having perpetrated the grandest and most imposing of all human crimes. That these deeds were really crimes there can be no doubt, when we consider that Alexander did not pretend to have any other motive in this invasion than love of conquest, which is, in other words, love of violence and plunder. They are only technically shielded from being called crimes by the fact that the earth has no laws and no tribunals high enough to condemn such enormous burglaries as that of one quarter of the globe breaking violently and murderously in upon and robbing the other.

Besides the treasures, Alexander found also at Susa a number of trophies which had been brought by Xerxes from Greece; for Xerxes had invaded Greece some hundred years before Alexander's day, and had brought to Susa the spoils and the trophies of his victories. Alexander sent them all back to Greece again.

Pass of Susa – The Mountaineers

From Susa the conqueror moved on to Persepolis, the great Persian capital. On his march he had to pass through a defile of the mountains. The mountaineers had been accustomed to exact tribute here of all who passed, having a sort of right, derived from ancient usage, to the payment of a toll. They sent to Alexander when they heard that he was approaching, and informed him that he could not pass with his army without paying the customary toll. Alexander sent back word that he would meet them at the pass, and give them *their due*.

They understood this, and prepared to defend the pass. Some Persian troops joined them. They built walls and barricades across the narrow passages. They collected great stones on the brinks of precipices, and on the declivities of the mountains, to roll down upon the heads of their enemies. By these and every other means they attempted to stop Alexander's passage. But he had contrived to send detachments around by circuitous and precipitous paths, which even the mountaineers had deemed impracticable, and thus attack his enemies suddenly and unexpectedly from above their own positions. As usual, his plan succeeded. The mountaineers were driven away, and the conqueror advanced toward the great Persian capital.

Chapter X
The Death of Darius, BCE 330

March to Persepolis – Reckless Cruelty

ALEXANDER'S MARCH FROM SUSA to Persepolis was less a march than a triumphal progress. He felt the pride and elation so naturally resulting from success very strongly. The moderation and forbearance which had characterized him in his earlier years, gradually disappeared as he became great and powerful. He was intoxicated with his success. He became haughty, vain, capricious and cruel. As he approached Persepolis, he conceived the idea that, as this city was the capital and centre of the Persian monarchy, and, as such, the point from which had emanated all the Persian hostility to Greece, he owed it some signal retribution. Accordingly, although the inhabitants made no opposition to his entrance, he marched in with the phalanx formed, and gave the soldiers liberty to kill and plunder as they pleased.

The Banquet – Thais Proposes to Burn the Persian Palace

There was another very striking instance of the capricious recklessness now beginning to appear in Alexander's character, which occurred soon after he had taken possession of Persepolis. He was giving a great banquet to his friends, the officers of the army, and to Persians of distinction among those who had submitted to him. There was, among other women at this banquet, a very beautiful and accomplished female named Thais. Alexander made her his favourite and companion, though she was not his wife. Thais did all in her power to captivate and please Alexander during the feast by her vivacity, her wit, her adroit attentions to him and the display of her charms, and at length, when he himself, as well as the other guests, were excited with wine, she asked him to allow her to have the pleasure of going herself and setting fire, with her own hands, to the great palace of the Persian kings in the city. Thais was a native of Attica in Greece, a kingdom of which Athens was the capital. Xerxes, who had built the great palace of Persepolis, had formerly invaded Greece and had burned Athens, and now Thais desired to burn his palace in Persepolis, to gratify her revenge, by making of its conflagration an evening spectacle to entertain the Macedonian party after their supper. Alexander agreed to the proposal, and the whole company moved forward. Taking the torches from the banqueting halls, they sallied forth, alarming the city with their shouts, and with the flashing of the lights they bore. The plan of Thais was carried fully into effect, every half-intoxicated guest assisting, by putting fire to the immense pile wherever they could get access to it. They performed the barbarous deed with shouts of vengeance and exultation.

Conflagration of the Palace

There is, however, something very solemn and awful in a great conflagration at night, and very few incendiaries can gaze upon the fury of the lurid and frightful flames which they have caused to ascend without some misgivings and some remorse. Alexander was sobered by the grand and sublime, but terrible spectacle. He was awed by it. He repented. He ordered the fire to be extinguished; but it was too late. The palace was destroyed, and one new blot, which has never since been effaced, was cast upon Alexander's character and fame.

Olympias

And yet, notwithstanding these increasing proofs of pride and cruelty, which were beginning to be developed, Alexander still preserved some of the early traits of character which had made him so great a favourite in the commencement of his career. He loved his mother, and sent her presents continually from the treasures which were falling all the time into his possession. She was a woman of a proud, imperious and ungovernable character, and she made Antipater, whom Alexander had left in command in Macedon, infinite trouble. She wanted to exercise the powers of government herself, and was continually urging this. Alexander would not comply with these wishes, but he paid her personally every attention in his power, and bore all her invectives and reproaches with great patience and good humour. At one time he received a long letter from Antipater, full of complaints against her; but Alexander, after reading it, said that they were heavy charges it was true, but that a single one of his mother's tears would outweigh ten thousand such accusations.

Her Letters to Alexander

Olympias used to write very frequently to Alexander, and in these letters she would criticise and discuss his proceedings, and make comments upon the characters and actions of his generals. Alexander kept these letters very secret, never showing them to anyone. One day, however, when he was reading one of these letters, Hephaestion, the personal friend and companion who has been already several times mentioned, came up, half playfully, and began to look over his shoulder. Alexander went on, allowing him to read, and then, when the letter was finished he took the signet ring from his finger and pressed it upon Hephaestion's lips, a signal for silence and secrecy.

Alexander's Kindness to Sisygambis

Alexander was very kind to Sisygambis, the mother of Darius, and also to Darius's children. He would not give these unhappy captives their liberty, but in every other respect he treated them with the greatest possible kindness and consideration. He called Sisygambis mother, loaded her with presents – presents, it is true, which he had plundered from her son, but to which it was considered, in those days, that he had acquired a just and perfect title. When he reached Susa, he established Sisygambis and the children there in great state. This had been their usual residence in most seasons of the year, when not at Persepolis, so that here they were, as it were, at home. Ecbatana was, as has been already mentioned, further north, among the mountains. After the battle of Arbela, while Alexander marched to Babylon and to Susa, Darius had fled to Ecbatana, and was now there, his family being thus at one of the royal palaces under the command of the conqueror, and he himself independent, but insecure, in the other. He had with him about forty thousand men, who still remained faithful to his fallen fortunes. Among these were several thousand Greeks, whom he had collected in Asia Minor and other Grecian countries, and whom he had attached to his service by means of pay.

Darius at Ecbatana – His Speech to His Army

He called the officers of his army together, and explained to them the determination that he had come to in respect to his future movements. 'A large part of those,' said he, 'who formerly served as officers of my government have abandoned me in my adversity, and gone over to Alexander's side. They have surrendered to him the towns, and citadels, and provinces which I intrusted to their fidelity. You alone remain faithful and true. As for myself, I might yield to the conqueror, and have him assign to me some province or kingdom to govern as his subordinate; but I will never submit to such a degradation. I can die in the struggle, but never will yield. I will wear no crown which another puts upon my brow, nor give up my right to reign over the empire of my ancestors till I give up my life. If you agree with me in this determination, let us act energetically upon it. We have it in our power to terminate the injuries we are suffering, or else to avenge them.'

Conspiracy Against Darius

The army responded most cordially to this appeal. They were ready, they said, to follow him wherever he should lead. All this apparent enthusiasm, however, was very delusive and unsubstantial. A general named Bessus, combining with some other officers in the army, conceived the plan of seizing Darius and making him a prisoner, and then taking command of the army himself. If Alexander should pursue him, and be likely to overtake and conquer him, he then thought that, by giving up Darius as a prisoner, he could stipulate for liberty and safety, and perhaps great rewards, both for himself and for those who acted with him. If, on the other hand, they should succeed in increasing their own forces so as to make head against Alexander, and finally to drive him away, then Bessus was to usurp the throne, and dispose of Darius by assassinating him, or imprisoning him for life in some remote and solitary castle.

Bessus and His Confederates

Bessus communicated his plans, very cautiously at first, to the leading officers of the army. The Greek soldiers were not included in the plot. They, however, heard and saw enough to lead them to suspect what was in preparation. They warned Darius, and urged him to rely upon them more than he had done; to make them his body-guard; and to pitch his tent in their part of the encampment. But Darius declined these proposals. He would not, he said, distrust and abandon his countrymen, who were his natural protectors, and put himself in the hands of strangers. He would not betray and desert his friends in anticipation of their deserting and betraying him.

Advance of Alexander – The Caspian Gates

In the meantime, as Alexander advanced toward Ecbatana, Darius and his forces retreated from it toward the eastward, through the great tract of country lying south of the Caspian Sea. There is a mountainous region here, with a steep narrow pass traversing it, through which it would be necessary for Darius to pass. This defile was called the Caspian Gates, the name referring to rocks on each side. The marching of an army through a narrow and dangerous pass like this always causes detention and delay, and Alexander hastened forward in hopes to overtake Darius before he should reach it. He advanced with such speed that only the strongest and most robust of his army could keep up. Thousands, worn out with exertion and toil, were left behind, and many of the horses sank down by the road side, exhausted with heat and fatigue, to die. Alexander pressed desperately on with all who were able to follow.

Foraging Parties

It was all in vain, however; it was too late when he arrived at the pass. Darius had gone through with all his army. Alexander stopped to rest his men, and to allow time for those behind to come up. He then went on for a couple of days, when he encamped, in order to send out foraging parties — that is to say, small detachments, dispatched to explore the surrounding country in search of grain and other food for the horses. Food for the horses of an army being too bulky to be transported far, has to be collected day by day from the neighbourhood of the line of march.

While halting for these foraging parties to return, a Persian nobleman came into the camp, and informed Alexander that Darius and the forces accompanying him were encamped about two days' march in advance, but that Bessus was in command – the conspiracy having been successful, and Darius having been deposed and made a prisoner. The Greeks, who had adhered to their fidelity, finding that all the army were combined against them, and that they were not strong enough to resist, had abandoned the Persian camp, and had retired to the mountains, where they were awaiting the result.

The Pursuit Continued

Alexander determined to set forward immediately in pursuit of Bessus and his prisoner. He did not wait for the return of the foraging parties. He selected the ablest and most active, both of foot soldiers and horsemen, ordered them to take two days' provisions, and then set forth with them that very evening. The party pressed on all that night, and the next day till noon. They halted till evening, and then set forth again. Very early the next morning they arrived at the encampment which the Persian nobleman had described. They found the remains of the campfires, and all the marks usually left upon a spot which has been used as the bivouac of an army. The army itself, however, was gone.

Alexander Stops to Rest His Army

The pursuers were now too much fatigued to go any further without rest. Alexander remained here, accordingly, through the day, to give his men and his horses refreshment and repose. That night they set forward again, and the next day at noon they arrived at another encampment of the Persians, which they had left scarcely twenty-four hours before. The officers of Alexander's army were excited and animated in the highest degree, as they found themselves thus drawing so near to the great object of their pursuit. They were ready for any exertions, any privation and fatigue, any measures, however extraordinary, to accomplish their end.

Want of Water – The Pursuit Grows More Exciting

Alexander inquired of the inhabitants of the place whether there were not some shorter road than the one along which the enemy were moving. There was one crossroad, but it led through a desolate and desert tract of land, destitute of water. In the march of an army, as the men are always heavily loaded with arms and provisions, and water cannot be carried, it is always considered essential to choose routes which will furnish supplies of water by the way. Alexander, however, disregarded this consideration here, and prepared at once to push into the crossroad with a small detachment. He had been now two years advancing from Macedon into the heart of Asia, always in quest of Darius as his great opponent and enemy. He had conquered his armies, taken his cities, plundered his palaces and made himself master of his whole realm. Still, so long as Darius himself remained at liberty and in the field, no victories could be considered as complete. To capture Darius himself would be the last and crowning act of his conquest. He had now been pursuing him for eighteen hundred miles, advancing slowly from province to province, and from kingdom to kingdom. During all this time the strength of his flying foe had been wasting away. His armies had been broken up, his courage and hope had gradually failed, while the animation and hope of the pursuer had been gathering fresh and increasing strength from his successes, and were excited to wild enthusiasm now, as the hour for the final consummation of all his desires seemed to be drawing nigh.

Guides Employed

Guides were ordered to be furnished by the inhabitants, to show the detachment the way across the solitary and desert country. The detachment was to consist of horsemen entirely, that they might advance with the utmost celerity. To get as efficient a corps as possible, Alexander dismounted five hundred of the cavalry, and gave their horses to five hundred men – officers and others – selected for their strength and courage from among the foot soldiers. All were ambitious of being designated for this service. Besides the honour of being so selected, there was an intense excitement, as usual toward the close of a chase, to arrive at the end.

The Persians Overtaken

This body of horsemen were ready to set out in the evening. Alexander took the command, and, following the guides, they trotted off in the direction which the guides indicated. They travelled all night. When the day dawned, they saw, from an elevation to which they had attained, the body of the Persian troops moving at a short distance before them, foot soldiers, chariots and horsemen pressing on together in great confusion and disorder.

Murder of Darius

As soon as Bessus and his company found that their pursuers were close upon them, they attempted at first to hurry forward, in the vain hope of still effecting their escape. Darius was in a chariot. They urged this chariot on, but it moved heavily. Then they concluded to abandon it, and they called upon Darius to mount a horse and ride off with them, leaving the rest of the army and the baggage to its fate. But Darius refused. He said he would rather trust himself in the hands of Alexander than in those of such traitors as they. Rendered desperate by their situation, and exasperated by this reply, Bessus and his confederates thrust their spears into Darius's body, as he sat in his chariot, and then galloped away. They divided into different parties, each taking a different road. Their object in doing this was to increase their chances of escape by confusing Alexander in his plans for pursuing them. Alexander pressed on toward the ground which the enemy were abandoning, and sent off separate detachments after the various divisions of the flying army.

Sufferings of Darius – Treachery of Friends

In the meantime, Darius remained in his chariot wounded and bleeding. He was worn out and exhausted, both in body and mind, by his complicated sufferings and sorrows. His kingdom lost; his family in captivity; his beloved wife in the grave, where the sorrows and sufferings of separation from her husband had borne her; his cities sacked; his palaces and treasures plundered; and now he himself, in the last hour of his extremity, abandoned and betrayed by all in whom he had placed his confidence and trust, his heart sunk within him in despair. At such a time the soul turns from traitorous friends to an open foe with something like a feeling of confidence and attachment. Darius's exasperation against Bessus was so intense, that his hostility to Alexander became a species of friendship in comparison. He felt that Alexander was a sovereign like himself, and would have some sympathy and fellow-feeling for a sovereign's misfortunes. He thought, too, of his mother, his wife and his children, and the kindness with which Alexander had treated them went to his heart. He lay there, accordingly, faint and bleeding in his chariot, and looking for the coming of Alexander as for that of a protector and friend, the only one to whom he could now look for any relief in the extremity of his distress.

Darius Found

The Macedonians searched about in various places, thinking it possible that in the sudden dispersion of the enemy Darius might have been left behind. At last the chariot in which he was lying was found. Darius was in it, pierced with spears. The floor of the chariot was covered with blood. They raised him a little, and he spoke. He called for water.

Darius Calls for Water

Men wounded and dying on the field of battle are tormented always with an insatiable and intolerable thirst, the manifestations of which constitute one of the greatest horrors of the scene. They cry piteously to all who pass to bring them water, or else to kill them. They crawl along the ground to get at the canteens of their dead companions, in hopes to find, remaining in them, some drops to drink; and if there is a little brook meandering through the battlefield, its bed gets filled and choked up with the bodies of those who crawled there, in their agony, to quench their horrible thirst, and die. Darius was suffering this thirst. It bore down and silenced, for the time, every other suffering, so that his first cry, when his enemies came around him with shouts of exultation, was not for his life, not for mercy, not for relief from the pain and anguish of his wounds – he begged them to give him some water.

The Interpreter

He spoke through an interpreter. The interpreter was a Persian prisoner whom the Macedonian army had taken sometime before, and who had learned the Greek language in the Macedonian camp. Anticipating some occasion for his services, they had brought him with them now, and it was through him that Darius called for water. A Macedonian soldier went immediately to get some. Others hurried away in search of Alexander, to bring him to the spot where the great object of his hostility, and of his long and protracted pursuit, was dying.

Darius's Message to Alexander

Darius received the drink. He then said that he was extremely glad that they had an interpreter with them, who could understand him, and bear his message to Alexander. He had been afraid that he should have had to die without being able to communicate what he had to say. 'Tell Alexander,' said he, then, 'that I feel under the strongest obligations to him which I can now never repay, for his kindness to my wife, my mother, and my children. He not only spared their lives, but treated them with the greatest consideration and care, and did all in his power to make them happy. The last feeling in my heart is gratitude to him for these favours. I hope now that he will go on prosperously, and finish his conquests as triumphantly as he has begun them.' He would have made one last request, he added, if he had thought it necessary, and that was, that Alexander would pursue the traitor Bessus, and avenge the murder he had committed; but he was sure that Alexander would do this of his own accord, as the punishment of such treachery was an object of common interest for every king.

Affecting Scene

Darius then took Polystratus, the Macedonian who had brought him the water, by the hand, saying, 'Give Alexander thy hand as I now give thee mine; it is the pledge of my gratitude and affection.'

Alexander's Grief at Darius's Death

Darius was too weak to say much more. They gathered around him, endeavouring to sustain his strength until Alexander should arrive; but it was all in vain. He sank gradually, and soon ceased to breathe. Alexander came up a few minutes after all was over. He was at first shocked at the spectacle before him, and then overwhelmed with grief. He wept bitterly. Some compunctions of conscience may have visited his heart at seeing thus before him the ruin he had made. Darius had never injured him or done him any wrong, and yet here he lay, hunted to death by a persevering and relentless hostility, for which his conqueror had no excuse but his innate love of dominion over his fellow-men. Alexander spread his own military cloak over the dead body. He immediately made arrangements for having the body embalmed, and then sent it to Susa, for Sisygambis, in a very costly coffin, and with a procession of royal magnificence. He sent it to her that she might have the satisfaction of seeing it deposited in the tombs of the Persian kings. What a present! The killer of a son sending the dead body, in a splendid coffin, to the mother, as a token of respectful regard!

Crossing the Oxus – Capture of the Traitor Bessus

Alexander pressed on to the northward and eastward in pursuit of Bessus, who had soon collected the scattered remains of his army, and was doing his utmost to get into a posture of defence. He did not, however, overtake him till he had crossed the Oxus, a large river flowing to the northward and westward into the Caspian Sea. He had great difficulty in crossing this river, as it was too deep to be forded, and the banks and bottom were so sandy and yielding that he could not make the foundations of bridges stand. He accordingly made floats and rafts, which were supported by skins made buoyant by inflation, or by being stuffed with straw and hay. After getting his army, which had been in the meantime greatly re-enforced and strengthened, across this river, he moved on. The generals under Bessus, finding all hope of escape failing them, resolved on betraying him as he had betrayed his commander. They sent word to Alexander that if he would send forward a small force where they should indicate, they would give up Bessus to his hands. Alexander did so, intrusting the command to an officer named Ptolemy. Ptolemy found Bessus in a small walled town whither he had fled for refuge, and easily took him prisoner. He sent back word to Alexander that Bessus was at his disposal, and asked for orders. The answer was, 'Put a rope around his neck and send him to me.'

When the wretched prisoner was brought into Alexander's presence, Alexander demanded of him how he could have been so base as to have seized, bound, and at last murdered his kinsman and benefactor. It is a curious instance in proof of the permanence and stability of the great characteristics of human nature, through all the changes of civilization and lapses of time, that Bessus gave the same answer that wrongdoers almost always give when brought to account for their wrongs. He laid the fault upon his accomplices and friends. It was not his act, it was theirs.

Mutilation of Bessus – He is Sent to Sisygambis

Alexander ordered him to be publicly scourged; then he caused his face to be mutilated in a manner customary in those days, when a tyrant wished to stamp upon his victim a perpetual mark of infamy. In this condition, and with a mind in an agony of suspense and fear at the thought of worse tortures which he knew were to come, Alexander sent him as a second present to Sisygambis, to be dealt with, at Susa, as her revenge might direct. She inflicted upon him the most extreme tortures, and finally, when satiated with the pleasure of seeing him suffer, the story is that they chose four very elastic trees, growing at a little distance from each other, and bent down the tops of them toward the central point between them. They fastened the exhausted and dying Bessus to these trees, one limb of his body to each, and then releasing the stems from their confinement, they flew upward, tearing the body asunder, each holding its own disservered portion, as if in triumph, far over the heads of the multitude assembled to witness the spectacle.

Chapter XI
Deterioration of Character, BCE 329

Alexander at the Summit of His Ambition – Sad Changes

ALEXANDER WAS NOW TWENTY-SIX years of age. He had accomplished fully the great objects which had been the aim of his ambition. Darius was dead, and he was himself the undisputed master of all western Asia. His wealth was almost boundless. His power was supreme over what was, in his view, the whole known world. But, during the process of rising to this ascendency, his character was sadly changed.

He lost the simplicity, the temperance, the moderation and the sense of justice which characterized his early years. He adopted the dress and the luxurious manners of the Persians. He lived in the palaces of the Persian kings, imitating all their state and splendour. He became very fond of convivial entertainments and of wine, and (according to some) often drank to excess. He provided himself a harem of three hundred and sixty young females, in whose company he spent his time, giving himself up to every form of vice and dissipation. In a word, he was no longer the same man. The decision, the energy of character, the steady pursuit of great ends by prudence, forethought, patient effort and self-denial, all disappeared; nothing now seemed to interest him but banquets, carousals, parties of pleasure and whole days and nights spent in dissipation and vice.

His Officers Became Estranged

This state of things was a great cause of mortification and chagrin to the officers of his army. Many of them were older than himself, and better able to resist these temptations to luxury, unmanly pastimes and vice. They therefore remained firm in their original simplicity and integrity, and after some respectful but ineffectual remonstrances, they stood aloof, alienated from their commander in heart, and condemning very strongly, among themselves, his wickedness and folly.

On the other hand, many of the *younger* officers followed Alexander's example, and became as vain, irregular and as fond of vicious indulgence as he. But then, though they joined him in his pleasures, there was no strong bond of union between him and them. The tie which binds mere companions in pleasure together is always very slight and frail. Thus Alexander gradually lost the confidence and affection of his old friends, and gained no new ones. His officers either disapproved his conduct, and were distant and cold, or else joined him in his dissipation and vice, without feeling any real respect for his character, or being bound to him by any principle of fidelity.

Character of Parmenio – His Services to Alexander

Parmenio and his son Philotas were, respectively, striking examples of these two kinds of character. Parmenio was an old general, now considerably advanced in life. He had served, as has already been stated, under Philip, Alexander's father, and had acquired great experience and great fame before Alexander succeeded to the throne. During the whole of Alexander's career Parmenio had been his principal lieutenant general, and he had always placed his greatest reliance upon him in all trying emergencies. He was cool, calm, intrepid, sagacious. He held Alexander back from many rash enterprises, and was the efficient means of his accomplishing most of his plans. It is the custom among all nations to give kings the glory of all that is effected by their generals and officers; and the writers of those days would, of course, in narrating the exploits of the Macedonian army, exaggerate the share which Alexander had in their performances, and underrate those of Parmenio. But in modern times, many impartial readers, in reviewing calmly these events, think that there is reason to doubt whether Alexander, if he had set out on his great expedition without Parmenio, would have succeeded at all.

Parmenio's Son, Philotas – His Dissolute Character

Philotas was the son of Parmenio, but he was of a very different character. The difference was one which is very often, in all ages of the world, to be observed between those who *inherit* greatness and those who acquire it for themselves. We see the same analogy reigning at the present day, when the sons of the wealthy, who are *born* to fortune, substitute pride, arrogance and vicious self-indulgence and waste for the modesty, prudence and virtue of their sires, by means of which the fortune was acquired. Philotas was proud, boastful, extravagant and addicted, like Alexander his master, to every species of indulgence and dissipation. He was universally hated. His father, out of patience with his haughty airs, his boastings and his pomp and parade, advised him, one day, to 'make himself less.' But Parmenio's prudent advice to his son was thrown away. Philotas spoke of himself as Alexander's great reliance. 'What would Philip have been or have done,' said he, 'without my father Parmenio? and what would Alexander have been or have done, without me?' These things were reported to Alexander, and thus the mind of each was filled with suspicion, fear and hatred toward the other.

Conspiracies

Courts and camps are always the scenes of conspiracy and treason, and Alexander was continually hearing of conspiracies and plots formed against him. The strong sentiment of love and devotion with which he inspired all around him at the commencement of his career, was now gone, and his generals and officers were continually planning schemes to depose him from the power which he seemed no longer to have the energy to wield; or, at least, Alexander was continually suspecting that such plans were formed, and he was kept in a continual state of uneasiness and anxiety in discovering and punishing them.

Plot of Dymnus

At last a conspiracy occurred in which Philotas was implicated. Alexander was informed one day that a plot had been formed to depose and destroy him; that Philotas had been made acquainted with it by a friend of Alexander's, in order that he might make it known to the king; that he had neglected to do so, thus making it probable that he was himself in league with the conspirators. Alexander was informed that the leader and originator of this conspiracy was one of his generals named Dymnus.

Dymnus Destroys Himself

He immediately sent an officer to Dymnus to summon him into his presence. Dymnus appeared to be struck with consternation at this summons. Instead of obeying it, he drew his sword, thrust it into his own heart, and fell dead upon the ground.

Philotas Suspected

Alexander then sent for Philotas, and asked him if it was indeed true that he had been informed of this conspiracy, and had neglected to make it known.

Philotas replied that he had been told that such a plot was formed, but that he did not believe it; that such stories were continually invented by the malice of evil-disposed men, and that he had not considered the report which came to his ears as worthy of any attention. He was, however, now convinced, by the terror which Dymnus had manifested, and by his suicide, that all was true, and he asked Alexander's pardon for not having taken immediate measures for communicating promptly the information he had received.

Alexander gave him his hand, said that he was convinced that he was innocent, and had acted as he did from disbelief in the existence of the conspiracy, and not from any guilty participation in it. So Philotas went away to his tent.

The Council of Officers – Philotas Accused

Alexander, however, did not drop the subject here. He called a council of his ablest and best friends and advisers, consisting of the principal officers of his army, and laid the facts before them. They came to a different conclusion from his in respect to the guilt of Philotas. They believed him implicated in the crime, and demanded his trial. Trial in such a case, in those days, meant putting the accused to the torture, with a view of forcing him to confess his guilt.

Alexander yielded to this proposal. Perhaps he had secretly instigated it. The advisers of kings and conquerors, in such circumstances as this, generally have the sagacity to discover what advice will be agreeable. At all events, Alexander followed the advice of his counsellors, and made arrangements for arresting Philotas on that very evening.

Arrest of Philotas

These circumstances occurred at a time when the army was preparing for a march, the various generals lodging in tents pitched for the purpose. Alexander placed extra guards in various parts of the encampment, as if to impress the whole army with a sense of the importance and solemnity of the occasion. He then sent officers to the tent of Philotas, late at night, to arrest him. The officers found their unhappy victim asleep. They awoke him, and made known their errand. Philotas arose, and obeyed the summons, dejected and distressed, aware, apparently, that his destruction was impending.

The next morning Alexander called together a large assembly, consisting of the principal and most important portions of the army, to the number of several thousands. They came together with an air of impressive solemnity, expecting, from the preliminary preparations, that business of very solemn moment was to come before them, though they knew not what it was.

The Body of Dymnus – Alexander's Address to the Army

These impressions of awe and solemnity were very much increased by the spectacle which first met the eyes of the assembly after they were convened. This spectacle was that of the dead body of Dymnus, bloody and ghastly, which Alexander ordered to be brought in and exposed to view. The death of Dymnus had been kept a secret, so that the appearance of his body was an unexpected as well as a shocking sight. When the first feeling of surprise and wonder had a little subsided, Alexander explained to the assembly the nature of the conspiracy, and the circumstances connected with the self-execution of one of the guilty participators in it. The spectacle of the body, and the statement of the king, produced a scene of great and universal excitement in the assembly, and this excitement was raised to the highest pitch by the announcement which Alexander now made, that he had reason to believe that Philotas and his father Parmenio, officers who had enjoyed his highest favour, and in whom he had placed the most unbounded confidence, were the authors and originators of the whole design.

Philotas Brought to Trial

He then ordered Philotas to be brought in. He came guarded as a criminal, with his hands tied behind him, and his head covered with a coarse cloth. He was in a state of great dejection and despondency. It is true that he was brought forward for trial, but he knew very well that trial meant torture, and that there was no hope for him as to the result. Alexander said that he would leave the accused to be dealt with by the assembly, and withdrew.

Defense of Philotas – He is Put to the Torture

The authorities of the army, who now had the proud and domineering spirit which had so long excited their hatred and envy completely in their power, listened for a time to what Philotas had to say in his own justification. He showed that there was no evidence whatever against him, and appealed to their sense of justice not to condemn him on mere vague surmises. In reply, they decided to put him to the torture. There was no evidence, it was true, and they wished, accordingly, to supply its place by his own confession, extorted by pain. Of course, his most inveterate and implacable enemies were appointed to conduct the operation. They put Philotas upon the rack. The rack is an instrument of wheels and pulleys, into which the victim is placed, and his limbs and tendons are stretched by it in a manner which produces most excruciating pain.

Philotas bore the beginning of his torture with great resolution and fortitude. He made no complaint, he uttered no cry: this was the signal to his executioners to increase the tension and the agony. Of course, in such a trial as this, there was no question of guilt or innocence at issue. The only question was, which could stand out the longest, his enemies in witnessing horrible sufferings, or he himself in enduring them. In this contest the unhappy Philotas was vanquished at last. He begged them to release him from the rack, saying he would confess whatever they required, on condition of being allowed to die in peace.

Confession of Philotas – He is Stoned to Death

They accordingly released him, and, in answer to their questions, he confessed that he himself and his father were involved in the plot. He said yes to various other inquiries relating to the circumstances of the conspiracy, and to the guilt of various individuals whom those that managed the torture had suspected, or who, at any rate, they wished to have condemned. The answers of Philotas to all these questions were written down, and he was himself sentenced to be stoned. The sentence was put in execution without any delay.

Parmenio Condemned to Death

During all this time Parmenio was in Media, in command of a very important part of Alexander's army. It was decreed that he must die; but some careful management was necessary to secure his execution while he was at so great a distance, and at the head of so great a force. The affair had to be conducted with great secrecy as well as dispatch. The plan adopted was as follows:

Mission of Polydamas

There was a certain man, named Polydamas, who was regarded as Parmenio's particular friend. Polydamas was commissioned to go to Media and see the execution performed. He was selected, because it was supposed that if any enemy, or a stranger, had been sent, Parmenio would have received him with suspicion or at least with caution, and kept himself on his guard. They gave Polydamas several letters to Parmenio, as if from his friends, and to one of them they attached the seal of his son Philotas, the more completely to deceive the unhappy father. Polydamas was eleven days on his journey into Media. He had letters to Cleander, the governor of the province of Media, which contained the king's warrant for Parmenio's execution. He arrived at the house of Cleander in the night. He delivered his letters, and they together concerted the plans for carrying the execution into effect.

Precautions

After having taken all the precautions necessary, Polydamas went, with many attendants accompanying him, to the quarters of Parmenio. The old general, for he was at this time eighty years of age, was walking in his grounds. Polydamas being admitted, ran up to accost him, with great appearance of cordiality and friendship. He delivered to him his letters, and Parmenio read them. He seemed much pleased with their contents, especially with the one which had been written in the name of his son. He had no means of detecting the imposture, for it was very customary in those days for letters to be written by secretaries, and to be authenticated solely by the seal.

Brutal Murder of Parmenio

Parmenio was much pleased to get good tidings from Alexander, and from his son, and began conversing upon the contents of the letters, when Polydamas, watching his opportunity, drew forth a dagger which he had concealed upon his person, and plunged it into Parmenio's side. He drew it forth immediately and struck it at his throat. The attendants rushed on at this signal, and thrust their swords again and again into the fallen body until it ceased to breathe.

The death of Parmenio and of his son in this violent manner, when, too, there was so little evidence of their guilt, made a very general and a very unfavourable impression in respect to Alexander; and not long afterward another case occurred, in some respects still more painful, as it evinced still more strikingly that the mind of Alexander, which had been in his earlier days filled with such noble and lofty sentiments of justice and generosity, was gradually getting to be under the supreme dominion of selfish and ungovernable passions: it was the case of Kleitus.

Story of Kleitus – He Saves Alexander's Life

Kleitus the Black was a very celebrated general of Alexander's army, and a great favourite with the king. He was the brother of Alexander's childhood nurse, and he had, in fact, on one occasion saved Alexander's life. It was at the battle of the Granicus. Alexander had exposed himself in the thickest of the combat, and was surrounded by enemies. The sword of one of them was actually raised over his head, and would have fallen and killed him on the spot, if Kleitus had not rushed forward and cut the man down just at the instant when he was about striking the blow. Such acts of fidelity and courage as this had given Alexander great confidence in Kleitus. It happened, shortly after the death of Parmenio, that the governor of one of the most important provinces of the empire resigned his post. Alexander appointed Kleitus to fill the vacancy.

The evening before his departure to take charge of his government, Alexander invited him to a banquet, made, partly at least, in honour of his elevation. Kleitus and the other guests assembled. They drank wine, as usual, with great freedom. Alexander became excited, and began to speak, as he was now often accustomed to do, boastingly of his own exploits, and to disparage those of his father Philip in comparison.

Services of Kleitus

Men half intoxicated are very prone to quarrel, and not the less so for being excellent friends when sober. Kleitus had served under Philip. He was now an old man, and, like other old men, was very tenacious of the glory that belonged to the exploits of his youth. He was very restless and uneasy at hearing Alexander claim for himself the merit of his father Philip's victory at Chaeronea, and began to murmur something to those who sat next to him about kings claiming and getting a great deal of glory which did not belong to them.

Occurrences at the Banquet

Alexander asked what it was that Kleitus said. No one replied. Kleitus, however, went on talking, speaking more and more audibly as he became gradually more and more excited. He praised the character of Philip, and applauded his military exploits, saying that they were far superior to any of the enterprises of *their* day. The different parties at the table took up the subject, and began to dispute, the old men taking the part of Philip and former days, and the younger defending Alexander. Kleitus became more and more excited. He praised Parmenio, who had been Philip's greatest general, and began to impugn the justice of his late condemnation and death.

Kleitus Reproaches Alexander – Alexander's Rage

Alexander retorted and Kleitus, rising from his seat, and losing now all self-command, reproached him with severe and bitter words. 'Here is the hand,' said he, extending his arm, 'that saved your life at the battle of the Granicus, and the fate of Parmenio shows what sort of gratitude and what rewards faithful servants are to expect at your hands.' Alexander, burning with rage, commanded Kleitus to leave the table. Kleitus obeyed, saying, as he moved away, 'He is right not to bear freeborn men at his table who can only tell him the truth. He is right. It is fitting for him to pass his life among barbarians and slaves, who will be proud to pay their adoration to his Persian girdle and his splendid robe.'

Alexander Assassinates Kleitus

Alexander seized a javelin to hurl at Kleitus's head. The guests rose in confusion, and with many outcries pressed around him. Some seized Alexander's arm, some began to hurry Kleitus out of the room, and some were engaged in loudly criminating and threatening each other. They got Kleitus out of the apartment, but as soon as he was in the hall he broke away from them, returned by another door, and began to renew his insults to Alexander. The king hurled his javelin and struck Kleitus down, saying, at the same time, 'Go, then, and join Philip and Parmenio.' The company rushed to the rescue of the unhappy man, but it was too late. He died almost immediately.

His Remorse

Alexander, as soon as he came to himself was overwhelmed with remorse and despair. He mourned bitterly, for many days, the death of his long-tried and faithful friend, and execrated the intoxication and passion, on his part, which had caused it. He could not, however, restore Kleitus to life, nor remove from his own character the indelible stains which such deeds necessarily fixed upon it.

Chapter XII
Alexander's End, DCE 326-319

❋

Alexander's Invasion of India – Insubordination of the Army

A FTER THE EVENTS narrated in the last chapter, Alexander continued, for two or three years, his expeditions and conquests in Asia, and in the course of them he met with a great variety of adventures which cannot be here particularly described. He penetrated into India as far as the banks of the Indus, and, not content with this, was preparing to cross the Indus and go on to the Ganges. His soldiers, however, resisted this design. They were alarmed at the stories which they heard of the Indian armies, with elephants bearing castles upon their backs, and soldiers armed with strange and unheard-of weapons. These rumours, and the natural desire of the soldiers not to go away any further from their native land, produced almost a mutiny in the army. At length, Alexander, learning how strong and how extensive the spirit of insubordination was becoming, summoned his officers to his own tent, and then ordering the whole army to gather around, he went out to meet them.

Alexander's Address to the Army

He made an address to them, in which he recounted all their past exploits, praised the courage and perseverance which they had shown thus far and endeavoured to animate them with a desire to proceed. They listened in silence, and no one attempted to reply. This solemn pause was followed by marks of great agitation throughout the assembly. The army loved their commander, notwithstanding his faults and failings. They were extremely unwilling to make any resistance to his authority; but they had lost that extreme and unbounded confidence in his energy and virtue which made them ready, in the former part of his career, to press forward into any difficulties and dangers whatever, where he led the way.

At last one of the army approached the king and addressed him somewhat as follows:

Address Made to Him – The Army Refuses to Go Further

'We are not changed, sir, in our affection for you. We still have, and shall always retain, the same zeal and the same fidelity. We are ready to follow you at the hazard of our lives, and to march wherever you may lead us. Still we must ask you, most respectfully, to consider the circumstances in which we are placed. We have done all for you that it was possible for man to do. We have crossed seas and land. We have marched to the end of the world, and you are now meditating the conquest of another, by going in search of new Indias, unknown to the Indians themselves. Such a thought may be worthy of your courage and resolution, but it surpasses ours, and our strength still more. Look at these ghastly faces, and these bodies covered with wounds and scars. Remember how numerous we were when first we set out with you, and see how few of us remain. The few who have escaped so many toils and dangers have neither courage nor strength to follow you any further. They all long to revisit their country and their homes, and to enjoy, for the remainder of their lives, the fruits of all their toils. Forgive them these desires, so natural to man.'

Alexander's Disappointment

The expression of these sentiments confirmed and strengthened them in the minds of all the soldiers. Alexander was greatly troubled and distressed. A disaffection in a small part of an army may be put down by decisive measures; but when the determination to resist is universal, it is useless for any commander, however imperious and absolute in temper, to attempt to withstand it. Alexander, however, was extremely unwilling to yield. He remained two days shut up in his tent, the prey to disappointment and chagrin.

Alexander Resolves to Return – He is Wounded in an Assault

The result, however, was that he abandoned plans of further conquest, and turned his steps again toward the west. He met with various adventures as he went on, and incurred many dangers, often in a rash and foolish manner, and for no good end. At one time, while attacking a small town, he seized a scaling ladder and mounted with the troops. In doing this, however, he put himself forward so rashly and inconsiderately that his ladder was broken, and while the rest retreated he was left alone upon the wall, whence he descended into the town, and was immediately surrounded by enemies. His friends raised their ladders again, and pressed on desperately to find and rescue him. Some gathered around him and defended him, while others contrived to open a small gate, by which the rest of the army gained admission. By this means Alexander was saved; though, when they brought him out of the city, there was an arrow three feet long, which could not be extracted, sticking into his side through his coat of mail.

The surgeons first very carefully cut off the wooden shaft of the arrow, and then, enlarging the wound by incisions, they drew out the barbed point. The soldiers were indignant that Alexander should expose his person in such a foolhardy way, only to endanger himself, and to compel them to rush into danger to rescue him. The wound very nearly proved fatal. The loss of blood was attended with extreme exhaustion; still, in the course of a few weeks he recovered.

Alexander's Excesses

Alexander's habits of intoxication and vicious excess of all kinds were, in the meantime, continually increasing. He not only indulged in such excesses himself, but he encouraged them in others. He would offer prizes at his banquets to those who would drink the most. On one of these occasions, the man who conquered drank, it is said, eighteen or twenty pints of wine, after which he lingered in misery for three days, and then died; and more than forty others, present at the same entertainment, died in consequence of their excesses.

He Abandons His Old Friends

Alexander returned toward Babylon. His friend Hephaestion was with him, sharing with him everywhere in all the vicious indulgences to which he had become so prone. Alexander gradually separated himself more and more from his old Macedonian friends, and linked himself more and more closely with Persian associates. He married Stateira, the oldest daughter of Darius, and gave the youngest daughter to Hephaestion. He encouraged similar marriages between Macedonian officers and Persian maidens, as far as he could. In a word, he seemed intent in merging, in every way, his original character and habits of action in the softness, luxury and vice of the Eastern world, which he had at first so looked down upon and despised.

Entrance Into Babylon

Alexander's entrance into Babylon, on his return from his Indian campaigns, was a scene of great magnificence and splendour. Ambassadors and princes had assembled there from almost all the nations of the earth to receive and welcome him, and the most ample preparations were made for processions, shows, parades and spectacles to do him honour. The whole country was in a state of extreme excitement, and the most expensive preparations were made to give him a reception worthy of one who was the conqueror and monarch of the world, and the son of a god.

The Astrologers – Study of the stars

When Alexander approached the city, however, he was met by a deputation of Chaldean astrologers. The astrologers were a class of philosophers who pretended, in those days, to foretell human events by means of the motions of the stars. The motions of the stars were studied very closely in early times, and in those Eastern countries, by the shepherds, who had often to remain in the open air, through the summer nights, to watch their flocks. These shepherds observed that nearly all the stars were *fixed* in relation to each other, that is, although they rose successively in the east, and, passing over, set in the west, they did not change in relation to each other. There were, however, a few that wandered about among the rest in an irregular and unaccountable manner. They called these stars the wanderers – that is, in their language, *the planets* – and they watched their mysterious movements with great interest and awe. They naturally imagined that these changes had some connection with human affairs, and they endeavoured to prognosticate from them the events, whether prosperous or adverse, which were to befall mankind. Whenever a comet or an eclipse appeared, they thought it portended some terrible calamity. The study of the motions and appearances of the stars, with a view to foretell the course of human affairs, was the science of astrology.

Warning of the Astrologers

The astrologers came, in a very solemn and imposing procession, to meet Alexander on his march. They informed him that they had found indubitable evidence in the stars that, if he came into Babylon, he would hazard his life. They accordingly begged him not to approach any nearer, but to choose some other city for his capital. Alexander was very much perplexed by this announcement. His mind, weakened by luxury and dissipation, was very susceptible to superstitious fears. It was not merely by the debilitating influence of vicious indulgence on the nervous constitution that this effect was produced. It was, in part, the moral influence of conscious guilt. Guilt makes men afraid. It not only increases the power of real dangers, but predisposes the mind to all sorts of imaginary fears.

Alexander was very much troubled at this announcement of the astrologers. He suspended his march, and began anxiously to consider what to do. At length the Greek philosophers came to him and reasoned with him on the subject, persuading him that the science of astrology was not worthy of any belief. The Greeks had no faith in astrology. They foretold future events by the flight of birds, or by the appearances presented in the dissection of beasts offered in sacrifice!

At length, however, Alexander's fears were so far allayed that he concluded to enter the city. He advanced, accordingly, with his whole army, and made his entry under circumstances of the greatest possible parade and splendour. As soon, however, as the excitement of the first few days had passed away, his mind relapsed again, and he became anxious, troubled, and unhappy.

Death of Hephaestion

Hephaestion, his great personal friend and companion, had died while he was on the march toward Babylon, while they were staying in Ectabana. He was brought to the grave by diseases produced by dissipation and vice. Alexander was very much moved by his death. It threw him at once into a fit of despondency and gloom. It was sometime before he could at all overcome the melancholy reflections and forebodings which this event produced. He determined that, as soon as he arrived in Babylon, he would do all possible honour to Hephaestion's memory by a magnificent funeral.

Funeral Honours to Hephaestion

He accordingly now sent orders to all the cities and kingdoms around, and collected a vast sum for this purpose. He had a part of the city wall pulled down to furnish a site for a monumental edifice. This edifice was constructed of an enormous size and most elaborate architecture. It was ornamented with long rows of prows of ships, taken by Alexander in his victories, and by statues, columns, sculptures and gilded ornaments of every kind. There were images of sirens on the entablatures near the roof, which, by means of a mechanism concealed within, were made to sing dirges and mournful songs. The expense of this edifice, and of the games, shows and spectacles connected with its consecration, is said by the historians of the day to have been a sum which, on calculation, is found to equal to about ten millions of dollars (or over three hundred million in 2022).

A Stupendous Project

There were, however, some limits still to Alexander's extravagance and folly. There was a mountain in Greece, Mount Athos, which a certain projector said could be carved and fashioned into the form of a man – probably in a recumbent posture. There was a city on one of the declivities of the mountain, and a small river, issuing from springs in the ground, came down on the other side. The artist who conceived of this prodigious piece of sculpture said that he would so shape the figure that the city should be in one of its hands, and the river should flow out from the other.

Alexander listened to this proposal. The name Mount Athos recalled to his mind the attempt of Xerxes, a former Persian king, who had attempted to cut a road through the rocks upon a part of Mount Athos, in the invasion of Greece. He did not succeed, but left the unfinished work a lasting memorial both of the attempt and the failure. Alexander concluded at length that he would not attempt such a sculpture. 'Mount Athos,' said he, 'is already the monument of one king's folly; I will not make it that of another.'

Alexander's Depression – Magnificent Plans

As soon as the excitement connected with the funeral obsequies of Hephaestion were over, Alexander's mind relapsed again into a state of gloomy melancholy. This depression, caused, as it was, by previous dissipation and vice, seemed to admit of no remedy or relief but in new excesses. The traces, however, of his former energy so far remained that he began to form magnificent plans for the improvement of Babylon. He commenced the execution of some of these plans. His time was spent, in short, in strange alternations: resolution and energy in forming vast plans one day, and utter abandonment to all the excesses of dissipation and vice the next. It was a mournful spectacle to see his former greatness of soul still struggling on, though more and more faintly, as it became gradually overborne by the resistless inroads of intemperance and sin. The scene was at length suddenly terminated in the following manner:

A Prolonged Carousal – Alexander's Excesses

On one occasion, after he had spent a whole night in drinking and carousing, the guests, when the usual time arrived for separating, proposed that, instead of this, they should begin anew, and commence a second banquet at the end of the first. Alexander, half intoxicated already, entered warmly into this proposal. They assembled, accordingly, in a very short time. There were twenty present at this new feast. Alexander, to show how far he was from having exhausted his powers of drinking, began to pledge each one of the company individually. Then he drank to them all together. There was a very large cup, called the bowl of Hercules, which he now called for, and, after having filled it to the brim, he drank it off to the health of one of the company present, a Macedonian named Proteas. This feat being received by the company with great applause, he ordered the great bowl to be filled again, and drank it off as before.

Alexander's Last Sickness

The work was now done. His faculties and his strength soon failed him, and he sank down to the floor. They bore him away to his palace. A violent fever intervened, which the physicians did all in their power to allay. As soon as his reason returned a little, Alexander aroused himself from his lethargy, and tried to persuade himself that he should recover. He began to issue orders in regard to the army, and to his ships, as if such a turning of his mind to the thoughts of power and empire would help bring him back from the brink of the grave toward which he had been so obviously tending. He was determined, in fact, that he would not die.

His Dying Words

He soon found, however, notwithstanding his efforts to be vigorous and resolute, that his strength was fast ebbing away. The vital powers had received a fatal wound, and he soon felt that they could sustain themselves but little longer. He came to the conclusion that he must die. He drew his signet ring off from his finger; it was a token that he felt that all was over. He handed the ring to one of his friends who stood by his bedside. 'When I am gone,' said he, 'take my body to the Temple of Jupiter Ammon, and inter it there.'

Alexander's Death

The generals who were around him advanced to his bedside, and one after another kissed his hand. Their old affection for him revived as they saw him about to take leave of them forever. They asked him to whom he wished to leave his empire. 'To the most worthy,' said he. He meant, doubtless, by this evasion, that he was too weak and exhausted to think of such affairs. He knew, probably, that it was useless for him to attempt to control the government of his empire after his death. He said, in fact, that he foresaw that the decision of such questions would give rise to some strange funeral games after his decease. Soon after this he died.

Alexander and Washington

The palaces of Babylon were immediately filled with cries of mourning at the death of the prince, followed by bitter and interminable disputes about the succession. It had not been the aim of Alexander's life to establish firm and well-settled governments in the countries that he conquered, to encourage order, peace and industry among men, and to introduce system and regularity in human affairs, so as to leave the world in a better condition than he found it. In this respect his course of conduct presents a strong contrast with that of George Washington. It was Washington's aim to mature and perfect organizations which would move on prosperously of themselves, without him; and he was continually withdrawing his hand from action and control in public affairs, taking a higher pleasure in the independent working of the institutions which he had formed and protected, than in exercising, himself, a high personal power. Alexander, on the other hand, was all his life intent solely on enlarging and strengthening his own personal power. *He* was all in all. He wished to make himself so. He never thought of the welfare of the countries which he had subjected to his sway, or did anything to guard against the anarchy and civil wars which he knew full well would break out at once over all his vast dominions, as soon as his power came to an end.

Calamitous Results Which Followed Alexander's Death

The result was as might have been foreseen. The whole vast field of his conquests became, for many long and weary years after Alexander's death, the prey to the most ferocious and protracted civil wars. Each general and governor seized the power which Alexander's death left in his hands, and endeavoured to defend himself in the possession of it against the others. Thus, the devastation and misery which the making of these conquests brought upon Europe and Asia were continued for many years, during the slow and terrible process of their return to their original condition.

Stormy Debates – Arrhidaeus Appointed King

In the exigency of the moment, however, at Alexander's death, the generals who were in his court at the time assembled forthwith, and made an attempt to appoint someone to take the immediate command. They spent a week in stormy debates on this subject. Alexander had left no legitimate heir, and he had declined when on his deathbed, as we have already seen, to appoint a successor. Among his wives – if, indeed, they may be called wives – there was one named Roxana, who had a son not long after his death. This son was ultimately named his successor; but, in the meantime, his older half-brother named Arrhidaeus was chosen by the generals to assume the command. The selection of Arrhidaeus was a sort of compromise. He had no talents or capacity whatever, and was chosen by the rest on that very account, each one thinking that if such a mentally impaired one as Arrhidaeus was nominally the king, he could himself manage to get possession of the real power. Arrhidaeus accepted the appointment, but he was never able to make himself king in anything but the name.

Effects of the News of Alexander's Death

In the meantime, as the tidings of Alexander's death spread over the empire, it produced very various effects, according to the personal feelings in respect to Alexander entertained by the various personages and powers to which the intelligence came. Some, who had admired his greatness, and the splendour of his exploits, without having themselves experienced the bitter fruits of them, mourned and lamented his death. Others, whose fortunes had been ruined, and whose friends and relatives had been destroyed, in the course, or in the sequel of his victories, rejoiced that he who had been such a scourge and curse to others, had himself sunk, at last under the just judgment of Heaven.

Death of Sisygambis

We should have expected that Sisygambis, the bereaved and widowed mother of Darius, would have been among those who would have exulted most highly at the conqueror's death; but history tells us that, instead of this, she mourned over it with a protracted and inconsolable grief. Alexander had been, in fact, though the implacable enemy of her son, a faithful and generous friend to her. He had treated her, at all times, with the utmost respect and consideration, had supplied all her wants, and ministered, in every way, to her comfort and happiness. She had gradually learned to think of him and to love him as a son; he, in fact, always called her mother; and when she learned that he was gone, she felt as if her last earthly protector was gone. Her life had been one continued scene of affliction and sorrow, and this last blow brought her to her end. She pined away, perpetually restless and distressed. She lost all desire for food, and refused, like others who are suffering great mental anguish, to take the sustenance which her friends and attendants offered and urged upon her. At length she died. They said she starved herself to death; but it was, probably, grief and despair at being thus left, in her declining years, so hopelessly friendless and alone, and not hunger, that destroyed her.

Rejoicings at Athens – Demosthenes

In striking contrast to this mournful scene of sorrow in the palace of Sisygambis, there was an exhibition of the most wild and tumultuous joy in the streets, and in all the public places of resort in the city of Athens, when the tidings of the death of the great Macedonian king arrived there. The Athenian commonwealth, as well as all the other states of Southern Greece, had submitted very reluctantly to the Macedonian supremacy. They had resisted Philip, and they had resisted Alexander. Their opposition had been at last suppressed and silenced by Alexander's terrible vengeance upon Thebes, but it never was really subdued. Demosthenes, the orator, who had exerted so powerful an influence against the Macedonian kings, had been sent into banishment, and all outward expressions of discontent were restrained. The discontent and hostility existed still, however, as inveterate as ever, and was ready to break out anew, with redoubled violence, the moment that the terrible energy of Alexander himself was no longer to be feared.

Joy of the Athenians – Phocion

When, therefore, the rumour arrived at Athens – for at first it was a mere rumour – that Alexander was dead in Babylon, the whole city was thrown into a state of the most tumultuous joy. The citizens assembled in the public places, and congratulated and harangued each other with expressions of the greatest exultation. They were for proclaiming their independence and declaring war against Macedon on the spot. Some of the older and more sagacious of their counsellors were, however, more composed and calm. They recommended a little delay, in order to see whether the news was really true. Phocion, in particular, who was one of the prominent statesmen of the city, endeavoured to quiet the excitement of the people. 'Do not let us be so precipitate,' said he. 'There is time enough. If Alexander is really dead to-day, he will be dead to-morrow, and the next day, so that there will be time enough for us to act with deliberation and discretion.'

Measures of the Athenians

Just and true as this view of the subject was, there was too much of rebuke and satire in it to have much influence with those to whom it was addressed. The people were resolved on war. They sent commissioners into all the states of the Peloponnesus to organize a league, offensive and defensive, against Macedon. They recalled Demosthenes from his banishment, and adopted all the necessary military measures for establishing and maintaining their freedom. The consequences of all this would doubtless have been very serious, if the rumour of Alexander's death had proved false; but, fortunately for Demosthenes and the Athenians, it was soon abundantly confirmed.

Triumphant Return of Demosthenes

The return of Demosthenes to the city was like the triumphal entry of a conqueror. At the time of his recall he was at the island of Aegina, which is about forty miles southwest of Athens, in one of the gulfs of the Aegean Sea. They sent a public galley to receive him, and to bring him to the land. It was a galley of three banks of oars, and was fitted up in a style to do honour to a public guest. Athens is situated some distance back from the sea, and has a small port, called the Piraeus, at the shore – a long, straight avenue leading from the port to the city. The galley by which Demosthenes was conveyed landed at the Piraeus. All the civil and religious authorities of the city went down to the port, in a grand procession, to receive and welcome the exile on his arrival, and a large portion of the population followed in the train, to witness the spectacle, and to swell by their acclamations the general expression of joy.

Preparations for Alexander's Funeral

In the meantime, the preparations for Alexander's funeral had been going on, upon a great scale of magnificence and splendour. It was two years before they were complete. The body had been given, first, to be embalmed, according to the Egyptian and Chaldean art, and then had been placed in a sort of sarcophagus, in which it was to be conveyed to its long home. Alexander, it will be remembered, had given directions that it should be taken to the temple of Jupiter Ammon, in the Egyptian oasis, where he had been pronounced the son of a god. It would seem incredible that such a mind as his could really admit such an absurd superstition as the story of his divine origin, and we must therefore suppose that he gave this direction in order that the place of his interment might confirm the idea of his superhuman nature in the general opinion of mankind. At all events, such were his orders, and the authorities who were left in power at Babylon after his death, prepared to execute them.

A Funeral on a Grand Scale

It was a long journey. To convey a body by a regular funeral procession, formed as soon after the death as the arrangements could be made, from Babylon to the eastern frontiers of Egypt, a distance of a thousand miles, was perhaps as grand a plan of interment as was ever formed. It has something like a parallel in the removal of Napoleon's body from St. Helena to Paris, though this was not really an interment, but a transfer. Alexander's was a simple burial procession, going from the palace where he died to the proper cemetery – a march of a thousand miles, it is true, but all within his own dominions The greatness of it resulted simply from the magnitude of the scale on which everything pertaining to the mighty here was performed, for it was nothing but a simple passage from the dwelling to the burial ground on his own estates, after all.

The Funeral Car

A very large and elaborately constructed carriage was built to convey the body. The accounts of the richness and splendour of this vehicle are almost incredible. The spokes and staves of the wheels were overlaid with gold, and the extremities of the axles, where they appeared outside at the centres of the wheels, were adorned with massive golden ornaments. The wheels and axletrees were so large, and so far apart, that there was supported upon them a platform or floor for the carriage twelve feet wide and eighteen feet long. Upon this platform there was erected a magnificent pavilion, supported by Ionic columns, and profusely ornamented, both within and without, with purple and gold. The interior constituted an apartment, more or less open at the sides, and resplendent within with gems and precious stones. The space of twelve feet by eighteen forms a chamber of no inconsiderable size, and there was thus ample room for what was required within. There was a throne, raised some steps, and placed back upon the platform, profusely carved and gilded. It was empty; but crowns, representing the various nations over whom Alexander had reigned, were hung upon it. At the foot of the throne was the coffin, made, it is said, of solid gold, and containing, besides the body, a large quantity of the most costly spices and aromatic perfumes, which filled the air with their odor. The arms which Alexander wore were laid out in view, also, between the coffin and the throne.

Ornaments and Basso Relievos – Column of Mules

On the four sides of the carriage were *basso relievos*, that is, sculptured figures raised from a surface, representing Alexander himself, with various military concomitants. There were Macedonian columns, Persian squadrons, elephants of India, troops of horse and various other emblems of the departed hero's greatness and power. Around the pavilion, too, there was a fringe or network of golden lace, to the pendants of which were attached bells, which tolled continually, with a mournful sound, as the carriage moved along. A long column of mules, sixty-four in number, arranged in sets of four, drew this ponderous car. These mules were all selected for their great size and strength, and were splendidly caparisoned. They had collars and harnesses mounted with gold, and enriched with precious stones.

Crowds of Spectators

Before the procession set out from Babylon an army of pioneers and workmen went forward to repair the roads, strengthen the bridges, and remove the obstacles along the whole line of route over which the train was to pass. At length, when all was ready, the solemn procession began to move, and passed out through the gates of Babylon. No pen can describe the enormous throngs of spectators that assembled to witness its departure, and that gathered along the route, as it passed slowly on from city to city, in its long and weary way.

The Body Deposited at Alexandria

Notwithstanding all this pomp and parade, however, the body never reached its intended destination. Ptolemy, the officer to whom Egypt fell in the division of Alexander's empire, came forth with a grand escort of troops to meet the funeral procession as it came into Egypt. He preferred, for some reason or other, that the body should be interred in the city of Alexandria. It was accordingly deposited there, and a great monument was erected over the spot. This monument is said to have remained standing for fifteen hundred years, but all vestiges of it have now disappeared. The city of Alexandria itself, however, is the conqueror's real monument; the greatest and best, perhaps, that any conqueror ever left behind him. It is a monument, too, that time will not destroy; its position and character, as Alexander foresaw, by bringing it a continued renovation, secure its perpetuity.

Alexander's True Character – Conclusion

Alexander earned well the name and reputation of THE GREAT. He was truly great in all those powers and capacities which can elevate one man above his fellows. We cannot help applauding the extraordinary energy of his genius, though we condemn the selfish and cruel ends to which his life was devoted. He was simply a robber, but yet a robber on so vast a scale, that mankind, in contemplating his career, have generally lost sight of the wickedness of his crimes in their admiration of the enormous magnitude of the scale on which they were perpetrated.

The Invasion of India by Alexander the Great, as described by Arrian *et. al.*

OTHE FOLLOWING EXCERPTS are from J.W. M'Crindle's *The Invasion of India by Alexander the Great as described by Arrian, Q. Curtius, Diodoros, Plutarch and Justin.* M'Crindle (1825–1913) was a Scottish classicist and educator. He attended the University of Edinburgh and taught in Edinburgh schools before moving to India where he was both a professor and principal at several colleges. His work mainly focused on the history and translation of sources related to ancient India.

We have chosen extracts primarily from Arrian's historical version of Alexander, but also some from Diodorus Siculus and Plutarch where relevant. The reason for focusing on Arrian is because Abbott, in his text, primarily focused on work from the Roman historians, which tends to skew negatively towards Alexander. Arrian, while not always approving of Alexander's actions, had less of this negative bias. The excerpts from the Roman authors describe incidents from Alexander's life which are not mentioned in Arrian, but give us a better sense of Alexander's character.

Arrian's *Anabasis*: Fourth Book

Chapter XXII
Alexander Crosses the Indian Caucasus to Invade India and Advances to the River Kophen

AFTER CAPTURING THE ROCK OF CHORIENES, Alexander went himself to Bactria, but despatched Krateros with six hundred of the Companion Cavalry and a force of infantry, consisting of his own brigade with that of Polyperchon and Attalos and that of Alcetas, against Katanes and Ostanes the only chiefs now left in the country of the Paraitakenai who still held out against him. In the battle which ensued Krateros after a severe struggle proved victorious. Katanes fell in the action, while Ostanes was made prisoner and brought to Alexander. Of the barbarians who had followed them to the field, there were slain one hundred and twenty horsemen and about fifteen hundred foot. Krateros after the victory led his troops also to Bactria. While Alexander was here the tragic incident in his history, the affair of Kallisthenes and the pages, occurred.

When spring was now past, he led his army from Bactria to invade the Indians, leaving Amyntas in the land of the Bactrians with thirty-five hundred horse and ten thousand. In ten days he crossed the Caucasus and arrived at the city of Alexandria which he had founded in the land of the Parapamisadai when he first marched to Bactria. The ruler whom he had then set over the city he dismissed from his office because he thought he had not discharged its duties well. He recruited the population of Alexandria with fresh settlers from the surrounding district, and also with such of his soldiers as were unfit for further service. He then ordered Nikanor, one of the Companions, to take charge of the city itself and regulate its affairs, but he appointed Tyriaspes satrap of the land of the Parapamisadai and the rest of the country as far as the river Kophen. Having reached the city of Nikaia and sacrificed to the goddess Athena, he despatched a herald to Taxiles and the chiefs on this side of the river Indus, directing them to meet him where it was most convenient for each. Taxiles accordingly and the other chiefs did meet him and brought him such presents as are most esteemed by the Indians. They offered also to give him the elephants which they had with them amounting in number to twenty-five.

Having here divided his army, he despatched Hephaestion and Perdiccas with the brigades of Gorgias, Kleitos, and Meleager, half of the companion cavalry, and the whole of the mercenary cavalry, to the land of Peukelaotis and the river Indus. He ordered them either to seize by force whatever places lay on their route or to accept their submission if they capitulated, and when they came to the Indus to make whatever preparations were necessary for the transport of the army across that river. They were accompanied on their march by Taxiles and the other chiefs. On reaching the river Indus they began to carry out the instructions which they had received from Alexander. One of the chiefs, however, Astes, a prince of the land of Peukelaotis, revolted, but perished in the attempt, besides involving in ruin the city to which he had fled for refuge, which the troops under Hephaestion captured in thirty days. Astes himself fell, and Sañjaya, who had some time before fled from Astes and deserted to Taxiles, a circumstance which guaranteed his fidelity to Alexander, was appointed governor of the city.

Chapter XXIII
Alexander Wars Against the Aspasians

ALEXANDER TOOK COMMAND in person of the other division of the army, consisting of the hypaspists (shield bearers), all the companion cavalry except what was with Hephaestion, the brigades of infantry called the foot-companions, the archers, the Agrianians and the horse lancers, and advanced into the country of the Aspasians and Guraeans and Assakenians. The route which he followed was hilly and rugged, and lay along the course of the river called the Khoes, which he had difficulty in crossing. This done he ordered the mass of the infantry to follow leisurely, while he rode rapidly forward, taking with him the whole of his cavalry, besides eight hundred Macedonian foot soldiers, whom he mounted on horseback with their infantry shields; for he had been informed that the barbarians inhabiting those parts had fled for refuge to their native mountains, and to such of their cities as were strongly fortified. When he proceeded to attack the first city of this kind that came in his way, he found men drawn up before it in battle order, and on these he fell at once, just as he was, put them to rout, and shut them up within the gates. He was wounded, however, in the shoulder by a dart which penetrated through his breastplate, but not severely, for the breastplate prevented the weapon from going right through his shoulder. Ptolemy, the son of Lagos, and Leonnatus were also wounded.

He then encamped near the city on the side where he thought the wall was weakest. Next day, as soon as there was light, the Macedonians attacked the outer of the two walls by which the city was encompassed, and as it was but rudely constructed they captured it without difficulty. At the inner wall, however, the barbarians made some resistance; but when the ladders were applied, and the defenders were galled with darts wherever they turned, they no longer stood their ground, but issued from the city through the gates and made for the hills. Some of them perished in the flight, while such as were taken alive were to a man put to death by the Macedonians, who were enraged against them for having wounded Alexander. Most of them, however, made good their escape to the mountains, which lay at no great distance from the city. Alexander razed it to the ground, and then marched forward to another city called Andaka, which surrendered on capitulation. When the place had thus fallen into his hands he left Krateros in these parts, with the other infantry officers, to take by force whatever other cities refused voluntary submission, and to settle the affairs of the surrounding district in the best way existing circumstances would permit, while he himself advanced to the river Euaspla, where the chief of the Aspasians was.

[Here we skip over what are mostly battle preparations of Chapter XXIV (Operations Against the Aspasians)]

Chapter XXV
Defeat of the Aspasians – The Assakenians and Guraeans Attacked

WHEN THEY SAW THE MACEDONIANS advancing against them they came down from the high ground which they had occupied into the plain below, confident in their numbers, and despising the Macedonians for the smallness of theirs. A sharp conflict followed, but Alexander without much trouble gained the victory. Ptolemy did not draw up his men in line upon the plain, but since the barbarians were posted on a small hill, he formed his battalions into column, and led them up the hill on the side where it was most assailable. He did not surround the entire circuit of the hill, but left an opening for the barbarians by which to escape if they meant flight. With these men also the conflict was sharp, not only from the difficult nature of the ground, but also because the Indians were of a different mettle from the other barbarians there, and were by far the stoutest warriors in that neighbourhood; but brave as they were they were driven from the hill by the Macedonians.

The men of the third division under Leonnatus were equally successful, as they also routed those with whom they engaged. Ptolemy states that the men taken prisoners were in all above forty thousand, and that there were also captured more than two hundred and thirty thousand oxen, from which Alexander chose out the best – those which he thought superior to the others both for beauty and size – with a view to send them to Macedonia to be employed in agriculture.

He marched thence to invade the country of the Assakenians, for they were reported to have under arms and ready for battle an army of twenty thousand cavalry and more than thirty thousand infantry, besides thirty elephants. Krateros had now completed the work of fortifying the city which he had been left to plant with colonists, and rejoined Alexander with the heavy armed troops and the engines which it might be necessary to employ in besieging towns. Alexander himself then proceeded to attack the Assakenians, taking with him the companion cavalry, the horse archers, the brigade of Coenus and Polysperchon, and the thousand Agrianians and the archers. He passed through the country of the Guraeans, where he had to cross the Gouraeas, the river named after that country. The passage was difficult on account of the depth and swiftness of the stream, and also because the stones at the bottom were so smooth and round that the men on stepping on them were apt to stumble. When the barbarians saw Alexander approaching they had not the courage to encounter him in the open field with their collective forces, but dispersed to their several cities, which they resolved to defend to the last extremity.

Chapter XXVI
Siege of Massaga

ALEXANDER MARCHED FIRST to attack Massaga, which was the greatest city in those parts. When he was now approaching the walls, the barbarians, supported by a body of Indian mercenaries brought from a distance, and no less than seven thousand strong, sallied out with a run against the Macedonians when they observed them preparing to encamp. Alexander thus saw that the battle would be fought close to the city, whereas he wished the enemy to be drawn away to a distance from the walls, so that, if they were defeated, as he was certain they would be, they might have less chance of escaping with their lives by a short flight into the city.

Alexander therefore ordered the Macedonians to fall back to a little hill which was about seven stadia (one stadia is equal to six hundred feet / one hundred and eighty-two meters) distant from the place where he had meant to encamp. This gave the enemy fresh courage as they thought the Macedonians had already given way before them, and so they charged them at a running pace and without any observance of order. But when once their arrows began to reach his men, Alexander immediately wheeled round at a signal agreed on and led the phalanx at a running pace to fall upon them. But his horse-lancers and the Agrianians and the archers darted forward, and were the first to come into conflict with the barbarians, while he was leading the phalanx in regular order into action. The Indians were confounded by this unexpected attack, and no sooner found themselves involved in a hand-to-hand encounter than they gave way and fled back to the city. About two hundred of them were killed, and the rest were shut up within the walls. Alexander brought up the phalanx against the fortifications, but was wounded in the ankle, though not severely, by an arrow shot from the battlements. The next day he brought up the military engines, and without much difficulty battered down a part of the wall. But when the Macedonians attempted to force their way through the breach which had been made, the Indians repelled all their attacks with so much spirit that Alexander was obliged for that day to draw off his forces. On the morrow the Macedonians renewed their assault with even greater vigour, and a wooden tower was brought up against the wall from which the archers shot at the Indians, while missiles were discharged against them from engines. They were thus driven back to a good distance, but still their assailants were after all unable to force their way within the walls.

On the third day Alexander led the phalanx once more to the assault, and causing a bridge to be thrown from an engine over to that part of the wall which had been battered down, by that gangway he led the hypaspists over to the breach – the same men who by a similar expedient had enabled him to capture Tyre. The bridge, however, broke down under the great throng which was pushing forward with eager haste, and the Macedonians fell with it. The barbarians on the walls, seeing what had happened, began amid loud cheering to ply the Macedonians with stones and arrows and whatever missiles they had ready at hand or could at the moment snatch up, while others sallying out from posterns in the wall between the towers, struck them at close quarters before they could extricate themselves from the confusion caused by the accident.

Chapter XXVII
Massaga Taken by Storm – Ora and Bazira Besieged

ALEXANDER THEN SENT Alcetas with his brigade to take up the wounded and recall to the camp the active combatants. On the fourth day another gangway on a different engine was despatched by him against the wall.

Now the Indians, as long as the chief of that place was still living, continued with great vigour to maintain the defence, but when he was struck by a missile from an engine and was killed by the blow, while some of themselves had fallen in the uninterrupted siege, and most of them were wounded and disabled for fighting, they sent a herald to treat with Alexander. To him it was always a pleasure to save the lives of brave men, and he came to an agreement with the Indian mercenaries to the effect that they should change their side and take service in his ranks. Upon this they left the city, arms in hand, and encamped by themselves on a small hill which faced the camp of the Macedonians. But as they had no wish to take up arms against their own countrymen, they resolved to arise by night and make off with all speed to their homes. When Alexander was informed of this he surrounded the hill that same night with all his troops, and having thus intercepted the Indians in the midst of their flight, cut them to pieces. The city now stripped of its defenders he took by storm, and captured the mother and daughter of Assakenos. Alexander lost in the siege from first to last twenty-five of his men in all.

He then despatched Coenus to Bazira, convinced that the inhabitants would capitulate on learning that Massaga had been captured. He, moreover, sent Attalos, Alcetas, and Demetrios, the captain of cavalry, to another city, Ora, instructing them to draw a rampart round it, and to invest it until his own arrival. The inhabitants of this place sallied out against the troops under Alcetas, but the Macedonians had no great difficulty in routing them, and driving them back within the walls of the city. As regards Coenus, matters did not go well with him at Bazira, for as it stood on a very lofty eminence, and was strongly fortified in every quarter, the people trusted to the strength of their position and made no proposals about surrendering.

Alexander, on learning this, set out for Bazira, but as he knew that some of the barbarians of the neighbouring country were going to steal unobserved into the city of Ora, having been sent by Abisares for this very purpose, he directed his march first to that city. He then sent orders to Coenus to fortify some strong position as a basis of operations against the city of the Bazirians, and to leave in it a sufficient garrison to prevent the inhabitants from going into the country around for provisions without fear of danger. He was then to join Alexander with the remainder of his troops. When the men of Bazira saw Coenus departing with the bulk of his troops they regarded the Macedonians who remained, as contemptible antagonists, and sallied out into the plain to attack them. A sharp conflict ensued in which five hundred of the barbarians were slain, and upwards of seventy taken prisoners. The rest fled together into the city and were more rigorously than ever debarred all access to the country by the garrison of the fort. The siege of Ora did not cost Alexander much labour, for he captured the place at the first assault, and got possession of all the elephants which had been left therein.

Chapter XXVIII
Bazira Captured – Alexander Marches to the Rock Aornos

WHEN THE INHABITANTS OF BAZIRA heard that Ora had fallen, they regarded their case as desperate, and at the dead of night fled from their city to the Rock, as all the other barbarians were doing, for, having left their cities, they were fleeing to the rock in that land called Aornos; for this is a mighty mass of rock in that part of the country, and a report is current concerning it that even Heracles, the son of Zeus, had found it to be impregnable. Now whether the Theban, or the Tyrian, or the Egyptian Heracles penetrated so far as to the Indians I can neither positively affirm nor deny, but I incline

to think that he did not penetrate so far; for we know how common it is for men when speaking of things that are difficult to magnify the difficulty by declaring that it would baffle even Heracles himself. And in the case of this rock my own conviction is that Heracles was mentioned to make the story of its capture all the more wonderful. The rock is said to have had a circuit of about two hundred stadia, and at its lowest elevation a height of eleven stadia. It was ascended by a single path cut by the hand of man, yet difficult. On the summit of the rock there was, it is also said, plenty of pure water which gushed out from a copious spring. There was timber besides, and as much good arable land as required for its cultivation the labour of a thousand men.

Alexander on learning these particulars was seized with an ardent desire to capture this mountain also, the story current about Heracles not being the least of the incentives. With this in view he made Ora and Massaga strongholds for bridling the districts around them, and at the same time strengthened the defences of Bazira. The division under Hephaestion and Perdiccas fortified for him another city called Orobatis in which they left a garrison and then marched on to the river Indus. On reaching it they began preparing a bridge to span the Indus in accordance with Alexander's orders.

Alexander now appointed Nikanor, one of the companions, satrap of the country on this side of the Indus, and then first marched himself towards that river and received the submission of the city of Peukelaotis which lay not far from the Indus. He placed in it a garrison of Macedonian soldiers under the command of Philip, and then occupied himself in reducing other towns – some small ones – situated near the river Indus. He was accompanied on this occasion by Kophaios and Assagetes the local chiefs. On reaching Embolima, a city close adjoining the rock of Aornos, he there left Krateros with a part of the army to gather into the city as much corn as possible and all other requisites for a long stay, that the Macedonians having this place as the basis of their operations might, during a protracted siege, wear out the defenders of the rock by famine, should it fail to be captured at the first assault. He himself then advanced to the rock, taking with him the archers, the Agrianians, the brigade of Coenus, the lightest and best-armed men selected from the remainder of the phalanx, two hundred of the companion cavalry and one hundred horse-archers. At the end of the day's march he encamped on what he took to be a convenient site. The next day he advanced a little nearer to the Rock, and again encamped.

Chapter XXIX
Siege of Aornos

❋

SOME MEN THEREUPON who belonged to the neighbourhood came to him, and after proffering their submission undertook to guide him to the most assailable part of the rock, that from which it would not be difficult to capture the place. With these men he sent Ptolemy, the son of Lagos, a member of the bodyguard, leading the Agrianians and the other light-armed troops and the selected hypaspists, and directed him, on securing the position, to hold it with a strong guard and to signal to him when he had occupied it.

Ptolemy, who followed a route which proved rough and otherwise difficult to traverse, succeeded in occupying the position without being perceived by the barbarians. The whole circuit of this he fortified with a palisade and a trench, and then raised a beacon on the mountain from which the flame was likely to be seen by Alexander. Alexander did see it, and next day moved forward with his army, but as the barbarians obstructed his progress he could do nothing more on account of the difficult nature of the ground. When the barbarians perceived that Alexander had found an attack to be impracticable, they turned round, and in full force fell upon Ptolemy's men. Between these and the Macedonians hard fighting ensued, the Indians making strenuous efforts to destroy the palisade by tearing up the stakes, and Ptolemy to guard and maintain his position. The barbarians were worsted in the skirmish and when night began to fall withdrew.

From the Indian deserters Alexander selected one who knew the country and could otherwise be trusted, and sent him by night to Ptolemy with a letter importing that when he himself assailed the rock, Ptolemy should no longer content himself with defending his position but should fall upon the barbarians on the mountain, so that the Indians, being attacked in front and rear, might be perplexed how to act. Alexander, starting at daybreak from his camp, led his army by the route followed by Ptolemy when he went up unobserved, being convinced that if he forced a passage that way, and effected a junction with Ptolemy's men, the work still before him would not then be difficult; and so it turned out; for up to midday there continued to be hard fighting between the Indians and the Macedonians – the latter forcing their way up the ascent, while the former plied them with missiles as they ascended. But as the Macedonians did not slacken their efforts, ascending the one after the other, while those in advance paused to rest, they gained with much pain and toil the summit of the pass early in the afternoon, and joined Ptolemy's men. His troops being now all united, Alexander put them again in motion and led them against the rock itself; but to get close up to it was not yet practicable. So came this day to its end.

Next day at dawn he ordered the soldiers to cut a hundred stakes per man. When the stakes had been cut he began piling them up towards the rock (beginning from the crown of the hill on which the camp had been pitched) to form a great mound, whence he thought it would be possible for arrows and for missiles shot from engines to reach the defenders. Everyone took part in the work helping to advance the mound. Alexander himself was present to superintend, commending those that were intent on getting the work done, and chastising anyone that at the moment was idling.

Chapter XXX
Capture of Aornos – Advance to the Indus

THE ARMY BY THE FIRST DAY'S WORK extended the mound the length of a stadium, and on the following day the slingers by slinging stones at the Indians from the mound just constructed, and the bolts shot at them from the engines, drove them back whenever they sallied out to attack the men engaged upon the mound. The work of piling it up thus went on for three days, without intermission, when on the fourth day a few Macedonians forced their

**way to a small hill which was on a level with the rock, and occupied
its crest. Alexander without ever resting drove the mound towards
the hill which the handful of men had occupied, his object being to
join the two together.**

But the Indians terror-struck both by the unheard-of audacity of the
Macedonians in forcing their way to the hill, and also by seeing that this position
was now connected with the mound, abstained from further resistance, and,
sending their herald to Alexander, professed they were willing to surrender
the rock if he granted them terms of capitulation. But the purpose they had
in view was to consume the day in spinning out negotiations, and to disperse
by night to their several homes. When Alexander saw this he allowed them to
start off as well as to withdraw the sentinels from the whole circle of outposts.
He did not himself stir until they began their retreat, but, when they did so, he
took with him seven hundred of the bodyguards and the hypaspists and scaled
the rock at the point abandoned by the enemy. He was himself the first to reach
the top, the Macedonians ascending after him pulling one another up, some
at one place and some at another. Then at a preconcerted signal they turned
upon the retreating barbarians and slew many of them in the flight, besides
so terrifying some others that in retreating they flung themselves down the
precipices, and were in consequence dashed to death. Alexander thus became
master of the rock which had baffled Heracles himself. He sacrificed upon it
and built a fort, giving the command of its garrison to Shashigupta, who long
before had in Bactria deserted from the Indians to Bessus, but after Alexander
had conquered the Bactrian land served in his army, and showed himself a man
worthy of all confidence.

He then set out from the rock and invaded the land of the Assakenians,
for he had been apprised that the brother of Assakenos, with the elephants
and a host of the barbarians from the adjoining country, had fled for refuge
to the mountains of that land. On reaching Dyrta he found there were no
inhabitants either in the city itself or the surrounding district. So next day he
sent out Nearchus and Antiochus, commanders of the hypaspists, the former
with the light-armed Agrianians, and the latter with his own regiment and other
two regiments besides. They were despatched to examine the nature of the
localities, and to capture, if possible, some of the barbarians who might give

information about the state of matters in the country, and particularly about the elephants, as he was very anxious to know where they were.

He himself now marched towards the river Indus, and the army going on before made a road for him, without which there would have been no means of passing through that part of the country. He there captured a few of the barbarians, from whom he learned that the Indians of the country had fled away for refuge to Abisares, but had left their elephants there at pasture near the river Indus. He ordered these men to show him the way to the elephants. Now many of the Indians are elephant hunters, and men of this class found favour with him and were kept in his retinue, and on this occasion he went with them in pursuit of the elephants. Two of these animals were killed in the chase by throwing themselves down a steep place, but the others on being caught suffered drivers to mount them, and were added to the army. He was further fortunate in finding serviceable timber along the river, and this was cut for him by the army and employed in building boats. These were taken down the river Indus to the bridge which a good while before this Hephaestion and Perdiccas had constructed.

Arrian's *Anabasis:* Fifth Book

Chapter I
Alexander at Nysa

IN THE COUNTRY traversed by Alexander between the Kophen and the river Indus, they say that besides the cities already mentioned, there stood also the city of Nysa, which owed its foundation to Dionysus, and that Dionysus founded it when he conquered the Indians, whoever this Dionysus in reality was, and when or from wherever he made his expedition against the Indians; for I have no

means of deciding whether the Theban Dionysus setting out either from Thebes or the Lydian Tmolus marched with an army against the Indians, passing through a great many warlike nations unknown to the Greeks of those days, but without subjugating any of them by force of arms except only the Indian nations; all I know is, that one is not called on to sift minutely the legends of antiquity concerning the gods; for things that are not credible, if one reasons as to their consistency with the course of nature, do not seem to be incredible altogether if one takes the divine agency into account.

When Alexander came to Nysa, the Nysaens sent out to him their president, whose name was Akouphis, and along with him thirty deputies of their most eminent citizens, to entreat him to spare the city for the sake of the god. The deputies, it is said, on entering Alexander's tent found him sitting in his armour, covered with dust from his journey, wearing his helmet and grasping his spear. They fell to the ground in amazement at the sight, and remained for a long time silent. But when Alexander had bidden them rise and to be of good courage, then Akouphis taking up speech thus addressed him.

'The Nysaens entreat you, O King! to permit them to be still free and to be governed by their own laws from reverence towards Dionysus; for when Dionysus after conquering the Indian nation was returning to the shores of Greece he founded with his war-worn soldiers, who were also his bacchanals, this very city to be a memorial to posterity of his wanderings and his victory, just as you have founded yourself an Alexandria near Caucasus, and another Alexandria in the land of the Egyptians, not to speak of many others, some of which you have already founded, while others will follow in the course of time, just as your achievements exceed in number those displayed by Dionysus. Now Dionysus called our city Nysa, and our land the Nysaian, after the name of his nurse Nysa; and he besides gave to the mountain which lies near the city the name of Meros, because according to the legend he grew, before his birth, in the thigh of Zeus. And from his time forth we inhabit Nysa as a free city, and are governed by our own laws, and are a well-ordered community. But that Dionysus was our founder, take this as a proof, that ivy which grows nowhere else in the land of the Indians, grows with us.'

Chapter II
Alexander Permits the Nysaens to Retain Their Autonomy – Visits Mount Meros

IT GRATIFIED ALEXANDER to hear all this, for he was desirous that the legends concerning the wanderings of Dionysus should be believed, as well as that Nysa owed its foundation to Dionysus, since he had himself reached the place to which that deity had come, and meant to penetrate farther than he; for the Macedonians, he thought, would not refuse to share his toils if he advanced with an ambition to rival the exploits of Dionysus.

He therefore confirmed the inhabitants of Nysa in the enjoyment of their freedom and their own laws; and when he enquired about their laws, he praised them because the government of their state was in the hands of the aristocracy. He moreover requested them to send with him three hundred of their horsemen, together with one hundred of their best men selected from the governing body, which consisted of three hundred members. He then asked Akouphis, whom he appointed governor of the Nysaian land, to make the selection. When Akouphis heard this, he is said to have smiled at the request, and when Alexander asked him why he laughed, to have replied, 'How, O King! can a single city if deprived of a hundred of its best men continue to be well-governed? But if you have the welfare of the Nysaens at heart, take with you the three hundred horsemen, or, if you wish, even more; but instead of the hundred of our best men you have asked me to select, take with you twice that number of our worst men, so that on your returning hither you may find the city as well governed as it is now.' By these words he persuaded Alexander, who thought he spoke sensibly, and who ordered him to send the horsemen without again asking for the hundred men who were to have been selected, or even for others to supply their place. He requested Akouphis, however, to send him his son and his daughter's son to attend him on his expedition.

Alexander felt a strong desire to see the place where the Nysaens boasted to have certain memorials of Dionysus. So he went, it is said, to Mount Meros with the companion cavalry and the body of footguards, and found that the mountain abounded with ivy and laurel and umbrageous groves of all manner of trees, and that it had also chases supplied with game of every description. The Macedonians, to whom the sight of the ivy was particularly welcome, as it was the first they had seen for a long time (there being no ivy in the land of the Indians, even where they have the vine), are said to have set themselves at once to weave ivy chaplets, and, accoutred as they were, to have crowned themselves with these, chanting the while hymns to Dionysus and invoking the god by his different names. Alexander, they say, offered while there sacrifice to Dionysus and feasted with his friends. Some even go so far as to allege, if anyone cares to believe such things, that many of his courtiers, Macedonians of no mean rank, while invoking Dionysus, and wreathed with ivy crowns, were seized with the inspiration of the god, raised in his honour shouts of Evoi, and revelled like Bacchanals celebrating the orgies.

Chapter III

How Eratosthenes Views the Legends Concerning Heracles and Dionysus – Alexander Crosses the Indus

ANYONE WHO HEARS THESE STORIES is free to believe them or disbelieve them as he chooses. For my own part, I do not altogether agree with Eratosthenes the Cyrenaean, who says that all these references to the deity were circulated by the Macedonians in connection with the deeds of Alexander, to gratify his pride by grossly exaggerating their importance. For, to take an instance, he says that the Macedonians, on seeing a cavern among the Parapamisadae, and either hearing some local legend about it, or inventing one themselves, spread a report that this was beyond doubt the cave in which Prometheus had been bound, and to which the eagle resorted to prey upon his vitals, until Heracles, coming that way, slew the eagle and freed Prometheus from his bonds. And again, he says that the Macedonians transferred the name of Mount Caucasus from Pontus to the eastern parts of the world and the land of the Parapamisadae adjacent to India (for they called Mount Paropamisos, Caucasus), to enhance the glory of Alexander as if he had passed over Caucasus. And again, he says that when the Macedonians saw in India itself oxen marked with a brand in the form of a club, they took this as a proof that Heracles had gone as far as the Indians. Eratosthenes has likewise no belief in similar stories about the wanderings of Dionysus. Whether or not the accounts about them are true, I cannot decide, and so leave them.

When Alexander arrived at the river Indus he found a bridge already made over it by Hephaestion, and two thirty-oared galleys, besides a great many small boats. He found also a present which had been sent by Taxiles the Indian, consisting of two hundred talents of silver, three thousand oxen fattened for the shambles, ten thousand sheep or more and thirty elephants. The same prince had also sent to his assistance a force of seven hundred horsemen, and these brought word that Taxiles surrendered into his hands his capital Taxila, the greatest of all the cities between the river Indus and the Hydaspes. Alexander there offered sacrifices to the gods to whom it was his custom to sacrifice, and entertained his army with gymnastic and equestrian contests on the banks of the river. The sacrifices proved to be favourable for his undertaking the passage.

Chapter IV
General Description of the Indus and of the People of India

T HAT THE INDUS is the greatest of all the rivers of Asia, except the Ganges, which is itself an Indian river; that its sources lie on this side of the Paropamisos or Caucasus; that it falls into the great sea which washes the shores of India towards the south wind; that it has two mouths, both of which outlets abound with shallows, like the five mouths of the Ister; and that it forms a delta in the land of the

Indians closely resembling the Egyptian Delta, and that this is called in the Indian tongue Pattala, let this be my description of the Indus, setting forth those facts which can least be disputed, since the Hydaspes and the Acesines and the Hydraotes and the Hyphasis, which are also Indian rivers, are considerably larger than any other rivers in Asia, but are smaller, I may even say much smaller, than the Indus, just as also the Indus itself is smaller than the Ganges. Indeed, Ctesias (if anyone thinks him a proper authority) states that where the Indus is narrowest its banks are forty stadia apart, and where broadest one hundred stadia, while its ordinary breadth is the mean between these two distances.

This river Indus Alexander began to cross at daybreak with his army to enter the country of the Indians. Concerning this people I have, in this present work, described neither under what laws they live, nor what strange animals their country produces, nor in what number and variety fish and water monsters are bred in the Indus, the Hydaspes, the Ganges and other Indian rivers. Nor have I described the ants which dig up gold for them, nor its guardians the griffins, nor other stories invented rather to amuse than to convey a knowledge of facts, since there was no one to expose the falsehood of any absurd stories told about the Indians. However, Alexander and those who served in his army did expose the falsehood of most of them, although some even of these very men invented lies of their own. They proved also, in contradiction of the common belief, that the Indians were goldless, those tribes at least, and they were many, which Alexander visited with his army; and that they were not at all luxurious in their style of living, while they were of so great a stature that they were amongst the tallest men in Asia, being five cubits (one cubit is equal to eighteen to twenty-two inches / forty-five to fifty centimeters) in height, or nearly so. They were blacker than any other men except the Ethiopians, while in the art of war they were far superior to the other nations by which Asia was at that time inhabited. For I cannot make any proper comparison between the Indians and the race of ancient Persians, who, under the command of Cyrus, the son of Cambyses, wrested the supremacy of Asia from the Medes, and added to their empire other nations, some by conquest and others by voluntary submission; for the Persians of those days were but a poor people, inhabiting a rugged country and approximating closely in the austerity of their laws and usages to the Spartan discipline. Then with regard to the discomfiture of the

Persians in the Scythian land, I cannot with certainty conjecture to what cause it was attributable, whether to the difficult nature of the country into which they were led, or to some other mistake made by Cyrus, or whether it was that the Persians were inferior in the art of war to those Scythians whose territories they invaded.

[Here we skip over the mostly geographic descriptions of Chapter V (The Rivers and Mountains of Asia) and VI (Position and Boundaries of India)]

Chapter VII
The Bridging of Rivers

IN WHAT MANNER Alexander made his bridge over the Indus neither Aristobulus nor Ptolemy, the authorities whom I chiefly follow, have given any account; nor can I decide for certain whether the passage was bridged with boats, as was the Hellespont by Xerxes and as were the Bosporos and the Ister by Darius, or whether the bridge he made over the river was one continuous piece of work. I incline, however, to think that the bridge must have been made of boats, for neither would the depth of the river have admitted the construction of an ordinary kind of bridge, nor could a work so vast and difficult have been executed in so short a time. But if the passage was bridged with boats I cannot decide whether the vessels being fastened together with cables and anchored in a row sufficed to form a bridge as did those by which, as Herodotus of Halicarnassus says, the Hellespont was joined, or whether the method was that which is used by the Romans in bridging the Ister and the Celtic Rhine, and by which they bridged the Euphrates and the Tigris as often as necessity required.**

Since, however, the Romans, as far as my knowledge goes, have found that the bridging of rivers by boats is the most expeditious method of crossing them, I think it worth a description here. The vessels at a preconcerted signal are let go from their moorings and rowed downstream not prow but stern foremost. The current of course carries them downward, but a small pinnace furnished with oars holds them back till they settle into their appointed place. Then baskets of wicker work, pyramid-shaped and filled with rough stones, are lowered into the river from the prow of each vessel to make it hold fast against the force of the current. As soon as one of those vessels has been held fast another is in the same way anchored with its prow against the stream as far from the first as is commensurate with their bearing the strain of what is put upon them. On both of them beams of wood are rapidly laid lengthwise, and on these again planks are placed crosswise to bind them together. In this manner the work proceeds through all the vessels which are required for bridging the passage. At each end of the structure firmly fixed railed gangways are thrown forward to the shore so that horses and beasts of burden may with the greater safety enter upon it. These gangways serve at the same time to bind the bridge to the shore. In a short time the whole is completed amid great noise and bustle, though discipline is by no means lost sight of as the work proceeds. In each vessel the occasional exhortations of the overseers and their rebukes of negligence neither prevent orders from being heard nor the work from being quickly executed.

Chapter VIII
Alexander Arrives at Taxila – Receives an Embassy from Abisares and Advances to the Hydaspes

THIS METHOD HAS BEEN PRACTISED by the Romans from of old, but how Alexander bridged the river Indus I cannot say, for even those who served in his army are silent on the matter. But the bridge was made, I should think, as nearly as possible in the way described, or if it was otherwise contrived let it be so.

When Alexander had crossed to the other side of the Indus he again offered sacrifice according to his custom. Then marching away from the Indus he arrived at Taxila, a great and flourishing city, the greatest indeed of all the cities which lay between the river Indus and the Hydaspes. Taxiles, the governor of the city, and the Indians who belonged to it received him in a friendly manner, and he therefore added as much of the adjacent country to their territory as they requested. While he was there Abisares, the king of the Indians of the hill-country, sent him an embassy which included his own brother and other grandees of his court. Envoys came also from Doxarcus, the chief of the province, and those like the others brought presents. Here again in Taxila Alexander offered his customary sacrifices and celebrated a gymnastic and equestrian contest. Having appointed Philip, the son of Makhatas, satrap of the Indians of that district, he left a garrison in Taxila and those soldiers who were invalided, and then moved on towards the river Hydaspes – for he had learned that Porus with the whole of his army lay on the other side of that river resolved either to prevent him from making the passage or to attack him when crossing. Upon learning this Alexander sent back Coenus, the son of Polemocrates, to the river Indus with orders to cut in pieces all the boats that had been constructed for the passage of the Indus and to bring them to the river Hydaspes. In accordance with these orders the smaller boats were cut each into two sections and the thirty-oared galleys into three, and the sections were then transported on wagons to the banks of the Hydaspes. There the boats were reconstructed, and appeared as a flotilla upon that river. Alexander then taking the forces which he had with him when he arrived at Taxila and five thousand of the Indians commanded by Taxiles and the chiefs of that country advanced towards the Hydaspes.

Extract from Plutarch

Chapter LXIV
Alexander's Interview with the Indian Gymnosophists

HE CAPTURED ten of the gymnosophists who had been principally concerned in persuading Sabbas to revolt, and had done much harm otherwise to the Macedonians. These

men are thought to be great adepts in the art of returning brief and pithy answers, and Alexander proposed for their solution some hard questions, declaring that he would put to death first the one who did not answer correctly and then the others in order.

He demanded of the first 'Which he took to be the more numerous, the living or the dead?' He answered, 'The living, for the dead are not.'

The second was asked, 'Which breeds the largest animals, the sea or the land?' He answered, 'The land, for the sea is only a part of it.'

The third was asked, 'Which is the cleverest of beasts?' He answered, 'That with which man is not yet acquainted.'

The fourth was asked, 'For what reason he induced Sabbas to revolt?' He answered, 'Because I wished him to live with honour or die with honour.'

The fifth was asked, 'Which he thought existed first, the day or the night?' He answered, 'The day was first by one day.' As the king appeared surprised at this solution, he added, 'Impossible questions require impossible answers.'

Alexander then turning to the sixth asked him 'How a man could best make himself beloved?' He answered, 'If a man being possessed of great power did not make himself to be feared.'

Of the remaining three, one being asked 'How a man could become a god?' replied, 'By doing that which is impossible for a man to do.'

The next being asked, 'Which of the two was stronger, life or death?' he replied, 'Life, because it bears so many evils.'

The last being asked, 'How long it was honourable for a man to live?' answered, 'As long as he does not think it better to die than to live.'

Upon this Alexander, turning to the judge, requested him to give his decision. He said they had answered each one worse than the other. 'Since such is your judgment,' Alexander then said, 'you shall be yourself the first to be put to death.'

'Not so,' said he, 'O king, unless you are false to your word, for you said that he who gave the worst answer should be the first to die.'

Chapter LXV
Onesikritos Confers with the Indian Gymnosophists Kalanos and Dandamis – Kalanos Visits Alexander and Shows Him a Symbol of His Empire

THE KING THEN GAVE THEM presents and dismissed them to their homes. He also sent Onesikritos to the most renowned of these sages, who lived by themselves in tranquil seclusion, to request that they would come to him. This Onesikritos was a philosopher who belonged to the school of Diogenes the Cynic. He tells us that one of these men called Kalanos ordered him with the most overbearing insolence and rudeness to take off his clothes, and listen naked to his discourse – otherwise he would not enter into conversation with him even if he came from Zeus himself.

Dandamis, however, was of a milder temper, and when he had been told about Socrates, Pythagoras and Diogenes, he said they appeared to him to have been men of genius, but from an excessive deference to the laws had subjected their lives too much to their requirements. But other writers tell us that he said nothing more than this, 'For what purpose has Alexander come all the way hither?' Taxiles, however, persuaded Kalanos to visit Alexander. His real name was Sphines, but as he saluted those whom he met with 'Kale,' which is the Indian equivalent of 'Chairein' (that is, 'All hail'), he was called by the Greeks Kalanos. This philosopher, we are told, showed Alexander a symbol of his empire. He threw down on the ground a dry and shrivelled hide and planted his foot on the edge of it. But when it was trodden down in one place, it started up everywhere else. He then walked all round it and showed that the same thing took place wherever he trod, until at length he stepped into the middle, and by doing so made it all lie flat. This symbol was intended to show Alexander that he should control his empire from its centre, and not wander away to its distant extremities.

Arrian's *Anabasis:*
Fifth Book, Continued...

Chapter IX
Alexander on Reaching the Hydaspes Finds Porus Prepared to Dispute Its Passage

ALEXANDER ENCAMPED on the banks of the river, and Porus was seen on the opposite side, with all his army and his array of elephants around him. Against the place where he saw Alexander had encamped, he remained himself to guard the passage, but he sent detachments of his men, each commanded by a captain, to guard all parts of the river where it could be easily forded, as he was resolved to prevent the Macedonians from effecting a landing.

When Alexander saw this, he thought it expedient to move his army from place to place, so that Porus might be at a loss to discover his real intentions. For this purpose he divided his army into many parts, and some of the troops he led himself in different directions, sometimes to ravage the enemy's country, and sometimes to find out where he could most easily ford the river. He placed various commanders at various times over different divisions of his army, and despatched them also in different directions. At the same time, he caused provisions to be conveyed to the camp from all parts of the country on this side of the river, to impress Porus with the conviction that he intended to remain where he was near the bank, till the waters of the river subsided in winter, and afforded him a large choice of passages. As the boats were constantly plying up and down the stream, and the skins were being filled with hay, while all the bank was lined, here with horse and there with foot, all this prevented Porus from resting and concentrating his preparations at anyone point selected in preference to any other as the best for defending the passage. At this time of the year besides, all the Indian rivers were swollen and flowing with turbid and rapid currents, for the sun is then wont to turn towards the summer tropic. At this season incessant rains deluge the soil of India, and the snows of the Caucasus then melting flood the numerous rivers to which they give birth. In winter they again subside and become small and clear, and in many places fordable, with the exception of the Indus and the Ganges, and perhaps some one or two others. The Hydaspes at all events does become fordable.

Chapter X
Alexander's Devices to Deceive Porus and Steal the Passage of the River

ALEXANDER THEREFORE publicly announced that he would remain where he was throughout that season of the year if his passage was for the present to be obstructed, but he continued as before waiting in ambush to see whether he could anywhere rapidly steal a passage to the other side without being observed. He clearly saw that it was impossible for him to cross where Porus himself had encamped near the bank of the Hydaspes, not only because he had so many elephants, but also because his large army arrayed for battle, and splendidly accoutred, was ready to attack his troops the moment they landed. He foresaw besides that his horses would refuse to mount the opposite bank, where the elephants would at once encounter them, and by their very aspect and their roaring would terrify them outright; nor did he think that even before they gained the shore they would remain upon the inflated hides during the passage; but that on seeing the elephants even at a distance off, they would become frantic and leap into the water.

He resolved therefore to steal the passage, and to do this in the following way. Leading out by night the greater part of his cavalry along the riverbank in different directions, he ordered them to set up a loud clamour, raise the war shout, and fill the shores with every kind of noise, as if they were really preparing to attempt the passage. Porus marched meanwhile along the opposite bank, in the direction of the noise, having his elephants with him, and Alexander gradually accustomed him to lead out his men in this way in opposition. When this had been done repeatedly, and the men did nothing more than make a great noise and shout the war cry, Porus no longer made any countermovement when the cavalry issued out from the camp, but remained within his own lines, his spies being, however, posted at numerous points along the bank. When Alexander had thus quieted the suspicions of Porus about his nocturnal attempts, he devised the following stratagem.

Chapter XI
Arrangements Made by Alexander for Crossing the Hydaspes Unobserved

THERE WAS A BLUFF ascending from the bank of the Hydaspes at a point where the river made a remarkable bend, and this was densely covered with all sorts of trees. Over against it lay an island in the river overspread with jungle, an untrodden and solitary place. Perceiving that this island directly faced the bluff, and that both places were wooded and adapted to screen his attempt to cross the river, he decided to take his army over this way.

Now the bluff and the island were one hundred and fifty stadia distant from the great camp. But along the whole of the bank he had posted running sentries at a proper distance for keeping each other in sight, and readily transmitting along the line any orders that might be received from any quarter. In every direction, moreover, shouts were raised by night, and fires were burnt for many nights together. But when he had made up his mind to attempt the passage, the preparations for crossing were made in the camp without any concealment. In the camp Krateros had been left with his own division of the cavalry, and the Arakhosian and Parapamisadan horsemen, together with the brigades of the Macedonian phalanx commanded by Alcetas and Polysperchon and the contingent of five thousand men under the chiefs of the hither Indians. He had ordered Krateros not to attempt to cross the river before Porus moved off against them, or before learning that he was flying from the field, and that they were victorious. 'If, however,' said he, 'Porus with one part of his army advances against me while he leaves the other part and his elephants in his camp, then please to remain where you are; but if Porus takes all his elephants with him, and a portion of the rest of his army is left behind in the camp, then do you cross the river with all possible speed; for,' added he, 'it is the elephants only which make it impossible for the horses to land on the other bank. The rest of the army can cross over without difficulty.'

Chapter XII
Alexander Crosses the Hydaspes

SUCH WERE THE INSTRUCTIONS **given to Krateros; but halfway between the island and the main camp in which he had been left, there were posted Meleager, Attalos and Gorgias, with the mercenary cavalry and infantry, who had received orders to cross to the other side in detachments, into which their ranks were to be separated as soon as they saw the Indians fairly engaged in battle.**

He then selected to be taken under his own command the corps of bodyguards called Companions, the regiments of cavalry under Hephaestion, Perdiccas and Demetrios, also the Bactrian, Sogdian and Scythian cavalry, and the Daan horse-archers, and from the phalanx of infantry the hypaspists, the brigade of Kleitos and Coenus, and the archers and the Agrianians, and with these troops he marched with secrecy, keeping at a considerable distance from the bank that he might not be seen to be moving towards the island and the bluff, from which he intended to cross over to the other side. There in the night the skins, which had long before been provided for the purpose, were stuffed with hay, and securely stitched up. During the night a violent storm of rain came on, whereby his preparations and the attempt at crossing were not betrayed to the enemy by the rattle of arms and the shouting of orders, since the thunder and rain drowned all other sounds. Most of the boats which he had ordered to be cut into sections had been conveyed to this place, and when secretly pieced together again were hidden away in the woods along with the thirty-oared galleys. Towards daybreak the wind had died down and the rain ceased. The rest of the army then crossed over in the direction of the island, the cavalry mounted on the skin pontoon rafts, and as many of the foot soldiers as the boats could hold embarked in them. They so proceeded, that they were not seen by the sentries posted by Porus till they had passed beyond the island, and were not far from the bank.

Chapter XIII
Incidents of the Passage of the River

ALEXANDER HIMSELF EMBARKED on a thirty-oared galley, and went over accompanied by Ptolemy, Perdiccas and Lysimachus, his bodyguards, and by Seleukos, one of the companions, who was afterwards king, and by one half of the hypaspists, the other half being on board of the other galleys of like size. As soon as the soldiers had passed beyond the island, they steered for the bank, being now full in view of the enemy, whose sentinels on seeing their approach galloped off at the utmost speed of each man's horse to carry the tidings to Porus.

Meanwhile Alexander was himself the first to disembark, and taking the horsemen who had been conveyed over in his own and the other thirty-oared galleys, he at once formed them into line as they kept landing, for the cavalry had orders to be the first to disembark. At the head of these duly marshalled he moved forward. Owing, however, to his ignorance of the locality he had unawares landed not on the mainland, but upon an island, the great size of which prevented it all the more from being recognised as an island. It was separated from the mainland by a branch of the river in which the water was shallow; but the violent storm of rain which had lasted most of the night had so swollen the stream that the horsemen could not find the ford, and he feared that the latter part of the passage would be as laborious as the first. When at last the ford was found he led his men through it with difficulty; for the water where deepest reached higher than the breasts of the foot soldiers, and as for the horses their heads only were above the river. When he had crossed this piece of water also, he selected the mounted corps of bodyguards, and the best men from the other squadrons of cavalry, and brought them from column into line upon the right wing. Then in front of all the cavalry he posted the horse archers, and next in line to the cavalry and in front of all the infantry the royal hypaspists commanded by Seleukos. Next to these again he placed the royal foot guards, and then the other hypaspists, each in what happened to be the order of his precedence for the time being. At each extremity of the phalanx were posted the archers and the Agrianians and the javelin men.

Chapter XIV
Skirmish With the Son of Porus at the Landing Place

ALEXANDER HAVING MADE these dispositions, ordered the infantry, which numbered nearly six thousand men, to follow him at the ordinary marching pace and in regular order, for when he saw that he was superior in cavalry, he took with himself only the horsemen, about five thousand in number, and led them forward at a rapid pace. Tauron, the captain of the archers, he ordered to hasten forward with his men to give support to the cavalry. He had come to the conclusion that if Porus engaged him with all his troops he would either, without difficulty, overpower him by charging with his cavalry, or would remain on the defensive till the infantry came up during the action, or that if the Indians, terrified by the marvellous audacity of his passage of the river, should take to flight, he would be able to pursue them closely, and the slaughter being thus all the greater there would not be left much more work for him to do.

Aristoboulos says that the son of Porus arrived with about sixty chariots before Alexander made the final passage from the large island, and that he could have hindered Alexander from landing (for he made the passage with difficulty even when no one opposed him), if the Indians had but leaped down from their chariots and fallen upon those who first stepped on shore. The prince, however, passed by with his chariots, and allowed Alexander to accomplish the passage in complete safety. Against these Indians Alexander, he says, despatched his horse archers, who easily put them to a rout which was by no means bloodless. Other writers say that while the troops were landing an encounter took place between the Indians who had come with the son of Porus and Alexander at the head of his cavalry, and that as the son of Porus had come with a superior force Alexander himself was wounded by the Indian prince, and that his favourite horse Bucephalus was killed, having been wounded, like his master, by the son of Porus. But Ptolemy, the son of Lagos, with whom I agree, gives a different account, for he states, like the others, that Porus sent off his son, but not in command of merely sixty chariots; and indeed it is not at all likely that Porus, on learning from the scouts that either Alexander himself, or, at all events, a part of his army, had made the passage of the Hydaspes, would have sent his own son with no more than sixty chariots, which, considered as a reconnoitring party, would have been too numerous, and not rapid in retreat, but considered as meant to repel such of the enemy as had not yet crossed the river, and to attack those who had already landed, an altogether inadequate force. He says that the son of Porus arrived at the head of two thousand men and one hundred and twenty chariots, and that Alexander had made even the final passage from the island before the prince appeared upon the scene.

Chapter XV
The Arrangements Made by Porus for the Conflict

PTOLEMY STATES FURTHER that Alexander at first despatched against the prince the horse archers, and led the cavalry himself, under the belief that Porus was advancing against him with the

whole of his army, and that this was a body of advanced cavalry thrown forward by Porus. But when he discovered what the real strength of the Indians was he then briskly charged them with what cavalry he had with him. When they noticed that Alexander himself and his body of cavalry did not charge them in an extended line, but by squadrons, their ranks gave way, and four hundred of their horsemen fell, and among them the son of Porus. Their chariots, moreover, were captured, horses and all, for they proved heavy in the retreat and useless in the action itself, by having stuck fast in the clay.

When the horsemen who had escaped from this rout reported one after another to Porus that Alexander himself had crossed the river with the strongest division of his army, and that his son had been slain in the fight, he was still at a loss what to determine, for the division which had been left with Krateros in the great camp right opposite to his own position appeared to be undertaking the passage, but he at last decided to march with all his forces against Alexander and fight it out with the strongest division of the Macedonians led by the king in person. He nevertheless left there in his camp a few of the elephants and a small force to deter the cavalry under the command of Krateros from landing. He then took all his cavalry, four thousand strong, all his chariots, three hundred in number, two hundred of his elephants, and thirty thousand efficient infantry and marched against Alexander. When he found a place where he saw there was no clay, but that the ground from its sandy nature was all flat and firm, and suited for the movements of cavalry whether charging or falling back, he then drew up his army in order of battle, posting his elephants in the front line at intervals of at least one hundred feet, so as to have his elephants ranged in front before the whole body of his infantry, and so to spread terror at all points among Alexander's cavalry. He took it for certain besides that none of the enemy would have the audacity to push in at the intervals between the elephants – not the cavalry, since their horses would be terrified by these animals, and much less the infantry, since they would be checked in front by his heavy-armed foot soldiers falling upon them, and trampled down when the elephants wheeled round upon them. Behind these he drew up his infantry, which did not close up in one line with the elephants, but formed a second line in their rear, so that the regiments were only partly pushed forward into the intervals. He had also troops of infantry posted on the wings beyond the elephants, and on both sides of the infantry the cavalry had been drawn up, and in front of it the chariots.

Chapter XVI
The Plan of Attack Adopted by Alexander

IN THIS MANNER had Porus arranged his troops. As soon as Alexander perceived that the Indians had been drawn up in battle order he made his cavalry halt, that he might get in hand each regiment of the infantry as it came up; and even when the phalanx by a rapid march had effected a junction with the cavalry he still did not at once marshal its ranks and lead it into action, and thus expose the men, while tired and out of breath, to the barbarians, who were quite fresh, but he gave them time, while he rode round their ranks, to rest until they could recover themselves.

When he had observed how the Indians were arranged he made up his mind not to advance against the centre, in front of which the elephants had been posted, while the intervals between them had been filled with compact masses of infantry, for he feared lest Porus should reap the advantage which he had calculated on deriving from that arrangement. But as he was superior in cavalry he took the greater part of that force, and marched along towards the left wing of the enemy to make his attack in this quarter. Coenus he sent at the head of his own regiment of horse and that of Demetrios to the right, and ordered him, when the barbarians on seeing what a dense mass of cavalry was opposed to them, should be riding along to encounter it, to hang close upon their rear. The command of the phalanx of infantry he committed to Seleukos, Antigenes and Tauron, who received orders not to take part in the action till they saw that the phalanx of infantry and the cavalry of the enemy were thrown into disorder by the cavalry under his own command.

When the Indians were now within reach of his missiles he despatched against their left wing the horse archers, who were one thousnd strong, to throw the enemy in that part of the field into confusion with storms of arrows and charges of their horses. He marched rapidly forward himself with the companion cavalry against the left wing of the barbarians, making haste to attack their cavalry in a state of disorder while they were still in column, and before they could deploy into line.

Chapter XVII
Description of the Battle of the Hydaspes – Defeat of Porus

THE INDIANS MEANWHILE had collected their horsemen from every quarter, and were riding forward to repulse Alexander's onset, when Coenus, in accordance with his orders, appeared with his cavalry upon their rear. Seeing this the Indians had to make their cavalry face both to front and rear – the largest and best part to oppose Alexander, and the remainder to wheel round against Coenus and his squadrons. This therefore at once threw their ranks into confusion, and disconcerted their plan of operations; and Alexander, seeing that now was his opportunity while their cavalry was in the very act of forming to front and rear, fell upon those opposed to him with such vigour that the Indians, unable to withstand the charge of his cavalry, broke from their ranks, and fled for shelter to the elephants as to a friendly wall. Upon this the drivers of the elephants urged these animals forward against the cavalry; but the Macedonian phalanx itself now met them face to face, and threw darts at the men on the elephants, and from one side and the other struck the elephants themselves as they stood around them.

This kind of warfare was different from any of which they had experience in former contests, for the huge beasts charged the ranks of the infantry, and wherever they turned went crushing through the Macedonian phalanx though in close formation; while the horsemen of the Indians, on seeing that the infantry was now engaged in the action, again wheeled round and charged the cavalry. But Alexander's men, being far superior in personal strength and military discipline, again routed them, and again drove them back upon the elephants, and cooped them up among them. Meanwhile the whole of Alexander's cavalry had now been gathered into one battalion, not in consequence of an order, but from being thrown together in the course of the struggle, and wherever they fell upon the ranks of the Indians they made great carnage before parting from them. The elephants being now cooped up within a narrow space, did no less damage to their friends than to their foes, trampling them under their hoofs as they wheeled and pushed about. There resulted in consequence a great slaughter of the cavalry, cooped up as it was in a narrow space around the elephants. Many of the elephant drivers, moreover, had been shot down, and of the elephants themselves some had been wounded, while others, both from exhaustion and the loss of their drivers, no longer kept to their own side in the conflict, but, as if driven frantic by their sufferings, attacked friend and foe quite indiscriminately, pushed them, trampled them down, and killed them in all manner of ways. But the Macedonians, who had a wide and open field, and could therefore operate as they thought best, gave way when the elephants charged, and when they retreated followed at their heels and plied them with darts; whereas the Indians, who were in the midst of the animals, suffered far more the effects of their rage. When the elephants, however, became quite exhausted, and their attacks were no longer made with vigour, they fell back like ships backing water, and merely kept trumpeting as they retreated with their faces to the enemy. Then did Alexander surround with his cavalry the whole of the enemy's line, and signal that the infantry, with their shields linked together so as to give the utmost compactness to their ranks, should advance in phalanx. By this means the cavalry of the Indians was, with a few exceptions, cut to pieces in the action. Such also was the fate of the infantry, since the Macedonians were now pressing upon them from every side. Upon this all turned to flight wherever a gap could be found in the cordon of Alexander's cavalry.

Chapter XVIII
Sequel of the Battle and Surrender of Porus

MEANWHILE KRATEROS and all the other officers of Alexander's army, who had been left behind on the opposite bank of the Hydaspes, crossed the river when they perceived that Alexander was winning a splendid victory. These men, being fresh, were employed in the pursuit, instead of Alexander's exhausted troops, and they made no less a slaughter of the Indians in the retreat than had been made in the engagement.

The loss of the Indians in killed fell little short of twenty thousand infantry and three thousand cavalry, and all their chariots were broken to pieces. Two sons of Porus fell in the battle, and also Spitaces, the chief of the Indians of that district. The drivers of the elephants and of the chariots were also slain and the cavalry officers and the generals in the army of Porus all.... The elephants, moreover, that escaped destruction in the field were all captured. On Alexander's side there fell about eighty of the six thousand infantry who had taken part in the first attack, ten of the horse archers who first began the action, twenty of the companion cavalry and two hundred of the other cavalry.

When Porus, who had nobly discharged his duties throughout the battle, performing the part not only of a general, but also that of a gallant soldier, saw the slaughter of his cavalry and some of his elephants lying dead, and others wandering about sad and sullen without their drivers, while the greater part of his infantry had been killed, he did not, after the manner of Darius, the great king, abandon the field and show his men the first example of flight, but, on the contrary, fought on as long as he saw any Indians maintaining the contest in a united body; but he wheeled round on being wounded in the right shoulder, where only he was unprotected by armour in the battle. All the rest of his person was rendered shot-proof by his coat of mail, which was remarkable for its strength and the closeness with which it fitted his person, as could afterwards be observed by those who saw him. When he found himself wounded he turned his elephant round and began to retire. Alexander, perceiving that he was a great man and valiant in fight, was anxious to save his life, and for this purpose sent to him first of all Taxiles the Indian. Taxiles, who was on horseback, approached as near the elephant which carried Porus as seemed safe, and entreated him, since it was no longer possible for him to flee, to stop his elephant and listen to the message he brought from Alexander. But Porus, on finding that the speaker was his old enemy Taxiles, turned round and prepared to smite him with his javelin; and he would probably have killed him had not Taxiles instantly put his horse to the gallop and got beyond the reach of Porus. But not even for this act did Alexander feel any resentment against Porus, but sent to him messenger after messenger, and last of all Meroes, an Indian, as he had learned that Porus and this Meroes were old friends. As soon as Porus heard the message which Meroes now brought just at a time when he was overpowered by thirst, he made his elephant halt and dismounted. Then, when he had taken a draught of water and felt revived, he requested Meroes to conduct him without delay to Alexander.

Chapter XIX
Alexander Makes Porus His Firm Friend and Ally – Founds Two Cities – Death of His Famous Horse Bucephalus

H E WAS THEN CONDUCTED to Alexander, who, on learning that Meroes was approaching with him, rode forward in front of his line with a few of the Companions to meet him. Then reining in his horse he beheld with admiration the handsome person and majestic stature of Porus, which somewhat exceeded five cubits. He saw, too, with wonder that he did not seem to be broken and abased in spirit, but that he advanced to meet him as a brave man would meet another brave man after gallantly contending with another king in defence of his kingdom. Then Alexander, who was the first to speak, requested Porus to say how he wished to be treated. The report goes that Porus said in reply, 'Treat me,

Alexander, like a king! Treat me, O Alexander! as befits a king;' and that Alexander, being pleased with his answer, replied, 'It shall be as you desire, Porus, for my part; do you for your part ask what you desire. For mine own sake, O Porus! thou shalt be so treated, but do thou, in thine own behalf, ask for whatever boon thou pleasest,' to which Porus replied that in what he had asked everything was included. Alexander was more delighted than ever with this rejoinder, and not only appointed Porus to govern his own Indians, but added to his original territory another of still greater extent.

Alexander thus treated this brave man as befitted a king, and he consequently found him in all respects faithful and devoted to his interests. Such, then, was the result of the battle in which Alexander fought against Porus and the Indians of the other side of the Hydaspes in the month of Mounychion of the year when Hegemon was archon in Athens.

Alexander founded two cities, one on the battlefield, and the other at the point whence he had started to cross the river Hydaspes. The former he called Nikaia in honour of his victory over the Indians, and the other Boucephala in memory of his horse Bucephalus, which died there, not from being wounded by anyone, but from toil and old age, for he was about thirty years old, and had heretofore undergone many toils and dangers along with Alexander. This Bucephalus was never mounted by anyone except Alexander only, for he disdained all other riders. He was of an uncommon size and of generous mettle. He had by way of a distinguishing mark the head of an ox impressed upon him, and some say that from this circumstance he got his name. But others say that though he was black, he had on his forehead a white mark which bore a close resemblance to the brow of an ox. In the country of the Ouxians this horse disappeared from Alexander, who sent a proclamation through the land that he would kill all the Ouxians if they did not bring him his horse, and brought back he was immediately after the proclamation had been issued – so great was Alexander's attachment to his favourite, and so great was the fear of Alexander which prevailed among the barbarians. Let so much honour be paid by me to this Bucephalus for Alexander's sake.

Chapter XX
Alexander Conquers the Glausai – Receives Embassies from Abisares and Other Chiefs – Crosses the Acesines

W HEN ALEXANDER HAD DULY honoured with splendid rites those who had been slain in the battle, he offered to the gods in acknowledgment of his victory the customary sacrifices, and celebrated athletic and equestrian contests on the bank of the river Hydaspes, at the place where he first crossed with his army. He then left Krateros behind with a part of the army to build and fortify the cities which he was founding there, while he advanced himself against the Indians whose country lay next to the dominions of Porus. Aristoboulos says that the name of the nation was the Glaukanikoi, but Ptolemy calls them the Glausai. By which of the names it was called I take to be a matter of no consequence. Alexander invaded their country with the half of the companion cavalry, picked men from each phalanx of the infantry, all the horse archers, the Agrianians and the other archers. The people everywhere surrendered on terms of capitulation. In this manner he took thirty-seven cities, the smallest of which contained not fewer than five thousand inhabitants, while many contained upwards of ten thousand. He took also a great many villages which were not less populous than the towns; and this country he gave to Porus to rule, and between him and Taxiles he effected a reconciliation. He then sent Taxiles home to his capital.

At this time envoys came from Abisares to say that their king surrendered himself and his whole realm to Alexander. Yet before the battle in which Alexander had defeated Porus, Abisares was ready with his army to fight on the side of Porus. But he now sent his brother along with the other envoys to Alexander, taking with them money and forty elephants as a present. Envoys also arrived from the independent Indians, and from another Indian ruler called Porus. Alexander ordered Abisares to come to him as quickly as possible, threatening that if he did not come he would see him and his army arriving where he would not rejoice to see them.

At this time Phratophernes, the satrap of Parthia and Hyrkania, at the head of the Thracians who had been left with him came to Alexander. There came also envoys from Shashigupta, the satrap of the Assakenians, reporting that these people had slain their governor and revolted from Alexander. Against these he sent Philip and Tiryaspes to quell the insurrection and restore tranquillity and order to the province.

Alexander himself advanced towards the river Acesines. This is the only Indian river of which Ptolemy, the son of Lagos, has mentioned the size. He states that where Alexander crossed it with his army in boats and on inflated hides the current was so rapid that the waters dashed with foam and fury against the large and jagged rocks with which the channel was bestrewn. He informs us also that it was fifteen stadia in breadth; and while the passage was easy for those who crossed upon inflated hides, not a few of those who were carried in boats perished in the waters, as many of the boats were dashed to pieces by striking against the rocks. From this description we may fairly conclude, if we institute a comparison, that the size of the river Indus has been pretty correctly stated by those who take it to have an average breadth of forty stadia, while, where narrowest and of course deepest, it contracts to a breadth of fifteen stadia, which I take to be its actual breadth in many parts of its course, for I conclude that Alexander selected a part of the Acesines where the passage was widest, and where the current would consequently be slower than elsewhere.

Chapter XXI
Pursuit After Porus, Nephew of the Great Porus – Conquest of the Country Between the Acesines and the Hydraotes – Passage of the Latter River

AFTER CROSSING THE RIVER he left Coenus there upon the bank with his own brigade, and ordered him to superintend the passage of the river by those troops which had been left behind

to collect corn and other supplies from the part of India which was now under his authority.

Porus he sent home to his capital with orders to select the best fighting men of the Indians, and to muster all the elephants he possessed, and to rejoin him with these. He resolved to pursue in person the other Porus – the bad one – with the lightest troops in his army, for word had been brought that he had fled from the country of which he was the ruler; for, while hostilities still subsisted between Alexander and the other Porus, this Porus had sent envoys to Alexander offering to surrender into his hands both his person and the country over which he ruled, but this more from enmity to Porus than friendliness to Alexander. On learning therefore that Porus had not only been set at liberty, but had his kingdom restored to him, and that too with a large accession of territory, he was overcome with fear, not so much of Alexander as of his namesake Porus, and fled from his country, taking with him as many fighting men as he could persuade to accompany him in his flight.

Alexander, while marching to overtake him, arrived at the Hydraotes – another Indian river, not less in breadth than the Acesines, but not so rapid. Over all the country which he overran he planted garrisons in the most suitable places, so that the troops under Krateros and Coenus might, while scouring it far and near for forage, traverse it in safety to join him. He then despatched Hephaestion with a force comprising two divisions of infantry, his own regiment of cavalry and that of Demetrios, and one-half of the archers, into the country of that Porus who had revolted. He received orders to hand over the country to the other Porus, and when he had reduced all the independent Indian tribes bordering on the banks of the Hydraotes, to place these also under the rule of Porus. He himself then crossed the river Hydraotes, where he met with none of the difficulties which had attended the passage of the Acesines. When he was advancing into the country beyond the Hydraotes he found most of the natives willing to surrender on capitulation, while some met him in arms, and others were captured when attempting to escape and reduced to submission.

Chapter XXII
Alexander Marches Against the Kathaians – Takes Pimprama, and Lays Siege to Sangala

ALEXANDER MEANWHILE HAD LEARNED that the Kathaians and other tribes of independent Indians were preparing to meet him in battle if he invaded their country, and were inviting the neighbouring tribes, which were independent like themselves, to cooperate with them. He learned also that the city near which they meant to engage him was strongly fortified, and was called Sangala.

The Kathaians themselves enjoyed the highest reputation for courage and skill in the art of war, and the same warlike spirit characterised the Oxydrakai, another Indian race, and the Malloi, who were also an Indian race, for when shortly before this time Porus and Abisares had marched against them with their armies, and had besides stirred up many of the independent Indians against them, they were obliged, as it turned out, to retreat without accomplishing anything at all adequate to the scale of their preparations.

Alexander, on receiving this intelligence, marched rapidly against the Kathaians, and on the second day after he had left the river Hydraotes arrived at a city named Pimprama, belonging to an Indian race called the Adraïstai, which surrendered on terms of capitulation. Alexander gave his troops rest the next day, and on the third day advanced to Sangala, where the Kathaians and the neighbouring tribes that had joined them were mustered before the city, and drawn up in battle order on a low hill, which was not on all sides precipitous. They lay encamped behind their wagons, which, by encircling the hill in three rows, protected the camp with a triple barricade. Alexander, on perceiving the great number of the barbarians, and the nature of the position they occupied, drew up his army in the order which seemed best suited to the circumstances, and at once despatched against them the horse archers just as they were, with orders to ride along and shoot at the Indians from a distance, so as not only to prevent them from making a sortie before his own dispositions should be completed, but to wound them within their stronghold even before the battle began. Upon his right wing he posted the corps of horseguards and the cavalry regiment of Kleitos, next to these the hypaspists and then the Agrianians. The left wing he assigned to Perdiccas, who commanded his own cavalry regiment and the battalions of the footguards. The archers he formed into two bodies, and placed them upon each wing. While he was making these dispositions the infantry and cavalry which formed the rearguard arrived upon the field. This cavalry he divided in two parts, and led one to each wing, and with the infantry that had arrived he closed up the ranks of the phalanx more densely. Then he took the cavalry which had been drawn up on the right and advanced against the wagons ranged on the left wing of the Indians, where the position seemed easier to assault, and where the wagons were not so closely packed together.

Chapter XXIII
Alexander Drives the Kathaians into Sangala, Which He Invests on Every Side

BUT WHEN THE INDIANS, instead of sallying out from behind their wagons to attack the cavalry as it advanced, mounted upon them, and began to shoot from the top of them, Alexander saw that this was not work for cavalry, and so, having dismounted, he led on foot the phalanx of infantry against them.

The Macedonians found no difficulty in driving the Indians from the first row of wagons, but on the other hand the Indians, having formed in line in front of the second row, were able to force back their assailants with greater ease, standing as they did more compactly together, and in a narrower circle, while the Macedonians had less room in which to operate against them. At this time, they quietly drew back the wagons of the first row, and through the gaps each man, as he found an opportunity, assailed the enemy in an irregular way. Yet even from these wagons they were forcibly driven by the phalanx of infantry, and even at the third row they no longer held ground, but fled with all the haste they could into the city and shut themselves up within its gates. Alexander that same day encamped with his infantry around the city, as far at least as the phalanx enabled him to surround it, for the wall was of such great extent that his camp did not completely environ it. Opposite the part where the gap was left, and where also was a lake not far from the walls, he posted the cavalry all around the lake, as he knew it not to be deep, and at the same time anticipated that the Indians, terrified by their previous defeat, would abandon the city during the night. The event showed he had conjectured aright, for about the second watch the most of them dropped down from the wall and came upon the outposts of the cavalry. The foremost of them were cut to pieces by the sentinels, but those in the rear, perceiving that the lake was guarded all round, withdrew into the city. Alexander now encompassed the city with a double stockade, except where the lake shut it in, and around the lake he posted guards to keep still stricter watch. He resolved also to bring up the military engines against the place for battering down the walls. Some deserters, however, came to him from the city and informed him that the Indians intended that very night to escape from the city by way of the lake where the gap occurred in the stockade. So at that point he stationed Ptolemy, the son of Lagos, with three divisions of the hypaspists, each one thousand strong, all the Agrianians, and a single line of archers, and pointed out to him the particular spot where the barbarians, as he conjectured, were likeliest to attempt forcing their passage. 'And now,' said he, 'when you perceive the barbarians forcing their way at this point, do thou with the army arrest their advance, and order the trumpets to sound the signal; and do you, sirs,' he added, turning to the officers, 'as soon as the signal is given, each of you with your men in battle-order, hasten towards the noise wherever the trumpet summons you. I shall not myself stand idly by away from the fight.'

Chapter XXIV
Alexander Captures Sangala, Razes It to the Ground, and Advances to the River Hyphasis

SUCH WERE THE DIRECTIONS he gave, and Ptolemy in that place collected as many as he could of the wagons which the enemy had left behind in their first flight, and placed them athwart so

that the fugitives might imagine there were many obstacles to their escaping by night. He ordered the stakes, which had been cut but not fixed in the ground, to be formed into stockades at different points between the lake and the wall.

All this was done by the soldiers during the night. But when it was now about the fourth watch the barbarians, in accordance with the information Alexander had received, opened the gates which fronted the lake and rushed towards it at full speed. They did not, however, escape the vigilance either of the guards posted there, or of Ptolemy who lay behind ready to support them; and just then the trumpeters gave him the signal, and he advanced against the barbarians with his troops which were under arms and drawn up ready for action. The wagons, moreover, as well as the stockade, which had been constructed between the wall and the lake, impeded the fugitives; and as soon as the trumpet sounded the alarm Ptolemy with his men fell upon them and killed them, one after another, as they slunk out from the wagons. Upon this the Indians fled back once more to the city for refuge, and as many as five hundred of them were slain in the retreat.

Meanwhile Porus also arrived, bringing with him the remainder of his elephants and a force of five thousand Indians, and the military engines which had been constructed by Alexander were now being brought up to the wall. But the Macedonians, before any part of it was battered down, took the city by storm, having undermined the wall, which was of brick, and planted ladders against it all round. In the capture seventeen thousand of the Indians were slaughtered, and more than seventy thousand were captured, together with three hundred wagons and five hundred horsemen. The loss in Alexander's army during all the siege was somewhat under one hundred killed, but the proportion of the wounded to the number killed was higher than usual, for there were twelve hundred wounded, including some officers, and among these Lysimachus, a member of the bodyguard.

Alexander having buried the dead according to custom, sent Eumenes, his secretary, in command of three hundred horsemen to the two cities which had revolted along with Sangala, to tell those who held them that Sangala had been captured, and that Alexander would not at all deal hardly with them if they remained where they were and received him in a friendly way, for that none of the independent Indians who had voluntarily surrendered themselves had received any ill treatment at his hands. But they had already learned that Sangala had been stormed by Alexander, and being terrified by the news had left the cities and were in flight. When Alexander was informed of their flight he hastened after them, but as they had a long start of him most of them baffled his efforts to overtake them. Those, however, who were left behind in the retreat when their strength failed were taken by the troops and slaughtered to the number of about five hundred. As he gave up the design of pursuing the fugitives any farther, he drew back to Sangala and razed the city to the ground. The land belonging to it he made over to those Indians who had formerly been independent, but who had voluntarily submitted to him. He then sent Porus with his own forces to the cities which had submitted to introduce garrisons within them, but he himself with his army advanced to the river Hyphasis to conquer the Indians who dwelt beyond it. Nor did there appear to him any end of the war as long as an enemy remained to be encountered.

Chapter XXV
Alexander Finding the Army Unwilling to Advance Beyond the Hyphasis, Convokes His Officers and Addresses Them on the Subject

IT WAS REPORTED that the country beyond the Hyphasis was exceedingly fertile, and that the inhabitants were good agriculturists, brave in war and living under an excellent system of internal government; for the multitude was governed by the aristocracy, who exercised their authority with justice and moderation. It was also reported that the people there had a greater number of elephants than the other Indians, and that those were of superior size and courage. This information only whetted Alexander's eagerness to advance farther, but the Macedonians now began to lose heart when they saw the king raising up without end toils upon toils and dangers upon dangers. The army, therefore, began to hold conferences at which the more moderate men bewailed their condition, while others positively asserted that they would follow no farther though Alexander himself should lead the way. When this came to Alexander's knowledge he convoked the officers in command of brigades, before the disorder and despondency should be further developed among the soldiers, and he thus addressed them:

'On seeing that you, O Macedonians and allies! no longer follow me into dangers with your customary alacrity, I have summoned you to this assembly that I may either persuade you to go farther, or be persuaded by you to turn back. If you have reason to complain of past labours, and of me your leader, I need say no more. But if by those labours you have acquired Ionia, and the Hellespont with the two Phrygias, Cappadocia, Paphlagonia, Lydia, Karia, Lykia and Pamphylia, as well as Phoenicia and Egypt, together with Hellenic Libya, part of Arabia, Lowland Syria, Mesopotamia, Babylon, Susia, Persia and Media, and all the provinces governed by the Medes and Persians, not to mention other states which were never subject to them; if in addition we have conquered the regions beyond the Caspian Gates, those beyond Caucasus, the Tanais also, and the country beyond, Bactria, Hyrkania and the Hyrkanian Sea; if we have driven the Scythians back into their deserts, and if besides, the Indus, Hydaspes, Acesines and Hydraotes flow through territories that are ours, why should you hesitate to pass the Hyphasis also and add the tribes beyond it to your Macedonian conquests? Are you afraid there are other barbarians who may yet successfully resist you, although of those we have already met some have willingly submitted, others have been captured in flight, while others have left us their deserted country to be distributed either to our allies or to those who have voluntarily submitted to us?'

Chapter XXVI
Continuation of Alexander's Speech

FOR MY PART, I think that to a man of spirit there is no other aim and end of his labours except the labours themselves, provided they be such as lead him to the performance of glorious deeds.

But if anyone wishes to know the limits of the present warfare, let him understand that the river Ganges and the Eastern Sea are now at no great distance off. This sea, I am confident, is connected with the Hyrkanian Sea, because the Great Ocean flows round the whole earth. I shall besides prove to the Macedonians and their allies that the Indian Gulf is connected with the Persian, and the Hyrkanian Sea with the Indian Gulf. From the Persian Gulf our fleet will sail round to Libya as far as the Pillars of Heracles. From these pillars all the interior of Libya becomes ours, and thus all Asia shall belong to us, and the boundaries of our empire in that direction will coincide with those which the deity has made the boundaries of the earth.

But, if we now turn back, many warlike nations extending beyond the Hyphasis to the Eastern Sea, and many others lying northwards between these and Hyrkania, to say nothing of their neighbours the Scythian tribes, will be left behind us unconquered, so that if we turn back there is cause to fear lest the conquered nations, as yet wavering in their fidelity, may be instigated to revolt by those who are still independent. Our many labours will in that case be all completely thrown away, or we must enter on a new round of toils and dangers. But persevere, O Macedonians and allies! glory crowns the deeds of those who expose themselves to toils and dangers. Life, signalised by deeds of valour, is delightful, and so is death, if we leave behind us an immortal name. Know ye not that it was not by staying at home in Tiryns or Argos, or even in Peloponnese or Thebes, that our ancestor was exalted to such glory, that from being a man he became, or was thought to be, a god. Nor were the labours few even of Dionysus, who ranks as a god far above Heracles. But we have advanced beyond Nysa, and the rock Aornos, which proved impregnable to Heracles, is in our possession. Add, then, the rest of Asia to our present acquisitions – the smaller part of it to the greater. Could we ourselves, think you, have achieved any great and memorable deeds if, sitting down at home in Macedonia, we had been content without exertion merely to preserve our own country, by repelling the attacks of the neighbouring Thracians, Illyrians and Triballians, or those Greeks whose disposition to us is unfriendly?

'If, indeed, while leading you, I had myself shrunk from the toils and dangers to which you were exposed, you would not without good reason be dispirited in prospect of undertaking fresh enterprises, seeing that while you alone shared the toils, it was for others you procured the rewards. But our labours are in common; I, equally with you, share in the dangers, and the rewards become the public property. For the land is yours, and you are its satraps; and among you the greater part of its treasures has already been distributed. And when all Asia is subdued then, by heaven, I will not merely satisfy, but exceed every man's hopes and wishes. Such of you as wish to return home I shall send back to your own country, or even myself will lead you back. But those who remain here I will make objects of envy to those who go back.'

Chapter XXVII
Coenus, Replying to Alexander, States the Grievances of the Army

WHEN ALEXANDER HAD SPOKEN to this and the like effect, a long silence followed, because those present neither dared to speak freely in opposition to the king, nor yet wished to assent to what he proposed. Alexander again and again requested that anyone who wished should speak, even if his views differed from those which he had himself expressed. But the silence was unbroken for a long time, till at last Coenus, the son of Polemocrates, summoned up courage and spoke to this effect:

'Since as you do not wish, O king! to rule Macedonians by constraint, but say that you will lead them by persuasion, or suffering yourself to be persuaded by them, will not have recourse to compulsion, I intend to speak, not on behalf of myself and fellow-officers who have been honoured above the other soldiers, and have most of us received splendid rewards of our labours, and from having been highly exalted above others are more zealous than others to serve you in all things, but in behalf of the great body of the army. Yet on behalf of this army I intend not to say what may be agreeable to the men, but what I think will be conducive to your present interests and safest for the future. I feel bound by my age not to conceal what appears to be the best course to follow; bound by the high authority conferred on me by yourself, and bound also by the unhesitating boldness which I have hitherto exhibited in all enterprises of danger. The more I look to the number and magnitude of the exploits performed under your command by us who set out with you from home, the more does it seem to me expedient to place some limit to our toils and dangers. For you see yourself how many Macedonians and Greeks started with you, and how few of us are left. From our ranks you sent away home from Bactria the Thessalians as soon as you saw they had no stomach for further toils, and in this you acted wisely. Of the other Greeks, some have been settled in the cities founded by you, where all of them are not willing residents; others still share our toils and dangers. They and the Macedonian army have lost some of their numbers in the fields of battle; others have been disabled by wounds; others have been left behind in different parts of Asia, but the majority have perished by disease. A few only out of many survive, and these few possessed no longer of the same bodily strength as before, while their spirits are still more depressed. All those, whose parents are still living, have a yearning to see them – a yearning to see their wives and children – a yearning to see were it but their native land itself – a desire pardonable in men who would return home in great splendour derived from your munificence, and raised from humble to high rank, and from indigence to wealth. Seek not, therefore, to lead them against their inclinations, for you will not find them the same men in the face of dangers, if they enter without heart into their contests with the enemy. But do you also, if it agree with your wishes, return home with us, see your mother once more, settle the affairs of the Greeks, and carry to the house of your fathers those your great and numerous victories. Then having so done, form, if you so wish, a fresh expedition against these same tribes of eastern Indians, or, if you prefer, against the shores of the Euxine Sea, or against Carchedon, and the parts of Libya beyond the Carchedonians. It will then be your part to unfold your purpose, and then other Macedonians and other Greeks will follow you – young men full of vigour instead of old men worn out with toils – men for whom war, through their inexperience of it, has no immediate terrors, and eager to set out from the hope of future rewards. They will also naturally follow you with the greater alacrity, from seeing that the companions of your former toils and dangers have returned home wealthy instead of poor, and raised to high distinction from their original obscurity. Moderation, in the midst of success, is, O king! the noblest of virtues, for though, at the head of so brave an army, you have nothing to dread from mortal foes, yet the visitations of the deity cannot be foreseen, and man cannot, therefore, guard against them.'

Chapter XXVIII
Alexander Mortified By the Refusal of His Army to Advance, Secludes Himself in His Tent, But in the End Resolves to Return

WHEN COENUS HAD CONCLUDED his address, those present are said to have signified their approval of what he said by loud applause, while many by their streaming tears showed still more expressively their aversion to encounter further dangers, and how welcome to them was the idea of returning.**

But Alexander, who resented the freedom with which Coenus had spoken, and the hesitation displayed by the other generals, broke up the conference; but next day while his wrath was still hot he summoned the same men again, and told them that he was going forward himself, but would not force any of the Macedonians to accompany him against their wishes, for he would find men ready to follow their king of their own free will. But those who wished to go away were free to go home, and might tell their friends there that they had returned, and left their king in the midst of his enemies. It is said that with these words he withdrew into his tent, and did not admit any of his companions to see him on that day, nor even till the third day after, waiting to see whether a change of mood, such as often takes place in an assemblage of soldiers, would manifest itself among the Macedonians and the allies, and make them readier to yield to his persuasions. But when a deep silence again reigned throughout the camp, and the soldiers were evidently offended by his wrath without their minds being changed by it, he began nonetheless, as Ptolemy, the son of Lagos, states, to offer there sacrifice for the passage of the river; but when on sacrificing he found the omens were against him, he then assembled the oldest of the Companions, and especially his intimate friends among them, and as everything indicated that to return was his most expedient course he intimated to the army that he had resolved to march back.

Chapter XXIX
Alexander Erects Altars on the Banks of the Hyphasis to Mark the Limits of His Advance, Recrosses the Hydraotes and Acesines and Regains the Hydaspes

THEN THEY SHOUTED, as a mixed multitude would shout when rejoicing, and many of them shed tears. Some of them even approached the royal pavilion, and invoked many blessings on Alexander, because by them and them only did he permit himself to be vanquished. He then divided the army into brigades, which he ordered to prepare twelve altars to equal in height the highest military towers, and to exceed them in point of breadth, to serve as thank-offerings to the gods who had led him so far as a conqueror, and also as a memorial of his own labours. When the altars had been constructed, he offered sacrifice upon them with the customary rites, and celebrated a gymnastic and equestrian contest. Having thereafter committed all the country west of the river Hyphasis to the government of Porus, he marched back to the Hydraotes. After crossing this river, he retraced his steps to the Acesines, and on arriving there found the city which he had ordered Hephaestion to fortify completely built. Herein he settled as many of the inhabitants of the neighbourhood as were willing to make it their domicile, and such also of the mercenary soldiers as were now unfit for further service. He then began to make preparations for the downward voyage to the Great Sea.

At this time Arsakes, ruler of the country adjoining the dominions of Abisares, together with the brother of Abisares and his other relatives, came to him, bringing presents such as the Indians consider the most valuable, and some thirty elephants sent by Abisares. They represented that Abisares was prevented from coming in person by illness – a statement which the ambassadors sent by Alexander to Abisares corroborated. Alexander, readily believing that such was the case, made Abisares satrap of his own dominions, and moreover placed Arsakes under his jurisdiction. Having then fixed the amount which was to be paid as tribute, he again offered sacrifice near the river Acesines. He then recrossed that river, and reached the Hydaspes, where he employed his army in repairing the damage caused by the rains to the cities of Nikaia and Boucephala, and set the other affairs of the country in order.

Arrian's *Anabasis*: Sixth Book

Chapter I
Alexander Mistakes the Indus for the Upper Nile – Prepares to Sail Downstream to the Sea

WHEN ALEXANDER HAD GOT READY upon the banks of the Hydaspes a large number of thirty-oared galleys, and others of one bank and a half of oars, besides numerous horse transports and every other requisite for the easy conveyance of an army by river, he resolved to sail down the Hydaspes to the Great Sea.

As he had before this seen crocodiles in the river Indus, and in no other river but the Nile only, and had besides seen beans of the same species as those which Egypt produces growing near the banks of the Acesines, and as he had heard that this river falls into the Indus, he was led to think that he had discovered the sources of the Nile. His idea was that this river rose somewhere among the Indians and pursued its course through a vast tract of desert country, where it lost the name of the Indus, and that from the time when it began to flow through the inhabited parts of the world it was called the Nile both by the Ethiopians, who lived there and by the Egyptians, just as Homer also changed its name, calling it the river Egypt after Egypt, the country where at last it discharges itself into the Inner Sea. Accordingly, when he was writing to his mother Olympias about the country of the Indians, he mentioned, it is said, among other things that he thought he had discovered the sources of the Nile, actually basing on such slight and contemptible evidence his judgements respecting questions of so much importance. When, however, he investigated with special care the facts relating to the river Indus, he ascertained from the natives that the Hydaspes unites with the Acesines, and the Acesines with the Indus, to which the other two rivers lose both their waters and their names. He learned further that the Indus discharges itself into the Great Sea by two mouths, and that it has no connection with the Egyptian country. He is said to have then deleted what he had written about the Nile in the letter to his mother, and as he had set his mind on sailing down the rivers to the Great Sea he ordered a fleet for this purpose to be prepared for him. Adequate crews for the vessels were supplied by the Phoenicians, Cyprians, Carians, and Egyptians who accompanied the army.

Chapter II
Description of the Voyage Down the Hydaspes

A T THIS TIME COENUS, who was one of Alexander's most faithful companions, took ill and died, and Alexander buried him with all the magnificence circumstances allowed. He then assembled the Companions and all the ambassadors of the Indians who had come to him, and in their presence appointed Porus king of all the Indian territories already subjugated – seven nations in all, containing more than two thousand cities.

He then made the following distribution of his army. He took in the ships along with himself all the hypaspists, and the archers, and the Agrianians, and the corps of horse-guards. Krateros commanding a division of the infantry and cavalry, conducted it along the right bank of the Hydaspes, while Hephaestion on the opposite bank advanced in command of the largest and best division of the army, to which the elephants, now about two hundred in number, were attached. These generals were instructed to march with all possible speed to where the palace of Sopeithes was situated. Philip, the satrap of the province lying west of the Indus in the direction of the Bactrians, received orders to follow them with his troops after an interval of three days, but the cavalry of the Nysaens he now sent back to Nysa. The command of the whole naval squadron was entrusted to Nearchus, while the pilot of Alexander's own ship was Onesicritos, who, in the narrative which he composed about the wars of Alexander, among his other lies, described himself as the commander of the fleet, although he was in reality only a pilot. According to Ptolemy, the son of Lagos, whose authority I principally follow, the ships numbered collectively eighty thirty-oared galleys, but the whole fleet, including the horse transports and the small craft and other river boats consisting of those that formerly plied on the rivers and those recently built for the present service, did not fall much short of two thousand.

Chapter III
Description of the Voyage Down the Hydaspes Continued

WHEN ALL THE PREPARATIONS had been completed, the army at break of day began to embark. Alexander himself sacrificed according to custom both to the gods and to the river Acesines as the seers directed. After he had embarked he poured a libation into the river, from his station on the prow, out of a golden bowl, and invoked not only the Hydaspes, but also the Acesines, as he had learned that the Acesines was the greatest of all the confluents of the Hydaspes, and that their point of junction was not far off. He invoked likewise the Indus, into which the Acesines falls after receiving the Hydaspes. He further poured out libations to his ancestor Heracles, and to Ammon and every other god to whom it was his custom to sacrifice, and then he ordered the signal for starting on the voyage to be given by sound of trumpet.

The fleet as soon as the signal sounded began the voyage in due order, for directions had been given at what distances the luggage boats, the horse transports, and the war galleys should keep apart from each other to prevent collisions which would be inevitable if the ships sailed at random down the channel. Even the fast boats were not allowed to break rank by outdistancing the others. The noise caused by the rowing was great beyond all precedent, proceeding as it did from a vast number of boats being rowed simultaneously, and swelled by the shouts of the officers directing the rowing to begin or to stop, commingled with the shouts of the rowers, which rung like the war cry when they joined together in keeping time to the dashing of the oars. The banks, moreover, being in many places higher than the ships, and compressing the sound within a narrow compass, sent the echoes, greatly increased by the compression itself, flying to and fro between them. The ravines also which occasionally opened on the river on either of its shores served further to swell the din by reverberating amid their solitudes the thuds of the oars. The appearance of the war-horses on the decks of the transports struck the barbarians, who saw them through the lattice work, with such wonder and astonishment, that the throng which lined the shores to witness the departure of the fleet accompanied it to a great distance, for in the country of the Indians horses had never before been seen on shipboard, nor was there any tradition to the effect that the Indian expedition of Dionysus as of a naval character. Those Indians also who had already submitted to Alexander, as soon as they heard the shouts of the rowers and the dashing of the oars, ran down to the edge of the river and followed the fleet, singing their own native songs, for the Indians have been peculiarly distinguished among the nations as lovers of dance and song, ever since Dionysus and his attendant Bacchanals made their festive progress through the realms of India.

Chapter IV
Alexander Accelerates His Voyage to Frustrate the Plans of the Malloi and Oxydrakai, and Reaches the Turbulent Confluence of the Hydaspes and Acesines

ALEXANDER SAILING THUS, halted on the third day at the place where he had ordered Hephaestion and Krateros to pitch their camps right opposite each other, each on his own side of the river. Having waited here for two days until Philip arrived with the rest of the army, he sent that general forward with the detachment he had brought with him to the river Acesines, with orders to continue his march along the banks of that river. He also sent Krateros and Hephaestion off again with instructions how they were to conduct the march.

He himself continued his voyage down the river Hydaspes, which was found throughout the passage to be nowhere less than twenty stadia in breadth. Mooring his boats wherever he could on the banks, he subjected the Indians who lived near the Hydaspes to his authority, some having surrendered on terms of capitulation, and such as resorted to arms, having been subdued by force. He then sailed rapidly to the country of the Malloi and Oxydracae, because he had ascertained that they were the most numerous and warlike of all the Indian tribes in those parts, and news had reached him that they had conveyed their children, and their wives for safety into their strongest cities, and that they meant themselves to give him a hostile reception. He in consequence prosecuted the voyage with still greater speed, so that he might attack them before they had settled their plans, and while their preparations were still incomplete and they were in a state of confusion and alarm. On the fifth day after he had started from the place where he had halted, and been joined by Krateros and Hephaestion, he reached the junction of the Hydaspes and Acesines. Where these rivers unite the one river formed from them is very narrow, and not only is the current swift from the narrowness of the channel, but the waters whirl round in monstrous eddies, curl up in great billows and dash so violently that the roar of the surge is distinctly heard by those who are still a great distance off. All this had been previously reported by the natives to Alexander, and he had repeated the information to the soldiers; but, notwithstanding, when the army in approaching the confluence caught the roar of the stream, the sailors simultaneously suspended the action of the oars, not at any order from the boatswains, who had become mute from astonishment, but because they were stunned with terror by the thundering noise.

Chapter V
Dangers Encountered by the Fleet at the Confluence – Plan of the Operations Which Followed – Voyage down the Acesines

WHEN THEY WERE NOT FAR from the meeting of the rivers, the pilots enjoined the rowers to put all their strength to the oars to clear the rapids, so that the vessels might not be caught and capsized in the eddies, but by the exertions of the rowers might overcome the whirling of the waters. The merchant vessels accordingly, if they happened to be whirled round by the current, suffered no damage from the eddy, beyond the alarm caused to the men on board, for these vessels, being of a round form, were kept upright by the current itself, and settled into the proper course.

But the ships of war did not escape so unscathed from the eddying stream, for, owing to their length, they were not upheaved in the same way as the others on the seething surges, and if they had two banks of oars, the lower oars were not raised much above the level of the water. When the broad sides, therefore, of these vessels were exposed to the eddying current, their oars, if not lifted in proper time, were caught by the water and the blades snapped asunder. Many of the ships were thus damaged, and two which fell foul of each other sunk with the greater part of their crews. But when the river began to widen out, the current was no longer so rapid and dangerous, and the impetuosity of the eddies diminished. Alexander therefore brought his fleet to moorings on the right bank where there was a protection from the strength of the current and a roadstead for the ships. Here was also a headland projecting into the river which afforded facilities for collecting the wrecks and whatever living freight they brought. He saved the survivors; and when he had repaired the damaged craft, ordered Nearchus to sail downward till he reached the confines of the nation called the Malloi. He made himself an inroad into the territories of the barbarians who refused their submission, and prevented them sending succours to the Malloi. He then rejoined the fleet.

Hephaestion, Krateros, and Philip had there already united their forces. He then transported to the other side of the river Hydaspes the elephants, the brigade of Polyperchon, the archers, and Philip with the troops under his command, and appointed Krateros to conduct this expedition. Nearchus he despatched in command of the fleet, and instructed him to start on the voyage three days before the departure of the army. The rest of his forces he divided into three parts. Hephaestion was directed to set out five days in advance, so that if any of the enemy fled forward before the division commanded by the king in person they might be captured, when endeavouring to escape in that direction, by falling into Hephaestion's hands. He gave also a part of the army to Ptolemy, the son of Lagos, with orders to follow him three days later, so that such of the enemy as fled backward from his own troops might fall into the hands of those under Ptolemy. The detachment that marched in advance he ordered to wait until he himself should come up at the confluence of the Acesines and Hydraotes, where Krateros and Ptolemy had orders to join him with their divisions.

Chapter VI
Alexander Invades the Territories of the Malloi

ALEXANDER SELECTED for his own division the hypaspists, the archers, the Agrianians, the corps of footguards under Peitho, all the horse-archers and the half of the companion cavalry, and

**led them through a waterless tract of country against the Malloi, a
race of independent Indians.**

On the first day he encamped near a small stream which was twenty stadia
distant from the river Acesines. Having dined there and allowed the army a
short time for repose, he ordered every man to fill whatever vessel he had
with water. He then marched during the remainder of the day and all night
a distance of about four hundred stadia, and with the dawn arrived before a
city to which many of the Malloi had fled for refuge. As they never imagined
that Alexander would come to attack them through the waterless desert,
most of them were abroad in the fields, and without their arms; and just as
it was manifest that he led his forces by this route because of the difficulties
it presented, so did it appear to the enemy past belief that he would conduct
an army by a way so perilous. He thus fell upon them unexpectedly, and slew
most of them without their even turning to offer resistance, since they were
unarmed. The rest he shut up within the city, and as the phalanx of infantry
had not yet arrived, he posted the cavalry in a cordon round the wall, thus
making it serve for a stockade. No sooner, however, did the infantry come
up than he despatched Perdiccas with his own cavalry regiment and that of
Kleitos, together with the Agrianians, to another city of the Malloi, into which
many of the Indians of that district had fled for refuge. He was enjoined to
blockade the men in the city, but not to attempt to storm the place until his
own arrival, so that no one might escape and carry the news of Alexander's
approach to the other barbarians. He then made an assault upon the wall,
which the barbarians abandoned on seeing it could no longer hold out, since
many had been killed during the siege, and others disabled for fighting by
reason of their wounds. They fled into the citadel, which, being seated on
a commanding height and difficult of access, they continued to defend for
some time. As the Macedonians, however, vigorously pressed the attack at
all points, while Alexander himself was seen everywhere urging forward the
work, the citadel was stormed, and all the men who had fled to it for refuge
were put to the sword to the number of two thousand.

Perdiccas meanwhile reached the city whither he had been sent, but on
learning that the inhabitants had not long before fled from it, he rode away
at full gallop on the track of the fugitives, while the light troops followed him

on foot as fast as they could. Some of the fugitives he overtook and killed, but such as had been too quick for him made their escape to the river marshes.

Chapter VII
Siege and Capture of Several Mallian Strongholds

ALEXANDER HAVING DINED and allowed his troops to rest till the first watch of the night, began to march forward, and having travelled a great distance in the night, arrived at the river Hydraotes at daybreak. There he learned that many of the Malloi had already crossed to the other bank, but he fell upon others who were in the act of crossing and slew many of them during the passage. He crossed the river along with them, just as he was, and by the same ford. He then closely pursued the fugitives who had outstripped him in their retreat. Many of these he slew and he captured others, but most of them escaped to a position of great natural strength which was also strongly fortified. But when the infantry came up with him, Alexander sent Peitho with his own brigade and two squadrons of cavalry against the fugitives. This detachment attacked the stronghold, captured it at the first assault and made slaves of all who had fled into it, except, of course, those who had fallen in the attack. Then Peitho and his men, their task fulfilled, returned to the camp.

Alexander himself next led his army against a certain city of the Brachmans, because he had learned that many of the Malloi had fled thither for refuge. On reaching it he led the phalanx in compact ranks against all parts of the wall. The inhabitants, on finding the walls undermined, and that they were themselves obliged to retire before the storm of missiles, left the walls and fled to the citadel, and began to defend themselves from thence. But as a few Macedonians had rushed in along with them, they rallied, and turning round in a body upon the pursuers, drove some from the citadel and killed twenty-five of them in their retreat. Upon this Alexander ordered his men to apply the scaling ladders to the citadel on all its sides, and to undermine its walls; and when an undermined tower had fallen and a breach had been made in the wall between two towers, thus exposing the citadel to attack in that quarter, Alexander was seen to be the first man to scale and lay hold of the wall. Upon seeing this, the rest of the Macedonians for very shame ascended the wall at various points, and quickly had the citadel in their hands. Some of the Indians set fire to their houses, in which they were caught and killed, but most part fell fighting. About five thousand in all were killed, and, as they were men of spirit, a few only were taken prisoners.

Chapter VIII
Alexander Defeats the Malloi at the Hydraotes

HE REMAINED THERE one day to give his army rest, and next day he moved forward to attack the rest of the Malloi. He found their cities abandoned, and ascertained that the inhabitants had fled into the desert. There he again allowed the army a day's rest, and next day sent Peitho and Demetrius, the cavalry commander, back to the river with their own troops, and as many battalions of light-armed infantry as the nature of the work required. He directed them to march along the edge of the river, and if they came upon any of those who had fled for refuge to the jungle, of which there were numerous patches along the riverbank, to put them all to death unless they voluntarily surrendered. The troops under these two officers captured many of the fugitives in these jungles and killed them.

He marched himself against the largest city of the Malloi, to which he was informed many men from their other cities had fled for safety. The Indians, however, abandoned this place also when they heard that Alexander was approaching. They then crossed the Hydraotes, and with a view to obstruct Alexander's passage, remained drawn up in order of battle upon the banks, because they were very steep. On learning this, he took all the cavalry which he had with him, and marched to that part of the Hydraotes where he had been told the Malloi were posted; and the infantry were directed to follow after him. When he came to the river and descried the enemy drawn up on the opposite bank, he plunged at once, just as he was after the march, into the ford, with the cavalry only. When the enemy saw Alexander now in the middle of the stream they withdrew in haste, but yet in good order, from the bank, and Alexander pursued them with the cavalry only. But when the Indians perceived he had nothing but a party of horse with him, they faced round and fought stoutly, being about fifty thousand in number. Alexander, perceiving that their phalanx was very compact, and his own infantry not on the ground, rode along all round them, and sometimes charged their ranks, but not at close quarters. Meanwhile the Agrianians and other battalions of light-armed infantry, which consisted of picked men, arrived on the field along with the archers, while the phalanx of infantry was showing in sight at no great distance off. As they were threatened at once with so many dangers, the Indians wheeled round, and with headlong speed fled to the strongest of all the cities that lay near. Alexander killed many of them in the pursuit, while those who escaped to the city were shut up within its walls. At first, therefore, he surrounded the place with his horsemen as soon as they came up from the march. But when the infantry arrived he encamped around the wall on every side for the remainder of this day – a time too short for making an assault, to say nothing of the great fatigue his army had undergone, the infantry from their long march, and the cavalry by the continuous pursuit, and especially by the passage of the river.

Chapter IX
Alexander Assails the Chief Stronghold of the Malloi, Scales the Wall of the Citadel, Into Which He Leaps Down Though Alone

ON THE FOLLOWING DAY, dividing his army into two parts, he himself assaulted the wall at the head of one division, while Perdiccas led forward the other. Upon this the Indians, without

waiting to receive the attack of the Macedonians, abandoned the walls and fled for refuge to the citadel.

Alexander and his troops therefore burst open a small gate, and entered the city long before the others. But Perdiccas and the troops under his command entered it much later, having found it no easy work to surmount the walls. The most of them, in fact, had neglected to bring scaling ladders, for when they saw the wall left without defenders they took it for granted that the city had actually been captured. But when it became clear that the enemy was still in possession of the citadel, and that many of them were drawn up in front of it to repel attack, the Macedonians endeavoured to force their way into it, some by sapping the walls, and others by applying the scaling ladders wherever that was practicable. Alexander, thinking that the Macedonians who carried the ladders were loitering too much, snatched one from the man who carried it, placed it against the wall, and began to ascend, cowering the while under his shield. The next to follow was Peukestas, who carried the sacred shield which Alexander had taken from the temple of Athena at Illium, and which he used to keep with him and have carried before him in all his battles. Next to him Leonnatus, an officer of the bodyguard, ascended by the same ladder; and by a different ladder Abreas, one of those soldiers who for superior merit drew double pay and allowances. The king was now near the coping of the wall, and resting his shield against it, was pushing some of the Indians within the fort, and had cleared the parapet by killing others with his sword. The hypaspists, now alarmed beyond measure for the king's safety, pushed each other in their haste up the same ladder and broke it, so that those who were already mounting it fell down and made the ascent impracticable for others.

Alexander, while standing on the wall, was then assailed on every side from the adjacent towers, for none of the Indians had the courage to come near him. He was assailed also by men in the city, who threw darts at him from no great distance off, for it so happened that a mound of earth had been thrown up in that quarter close to the wall. Alexander was, moreover, a conspicuous object both by the splendour of his arms and the astonishing audacity he displayed. He then perceived that if he remained where he was, he would be exposed to danger without being able to achieve anything noteworthy, but if he leaped down into the citadel he might perhaps by this very act paralyse the Indians with terror, and if he did not, but necessarily incurred danger, he would in that case not die ignobly, but after performing great deeds worth being remembered by the men of after times. Having so resolved, he leaped down from the wall into the citadel. Then, supporting himself against the wall, he slew with his sword some who assailed him at close quarters, and in particular the governor of the Indians, who had rushed upon him too boldly. Against another Indian whom he saw approaching, he hurled a stone to check his advance, and another he similarly repelled. If anyone came within nearer reach, he again used his sword. The barbarians had then no further wish to approach him, but standing around assailed him from all quarters with whatever missiles they carried or could lay their hands on.

Chapter X
Alexander is Dangerously Wounded Within the Citadel

A T THIS CRISIS Peukestas, Abreas the dimoirite (low ranking soldier) and after them Leonnatus, the only men who succeeded in reaching the top of the wall before the ladder broke, leaped down and began fighting in front of the king. But there Abreas fell, pierced in the forehead by an arrow. Alexander himself was also struck by one which pierced through his cuirass (breastplate) into his chest above the pap (nipple), so that, as Ptolemy says, air gurgled from the wound along with the blood. But sorely wounded as he was, he continued to defend himself as long as his blood was still warm. Since much blood, however, kept gushing out with every breath he drew, a dizziness and faintness seized him, and he fell where he stood in a collapse upon his shield. Peukestas then bestrode him where he fell, holding up in front of him the sacred shield which had been taken from Ilion, while Leonnatus protected him from side attacks. But both these men were severely wounded, and Alexander was now on the point of swooning away from the loss of blood.

As for the Macedonians, they were at a loss how to make their way into the citadel, because those who had seen Alexander shot at upon the wall and then leap down inside it had broken down the ladders up which they were rushing in all haste, dreading lest their king, in recklessly exposing himself to danger, should come by some hurt. In their perplexity they devised various plans for ascending the wall. It was made of earth, and so some drove pegs into it, and swinging themselves up by means of these, scrambled with difficulty to the top. Others ascended by mounting one upon the other. The man who first reached the top flung himself headlong from the wall into the city, and was followed by the others. There, when they saw the king fallen prostrate, they all raised loud lamentations and outcries of grief. And now around his fallen form a desperate struggle ensued, one Macedonian after another holding his shield in front of him. In the meantime, some of the soldiers having shattered the bar by which the gate in the wall between the towers was secured, made their way into the city a few at a time, and others, when they saw that a rift was made in the gate, put their shoulders under it, and having then pushed it into the space within the wall, opened an entrance into the citadel in that quarter.

Chapter XI
Dangerous Nature of Alexander's Wound – Arrian Refutes Some Current Fictions Relating to This Accident

UPON THIS SOME BEGAN to kill the Indians, and in the massacre spared none, neither man, woman nor child. Others bore off the king upon his shield. His condition was very low, and they could not yet tell whether he was likely to survive. Some writers have asserted that Kritodemos, a physician of Cos, of the family of Asclepius, extracted the weapon from the wound by making an incision where the blow had struck. Other writers, however, say that as no surgeon was present at this terrible crisis, Perdiccas, an officer of the bodyguard, at Alexander's own desire, made an incision into the wound with his sword and removed the weapon. Its removal was followed by such a copious effusion of blood that Alexander again

swooned, and the swoon had the effect of staunching the flow (flux). Many fictions also have been recorded by historians concerning this accident, and Fame, receiving them from the original inventors, has preserved them to our own day, nor will she cease to transmit the falsehoods to one generation after another except they be finally suppressed by this history.

The common account, for example, is that this accident befell Alexander among the Oxydrakai, but in fact it occurred among the Malloi an independent Indian nation. The city belonged to the Malloi, and the men who wounded Alexander were Malloi. They had certainly agreed to combine with the Oxydrakai and give battle to the common enemy, but Alexander had thwarted this design by his sudden and rapid march through the waterless country, whereby these tribes were prevented from giving each other mutual help. To take another instance, according to the common account, the last battle fought with Darius (that at which he fled, nor paused in his flight till he was seized by the soldiers of Bessos and murdered at Alexander's approach) took place at Arbela, just as the previous battle came off at Issus, and the first cavalry action at the Granicus. Now this cavalry action was really fought at the Granicus, and the next battle with Darius at Issus. But Arbela is distant from the field where Darius and Alexander had their last battle six hundred stadia according to those authors who make the distance greatest, and five hundred stadia according to those who make it least. But Ptolemy and Aristoboulos say that the battle took place at Gaugamela near the river Boumodos. Gaugamela, however, was not a city, but merely a good-sized village, a place of no distinction, and bearing a name which offends the ear. This seems to me the reason why Arbela, which was a city, has carried off the glory of the great battle. But if we must perforce consider that this battle took place near Arbela, though fought at so great a distance off, then we may as well say that the sea fight at Salamis came off near the Isthmus of Corinth, and the sea fight at Artemisium in Euboea, near Aegina or Sunium.

With regard again to those who protected Alexander with their shields in his peril, all agree that Peukestas was of the number, but with respect to Leonnatus and Abreas the dimoirite, they are no longer in harmony. Some say that Alexander received a blow on his helmet from a bludgeon and became dizzy and fell down, and that on regaining his feet he was hit by a dart which pierced through his breastplate into his chest. But Ptolemy, the son of Lagos, says that this wound in his chest was the only one he received. I take, however, the following to be the greatest error into which the historians of Alexander have fallen. Some have written that Ptolemy, the son of Lagos, along with Peukestas mounted the ladder together with Alexander; that Ptolemy held his shield over him when he was lying on the ground, and that he thence received the surname of Soter. And yet Ptolemy himself has recorded that he was not present at this conflict, but was fighting elsewhere against other barbarians, in command of a different division of the army. Let me mention these facts in digressing from my narrative that the men of after times may not regard it as a matter of indifference how these great deeds and great sufferings are reported.

Chapter XII
Distress and Anxiety of the Army at the Prospect of Alexander's Death

WHILE ALEXANDER REMAINED at this place to be cured of his wound, the first news which reached the camp whence he had started to attack the Malloi was that he had died of his wound. Then there arose at first a loud lamentation from the whole army, as the mournful tidings spread from man to man.

But when their lamentation was ended, they gave way to despondency and anxious doubts about the appointment of a commander to the army, for among the officers many could advance claims to that dignity which both to Alexander and the Macedonians seemed of equal weight. They were also in fear and doubt how they could be conducted home in safety, surrounded as they were on all hands by warlike nations, some not yet reduced, but likely to fight resolutely for their freedom, while others would to a certainty revolt when relieved from their fear of Alexander. They seemed besides to be just then among impassable rivers, while the whole outlook presented nothing but inextricable difficulties when they wanted their king. But on receiving word that he was still alive, they could hardly think it true, or persuade themselves that he was likely to recover. Even when a letter came from the king himself intimating that he would soon come down to the camp, most of them from the excess of fear which possessed them distrusted the news, for they fancied that the letter was a forgery concocted by his bodyguards and generals.

Chapter XIII
Joy of the Army on Seeing Alexander After His Recovery – His Officers Rebuke Him for His Rashness

ON COMING TO KNOW this, Alexander, anxious to prevent any commotions arising in the army, as soon as he could bear the fatigue, had himself conveyed to the banks of the river Hydraotes, and embarking there, he sailed down the river to reach the camp, at the junction of the Hydraotes and the Acesines, where Hephaestion commanded the land forces and Nearchus the fleet. When the vessel which carried the king was now approaching the camp, he ordered the awning to be removed from the stern that he might be visible to all. They were, however, even yet incredulous, supposing that the freight of the vessel was Alexander's dead body, until he neared the bank, when he raised his arm and stretched out his hand to the multitude.

Then the men raised a loud cheer, and lifted up their hands, some towards heaven and some towards Alexander himself. Tears even started involuntarily to the eyes of not a few at the unexpected sight. Some of the hypaspists brought him a litter where he was carried ashore from the vessel, but he called for his horse. When he was seen once more on horseback, the whole army greeted him with loud acclamations, which filled with their echoes the shores and all the surrounding hills and dales. On approaching his tent he dismounted that he might be seen walking. Then the soldiers crowded round him, touching some his hands, others his knees, and others nothing but his clothing. Some, satisfied with nothing more than a near view, went away with expressions of admiration. Others again covered him with garlands, and others with the flowers of the clime and the season.

Nearchus says that he was offended with certain of his friends who reproached him for exposing himself to danger when leading the army, for this, they said, was not the duty of a commander, but of a common soldier, and it seems to me that Alexander resented these remarks because he felt their truth, and knew he had laid himself open to censure. Owing, however, to his prowess in fighting and his love of glory, he, like other men who are swayed by some predominant pleasure, yielded to temptation, lacking sufficient force of will to hold aloof from dangers. Nearchus also says that a certain elderly Boeotian (whose name he does not give) observing that Alexander resented the censures of his friends, and was giving them sour looks, approached him, and in the Boeotian tongue thus addressed him: 'O Alexander, it is for heroes to do great deeds,' and then he subjoined an Iambic verse, the purport of which was that he who did any great deed was bound also to suffer. The man, it is said, not only found favour with Alexander, but was admitted afterwards to closer intimacy.

Chapter XIV
Submission of the Malloi, Oxydrakai, and Others – Voyage Down the Hydraotes and Acesines to the Indus

AT THIS TIME, envoys came to Alexander from the Malloi who still survived, tendering the submission of the nation; and from the Oxydrakai came the leading men of their cities and their provincial governors, besides one hundred and fifty of their most eminent men, entrusted with full powers to conclude a treaty. They brought with them those presents which the Indians consider the choicest, and, like the Malloi, tendered the submission of their

nation. Their error in so long delaying to send an embassy was, they said, pardonable, for they were attached more than others to freedom and autonomy, and their freedom they had preserved intact from the time Dionysus came to India until Alexander's arrival. Since, however, Alexander was also, according to current report, of the race of the gods, they were willing, if he so pleased, to receive whatever satrap Alexander might appoint, pay the tribute he chose to impose, and give as many hostages as he required. Upon this he asked for one thousand men, the flower of the nation, to be retained, if he thought good, as hostages, but, if not, to be employed as auxiliaries until he had finished the war against the other Indians. They selected accordingly one thousand men, their best and tallest, and sent them to him, together with five hundred chariots and their charioteers, though these were not demanded. Alexander appointed Philip as satrap over that nation and over the Malloi who still survived. The hostages he sent back, but he kept the chariots.

When these arrangements had been completed, and many vessels had been built in the interval while his wound was healing, he put on board the fleet seventeen hundred of the cavalry companions, the same number of light-armed troops as before, and about ten thousand infantry, and sailed a short distance down the river Hydraotes. But when the Hydraotes fell into the Acesines he continued the voyage down the latter river (which in preference to the Hydraotes gives its name to the united stream) until he reached the junction of the Acesines with the Indus. For these four vast rivers which are all navigable yield up their waters to the river Indus, but not each of them under its own special name. For the Hydaspes discharges into the Acesines, and the single stream then forms what is called the Acesines. But this Acesines again unites with the Hydraotes, and after absorbing this river is still the Acesines. The Acesines after this receives the Hyphasis, and still keeping its own name falls into the Indus, but after the junction it resigns its name to that river. Hence I am ready to believe that the Indus from this point to where it bifurcates to form the Delta expands to a breadth of one hundred stadia or even more in places where it spreads out more like a lake than a river.

Chapter XV
Appointment of Satraps – Voyage Down the Indus to the Dominions of Mousikanos, Who Tenders His Submission

THERE AT THE CONFLUENCE of the Acesines and Indus he waited until Perdiccas arrived with his forces. This general in the course of his march had subjugated the Abastanoi, one of the independent tribes. Meanwhile there arrived at the camp other thirty-oared galleys and transport vessels which had been built for him among the Abastanes and Xathrians, another independent tribe of Indians whose submission he had received. From the Ossadioi also, another independent tribe, came envoys offering the submission of their nation.

Alexander then fixed the confluence of the Acesines and Indus as the boundary of the satrapy of Philip, and left with him all the Thracians and as many foot-soldiers as seemed sufficient for the defence of his province. Then he ordered a city to be founded there at the very confluence of the rivers, hoping it would become a great city and make a name for itself in the world. He ordered also the construction of dockyards. At this time the Bactrian Oxyartes, the father of Alexander's wife Roxana, arrived, and on him he bestowed the satrapy of the Parapamisadai after dismissing the previous satrap Tiryaspes, who had been reported guilty of irregularities in the exercise of his authority.

Then he transported Krateros, with the bulk of the army and the elephants, to the left side of the river Indus, because the route along that bank of the river seemed easier for an army heavily accoutred, and because the tribes inhabiting those parts were not quite friendly. He sailed himself down to the capital of the Sogdia, where he fortified another city, constructed other dockyards and repaired his damaged vessels. He then appointed Oxyartes and Peitho satraps of the country which extended from the confluence of the Indus and Acesines to the sea, together with the whole seaboard of India.

Krateros he again despatched with the army through the country of the Arachotians and Drangians; while he sailed down himself to the realm of

Mousikanos, which was reported to be the most opulent in India, because that sovereign had neither come to surrender himself and his country, nor sent envoys to seek his friendship. He had not even sent presents to show the respect due to a mighty king, nor had he asked any favour from Alexander. He therefore made the voyage down the river so rapidly that he reached the frontiers of the country of Mousikanos before that prince had even heard that Alexander had started to attack him. Mousikanos, dismayed by his sudden arrival, hastened to meet him, taking the choicest presents India could offer and all his elephants with him. He offered to surrender both his nation and himself, and acknowledged his error, which was the most effective way with Alexander to obtain from him whatever one wanted. Alexander therefore granted Mousikanos a full pardon on account of his submission and penitence, expressed much admiration of his capital and his realm, and confirmed him in his sovereignty. Krateros was then ordered to fortify the citadel which protected the capital, and this work was executed while Alexander was still on the spot. A garrison was placed in the fortress, which he thought suitable for keeping the surrounding tribes in subjection.

Chapter XVI
Campaign Against Oxykanos and Sambus

THEN HE TOOK the archers and the Agrianians and the cavalry which was sailing with him, and marched against the governor of a district in that part of the country whose name was Oxykanos, because he neither came himself nor sent envoys to offer the surrender of himself and his country. At the first assault he took by storm the two largest cities under the rule of Oxykanos, in the second of which that chief himself was taken prisoner. The booty he gave to the army, but the elephants he led away and reserved for himself. The other cities in the same country surrendered without attempting resistance wherever he advanced; so much were the minds of all the Indians paralysed with abject terror by Alexander and the success of his arms.

He then advanced against Sambus, whom he had appointed satrap of the Indian mountaineers, and who was reported to have fled on hearing that Mousikanos had been pardoned by Alexander, and was ruling his own land, for he and Mousikanos were on hostile terms. But when Alexander approached the city called Sindimana, which formed the metropolis of the country of Sambus, the gates were thrown open on his arrival, and the members of the household of Sambus with his treasure (of which they had reckoned up the amount) and his elephants went forth to meet him. Sambus, these men informed him, had fled, not from hostility to Alexander, but from fears to which the pardon of Mousikanos had given rise. He captured besides another city, which had at this time revolted, and he put to death all those Brachmans who had instigated the revolt. These Brachmans are the philosophers of the Indians, and of their philosophy, if so it may be called, I shall give an account in my work which describes India.

Chapter XVII
Mousikanos is Captured by Peitho and Executed – Alexander Reaches Pattala at the Apex of the Indus Delta

MEANTIME, HE RECEIVED word that Mousikanos had revolted. Thereupon he despatched the satrap Peitho, the son of Agenor, against him with an adequate force, while he marched himself against the cities which had been placed under the rule of Mousikanos. Some of these he razed to the ground after reducing the inhabitants to slavery; into others he introduced garrisons and fortified their citadels.

When these operations were finished he returned to the camp and the fleet – whither Mousikanos was conducted, who had been taken prisoner by Peitho. Alexander ordered the rebel to be taken to his own country and hanged there, together with all those Brachmans who had instigated him to revolt. Then there came to him the ruler of the country of the Pattala, which, as I have stated, consists of the Delta formed by the river Indus, and is larger than the Egyptian Delta. This chief surrendered to him the whole of his land, and entrusted both himself and all his possessions to him. Alexander sent him back to his government with orders to make all due preparations for the reception of his expedition. He then sent away Krateros into Karmania by the route through the Arachotians and the Sarangians, leading the brigades of Attalos, Meleager and Antigenes, along with some of the archers and such of the companions and other Macedonians as he was sending home to Macedonia as unfit for further service. He also sent away the elephants with him. The rest of the army, except that portion which with himself was sailing down to the sea, was placed under the command of Hephaestion. Peitho, who led the horse lancers and the Agrianians, he transported to the opposite bank so that he might not be on that side of the river by which Hephaestion was to advance. Peitho was instructed to put colonists into the cities which had just been fortified, to suppress any insurrection which the Indians might attempt, to introduce settled order among them and then to join him at Pattala.

On the third day after Alexander had started on the voyage, he was informed that the Prince of Pattala was fleeing from that city, taking with him most of its inhabitants, and leaving the country deserted. He accordingly accelerated his voyage down the river, and on reaching Pattala found that both the city itself and the cultivated lands which lay around it had been deserted by the inhabitants. But he despatched his lightest troops in pursuit of the fugitives, and when some of these had been captured sent them on to their countrymen to bid them take courage and return, for they were free to inhabit their city and cultivate their lands as formerly; and so most of them did return.

Chapter XVIII
Alexander Orders Wells to Be Dug in the District Round Pattala, and Sails Down the Western Arm of the Indus

AFTER DIRECTING HEPHAESTION to construct a citadel in Pattala, he sent out men into the adjacent country, which was waterless, to dig wells and make it habitable. Some of

the barbarians in the neighbourhood attacked them, and, as they fell upon them quite unexpectedly, killed several of their number, but as the assailants lost many on their own side, they fled to the desert. The men were thus able to complete the work they were sent to execute, especially as Alexander, on learning that they had been attacked by the barbarians, had sent additional troops to take part in the work.

Near Pattala the stream of the Indus is divided into two large rivers, both of which retain the name of the Indus till they enter the sea. Here Alexander set about the construction of a roadstead and dock, and when some satisfactory progress had been made with these undertakings, he resolved to sail down to the mouth of the right arm of the river.

To Leonnatus he gave the command of about one thousand cavalry and eight thousand heavy and light infantry, and despatched him to move down the island of Pattala, holding along the shore in a line with the squadron of ships. He set out himself on a voyage down the right arm of the river, taking with him the fastest vessels with one-and-a-half bank of oars, all the thirty-oared galleys and several of the smaller craft. As the Indians of that region had fled, he had no pilot to direct his course, and this made the navigation all the more difficult.

Then on the second day after he had started a storm arose, and the gale blowing against the current made deep furrows in the river, and battered the hulls of the vessels so violently that most of his ships were damaged, while some of the thirty-oared galleys were completely wrecked, though the sailors managed to run them on shore before they went all to pieces in the water. Other vessels were therefore constructed; and Alexander, having despatched the quickest of the light-armed troops some distance into the interior, captured some Indians, whom he employed in piloting his fleet for the rest of the voyage. But when they found themselves where the river expands to the vast breadth of two hundred stadia the wind blew strong from the outer sea, and the oars could scarcely be raised in the swell. They therefore again drew toward the shore for refuge, and the fleet was steered by the pilots into the mouth of a canal.

Chapter XIX
The Fleet is Damaged by the Tide, Halts at an Island in the Indus, and Thence Reaches the Open Sea

WHILE THE FLEET WAS AT ANCHOR here, a vicissitude to which the Great Sea is subject occurred, for the tide ebbed, and their ships were left on dry ground. This phenomenon, of which Alexander and his followers had no previous experience, caused them no little alarm, and greater still was their dismay, when in due course of time the tide advanced, and the hulls of the vessels were floated aloft. Those vessels which it found settled in the soft mud were uplifted without damage, and floated again, nothing the worse for the strain; but as for those vessels which had been left on a drier part of the beach, and were not firmly embedded, some on the advance of a massive wave fell foul of each other, while others were dashed upon the strand and shattered in pieces.

Alexander caused these vessels to be repaired as well as circumstances allowed, and despatched men in advance down the river in two boats to explore an island at which the natives informed him he must anchor on his way to the sea. They said that the name of the island was Killouta. When he learned that the island had harbours, was of great extent, and yielded water, he ordered the rest of the fleet to make its way thither, but he himself with the fastest sailing ships advanced beyond the island to see the mouth of the river, and ascertain whether it offered a safe and easy passage out into the open main. When they had proceeded about two hundred stadia beyond the island, they descried another which lay out in the sea. Then they returned to the island in the river, and Alexander, having anchored his ships near its extremity, offered sacrifice to those gods to whom, he said, Ammon had enjoined him to sacrifice. On the following day he sailed down to the other island which lay in the ocean, and approaching close to it also, offered other sacrifices to other gods and in another manner. These sacrifices, like the others, he offered under sanction of an oracle given by Ammon. He then advanced beyond the mouths of the river

Indus, and sailed out into the great main to discover, as he declared, whether any land lay anywhere near in the sea, but, in my opinion, chiefly that it might be said that he had navigated the great outer sea of India. He then sacrificed bulls to the god Poseidon, which he threw into the sea; and following up the sacrifice with a libation, he threw the goblet and bowls of gold into the bosom of the deep as thanks-offerings, beseeching the god to conduct in safety the naval expedition which he intended to despatch under Nearchus to the Persian Gulf and the mouths of the Euphrates and Tigris.

Chapter XX
Alexander After Returning to Pattala Sails Down the Eastern Arm of the Indus

ON HIS RETURN to Pattala, he found the citadel fortified, and Peitho arrived with his troops after completing the objects of his expedition. Hephaestion was then ordered to prepare what was requisite for the fortification of the harbour, and the construction of a dockyard, for here at the city of Pattala, which stands where the river Indus bifurcates, he meant to leave behind him a very considerable naval squadron.

He himself sailed down again to the Great Sea by the other mouth of the Indus, to ascertain by which of the mouths it was easier to reach the ocean. The mouths of the river Indus are about eighteen hundred stadia distant from each other. When he was approaching the mouth, he came to a large lake formed by the river in widening out, unless, indeed, this watery expanse be due to rivers which discharge their streams into it from the surrounding districts, and give it the appearance of a gulf of the sea; for saltwater fish were now seen in it of larger size than the fish in our sea. Having anchored in the lake, at a place selected by the pilots, he left there most of the soldiers under the command of Leonnatus and all the boats, while he himself with the thirty-oared galleys, and the vessels with one and a half bank of oars passed beyond the mouth of the Indus, and sailing out into the sea by this other route, satisfied himself that the mouth of the Indus on this side was easier to navigate than the other. He then anchored his fleet near the beach, and taking with him some of the cavalry, proceeded along the shore a three days' journey, examining what sort of a country it was for a coasting voyage, and ordering wells to be sunk for supplying seafarers with water. He then returned to the fleet, and sailed back to Pattala. He sent, however, a part of the army to complete the work of digging wells along the shore, with instructions to return to Pattala on their completing this service. Sailing down again to the lake, he constructed there another harbour and other docks, and, having left a garrison in the place, he collected sufficient food to supply the army for four months, and made all other necessary preparations for the voyage along the coast.

Chapter XXI
Alexander Crosses the River Arabios and Invades the Oreitai

THE SEASON OF THE YEAR was impracticable for navigation from the prevalence of the Etesian winds, which do not blow there as with us from the north, but come as a south wind from the Great Ocean. It was ascertained that from the beginning of winter, that is from the setting of the Pleiades, till the winter solstice, the weather was suitable for making voyages, because the mild breezes which then blow steadily seaward from the land, which is drenched by this time with heavy rains, favour coasting voyages, whether made by oar or by sail.

Nearchus, who had been appointed to the command of the fleet, was waiting for the season for coasting, but Alexander set out from Pattala, and advanced with the whole of his army to the river Arabios. He then took half of the hypaspists and archers, the infantry brigades called foot companions, the corps of companion cavalry, and a squadron from each division of the other cavalry, and all the horse archers, and turned towards the sea, which lay on the left, not only to dig as many wells as possible for the use of the expedition while coasting those shores, but also to fall suddenly upon the Oreitans (an Indian tribe in those parts which had long been independent), because they had rendered no friendly service either to himself or the army. The command of the troops which he did not take with him was entrusted to Hephaestion. There was settled near the river Arabios another independent tribe called the Arabitai, and, as these neither thought themselves a match for Alexander, nor yet wished to submit to him, they fled into the desert when they learned that he was marching against them. But Alexander having crossed the Arabios, which was neither broad nor deep, traversed most of the desert, and found himself by daybreak near the inhabited country. Then leaving orders with the infantry to follow him in regular line, he set forward with the cavalry, which he divided into squadrons, to be spread over a wide extent of the plain, and it was thus he marched into the country of the Oreitans. All who turned to offer resistance were cut down by the cavalry, but many were taken prisoners. He then encamped near a small sheet of water, and on being joined by the troops under Hephaestion still continued his progress, and arrived at the village called Rambakia, which was the largest in the dominions of the Oreitans. He was pleased with the situation, and thought that if he colonised it, it would become a great and prosperous city. He therefore left Hephaestion behind him to carry this scheme into effect.

Chapter XXII
Submission of the Oreitai – Description of the Gedrosian Desert

HE THEN TOOK AGAIN the half of the hypaspists and Agrianians, and the corps of cavalry and the horse-archers, and marched forward to the frontiers of the Gedrosians and the Oreitans, where he was informed his way would lie through a narrow defile before which the combined forces of the Oreitans and the Gedrosians were lying encamped, resolved to prevent his passage. They were in

fact drawn up there, but when they were apprised of Alexander's approach most of them deserted the posts they were guarding and fled from the pass.

Then the leaders of the Oreitans came to him to surrender themselves and their nation. He ordered them to collect the multitude of the Oreitans, and send them away to their homes, since they were not to be subjected to any bad treatment. Over these people he placed Apollophanes as satrap. Along with him he left Leonnatus, an officer of the bodyguard in Ora, in command of all the Agrianians, some of the archers and cavalry, and the rest of the Grecian mercenary infantry and cavalry, and instructed him to remain in the country till the fleet sailed past its shores, to settle a colony in the city and establish order among the Oreitans, so that they might be readier to pay respect and obedience to the satrap. He himself with the great bulk of the army (for Hephaestion had now rejoined him with his detachment) advanced to the country of the Gedrosians by a route mostly desert.

Aristoboulos says that myrrh trees larger than the common kind grow plentifully in this desert, and that the Phoenicians who followed the army as suttlers collected the drops of myrrh which oozed out in great abundance from the trees (their stems being large and hitherto uncropped), and conveyed away the produce loaded on their beasts of burden. He says also that this desert yields an abundance of odoriferous roots of nard, which the Phoenicians likewise collected; but much of it was trodden down by the army, and the sweet perfume thus crushed out of it was from its great abundance diffused far and wide over the country. Other kinds of trees are found in the desert, one in particular which had a foliage like that of the laurel, and grew in places washed by the waves of the sea. These trees when the tide ebbed were left in dry ground, but when it returned they looked as if they grew in the sea. The roots of some were always washed by the sea, since they grew in hollows from which the water never receded, and yet trees of this kind were not destroyed by the brine. Some of these trees attained here the great height of thirty cubits. They happened to be at that season in bloom, and their flower closely resembled the white violet, which, however, it far surpassed in the sweetness of its perfume. Another kind of thorny stalk is mentioned, which grew on dry land, and was armed with a thorn so strong that when it got entangled in the dress of some who were riding past, it rather pulled the rider down from his horse than was itself torn away from its stalk. When hares are running past these bushes the thorns are said to fasten themselves in the fur so that the hares are caught like birds with birdlime or fish with hooks. These thorns were, however, easily cut through with steel, and when severed the stalk yielded juice even more abundant and more acid than what flows from fig trees in springtime.

Chapter XXIII
Alexander Marching Through Gedrosia
Endeavours to Collect Supplies for the Fleet

THENCE HE MARCHED through the country of the Gedrosians by a difficult route, on which it was scarcely possible to procure the necessaries of life, and which often failed to yield water for the army. They were besides compelled to march most of the way by night, and at too great a distance from the sea; for Alexander wished to go along the seacoast, both to see what harbours it had, and to make in the course of his march whatever preparations were possible for the benefit of the fleet, either by making his men dig wells or seek out markets and anchorages. The maritime parts of Gedrosia were, however, entirely desert.

Nevertheless he sent Thoas, the son of Mandradorus, down to the sea with a few horsemen to see if there happened to be any anchorage or water not far from the sea, or anything else that could supply the wants of the fleet. This man on returning reported that he found some fishermen upon the beach living in stifling huts, which had been constructed by heaping up mussel shells, while the roofs were formed of the backbones of fish. He also reported that these fishermen had only scanty supplies of water, obtained with difficulty by their digging through the shingle, and that what they got was not always fresh water.

When Alexander came to a district of the Gedrosian country where corn was more abundant, he seized it, placed it upon the beasts of burden, and having marked it with his own seal ordered it to be conveyed to the sea. But when he was coming to the halting station nearest the sea, the soldiers paid but little regard to the seal, and even the guards themselves made use of the corn and gave a share of it to such as were most pinched with hunger. Indeed, they were so overcome by their sufferings, that, as reason dictated, they took more account of the impending danger with which they now stood face to face than of the unseen and remote danger of the king's resentment. Alexander, however, forgave the offenders when made aware of the necessity which had prompted their act. He himself scoured the country in search of provisions, and sent Kretheus the Kallatian with all the supplies he could collect for the use of the army which was sailing round with the fleet. He also ordered the natives to grind all the corn they could collect in the interior districts, and convey it, for sale to the army, along with dates and sheep. He besides sent Telephos, one of the companions, to another locality with a small supply of ground corn.

Chapter XXIV
Difficulties Encountered on the March Through Gedrosia

HE THEN ADVANCED towards the capital of the Gedrosians, called Poura, and arrived there in sixty days after he had started from Ora. Most of Alexander's historians admit that all the hardships which his army suffered in Asia are not to be compared with the miseries which it here experienced. Nearchus is the only author who says that Alexander did not take that route in ignorance of its difficulty, but that he chose it on learning that no one had as yet traversed it with an army except Semiramis when she fled from India. The natives of the country say that she escaped with only twenty men of all her army, while even Cyrus, the son of Cambyses, escaped with only seven. For Cyrus, they say, did in truth enter this region to invade India, but lost, before reaching it, the greater part of his army from the difficulties which beset his march through the desert.

When Alexander heard these accounts he was seized, it is said, with an ambition to outrival both Cyrus and Semiramis. Nearchus says that this motive, added to his desire to be near the coast in order to keep the fleet supplied with provisions, induced him to march by this route; but that the blazing heat and want of water destroyed a great part of the army, and especially the beasts of burden, which perished from the great depth of the sand, and the heat which scorched like fire, while a great many died of thirst. For they met, he says, with lofty ridges of deep sand not hard and compact, but so loose that those who stepped on it sunk down as into mud or rather into untrodden snow. The horses and mules besides suffered still more severely both in ascending and descending the ridges, because the road was not only uneven, but wanted firmness. The great distances also between the stages were most distressing to the army, compelled as it was at times from want of water to make marches above the ordinary length. When they traversed by night all the stage they had to complete and came to water in the morning, their distress was all but entirely relieved. But if as the day advanced they were caught still marching owing to the great length of the stage, then suffer they did, tortured alike by raging heat and thirst unquenchable.

Chapter XXV
Sufferings of the Army in the Gedrosian Desert

THE SOLDIERS DESTROYED many of the beasts of burden of their own accord. For when their provisions ran short they came together and killed most of the horses and mules. They ate the flesh of these animals, which they professed had died of thirst and perished from the heat. No one cared to look very narrowly into the exact nature of what was doing, both because of the prevailing distress and also because all were alike implicated in the same offence. Alexander himself was not unaware of what was going on, but he saw that the remedy for the existing state of things was to pretend ignorance of it rather than permit it as a matter that lay within his

cognisance. It was therefore no longer easy to convey the soldiers labouring under sickness, nor others who had fallen behind on the march from exhaustion. This arose not only from the want of beasts of burden, but also because the men themselves took to destroying the wagons when they could no longer drag them forward owing to the deepness of the sand. They had done this even in the early stages of the march, because for the sake of the wagons they had to go not by the shortest roads, but those easiest for carriages.

Thus, some were left behind on the road from sickness, others from fatigue or the effects of the heat or intolerable thirst, while there were none who could take them forward or remain to tend them in their sickness. For the army marched on apace, and in the anxiety for its safety as a whole the care of individuals was of necessity disregarded. As they generally made their marches by night, some of the men were overcome by sleep on the way, but on awaking afterwards those who still had some strength left followed close on the track of the army, and a few out of many saved their lives by overtaking it. The majority perished in the sand like shipwrecked men at sea.

Another disaster also befell the army which seriously affected the men themselves as well as the horses and the beasts of burden. For the country of the Gedrosians, like that of the Indians, is supplied with rains by the Etesian winds; but these rains do not fall on the Gedrosian plains, but on the mountains to which the clouds are carried by the wind, where they dissolve in rain without passing over the crests of the mountains. When the army on one occasion lay encamped for the night near a small winter torrent for the sake of its water, the torrent which passes that way about the second watch of the night became swollen by rains which had fallen unperceived by the army, and came rushing down with so great a deluge that it destroyed most of the women and children of the camp followers, and swept away all the royal baggage and whatever beasts of burden were still left. The soldiers themselves, after a hard struggle, barely escaped with their lives, and a portion only of their weapons. Many of them besides came by their death through drinking, for if when jaded by the broiling heat and thirst they fell in with abundance of water, they quaffed it with insatiable avidity till they killed themselves. For this reason Alexander generally pitched his camp not in the immediate vicinity of the watering places, but some twenty stadia off to prevent the men and beasts from rushing in crowds into the water to the danger of their lives, as well as to prohibit those who had no self-control from polluting the water for the rest of the troops by their stepping into the springs or streams.

Chapter XXVI
Incidents of the March Through Gedrosia

HERE I FEEL MYSELF BOUND not to pass over in silence a noble act performed by Alexander, perhaps the noblest in his record, which occurred either in this country or, as some other authors have asserted, still earlier, among the Parapamisadai. The story is this.

The army was prosecuting its march through the sand under a sun already blazing high because a halt could not be made till water, which lay on the way farther on was reached, and Alexander himself, though distressed with thirst, was nevertheless with pain and difficulty marching on foot at the head of his army, that the soldiers might, as they usually do in a case of the kind, more cheerfully bear their hardships when they saw the misery equalised. But in the meantime some of the light-armed soldiers, starting off from the army, found water collected in the shallow bed of a torrent in a small and impure spring. Having, with difficulty, collected this water they hastened off to Alexander as if they were the bearers of some great boon. As soon as they came near the king they poured the water into a helmet, and offered it to him. He took it and thanked the men who brought it, but at once poured it upon the ground in the sight of all. By this deed the whole army was inspired with fresh vigour to such a degree that one would have imagined that the water poured out by Alexander had supplied a draught to the men all round. This deed I commend above all others, as it exhibits Alexander's power of endurance as well as his wonderful tact in the management of an army.

The army met also with the following adventure in this country. The guides, becoming uncertain of the way, at last declared that they could no longer recognise it, because all its tracks had been obliterated by the sands which the wind blew over them. Amid the deep sands, moreover, which had been everywhere heaped up to a uniform level, nothing rose up from which they could conjecture their path, not even the usual fringe of trees, nor so much as the sure landmark of a hillcrest. Nor had they practised the art of finding their way by observation of the stars by night or of the sun by day, as sailors do by watching one or other of the Bears – the Phoenicians the Lesser Bear, and all other nations the Greater. Alexander, at last perceiving that he should direct his march to the left, rode away forward, taking a small party of horsemen with him. But when their horses were tired out by the heat, he left most of his escort behind, and rode on with only five men and found the sea. Having scraped away the shingle on the beach, he found water, both fresh and pure, and then went back and brought his whole army to this place. And for seven days they marched along the seacoast, and procured water from the beach. As the guides by this time knew the way, he led his expedition thence into the interior parts.

Chapter XXVII
Appointment of Satraps – Alexander Learns That the Satrap Philip Had Been Murdered in India – Punishes Satraps Who Had Misgoverned

WHEN HE ARRIVED at the capital of the Gedrosians he then gave his army a rest. Apollophanes he deposed from his satrapy because he found out that he had utterly disregarded his instructions. He appointed Thoas to be satrap over the people of this district, but, as he took ill and died, Sibyrtius received the vacant office. The same man had also recently been appointed by Alexander satrap of Karmania, but now the government of the Arachotians and Gedrosians was committed to him, and Tlepolemos, the son of Pythophanes, got Karmania. The king was already advancing into Karmania when tidings reached him that Philip, the satrap of the

Indian country, had been plotted against by the mercenaries and treacherously murdered; but that the Macedonian bodyguards of Philip had put to death his murderers whom they had caught in the very act, and others whom they had afterwards seized. On learning what had occurred he sent a letter to India addressed to Eudemos and Taxiles directing them to assume the administration of the province previously governed by Philip until he could send a satrap to govern it.

When he arrived in Karmania, Krateros joined him, bringing the rest of the army and the elephants. He brought also Ordanes, whom he had made prisoner for revolting and attempting to make a revolution. Thither came also Stasanor, the satrap of the Areians and Zarangians, accompanied by Pharismanes, the son of Phrataphernes, the satrap of the Parthyaians and Hyrkanians. There came besides the generals who had been left with Parmenion over the army in Media, Cleander and Sitacles and Heracon, who brought with them the greater part of their army. Against Kleander and Sitacles both the natives and the soldiers themselves brought many accusations, as that they had pillaged temples, despoiled ancient tombs and perpetrated other outrageous acts of injustice and tyranny against their subjects. When these charges were proved against them, he put them to death, to make others who might be left as satraps, governors or chiefs of districts, stand in fear of suffering a like punishment if they violated their duty. This was the means which above all others served to keep in due order and obedience the nations which Alexander had conquered in war or which had voluntarily submitted to him, numerous as they were, and so far remote from each other, because under his sceptre the ruled were not allowed to be unjustly treated by their rulers. Heracon on this occasion was acquitted of the charge, but was soon afterwards punished, because he was convicted by the men of Sousa of having plundered the temple of their city. Stasanor and Phrataphernes in setting out to join Alexander, took with them a multitude of beasts of burden and many camels, because they learned that he was taking the route through the Gedrosians, and conjectured that his army would suffer, as it actually did. These men arrived therefore very opportunely, as did also their camels and their beasts of burden. For Alexander distributed all these animals to the officers one by one, to the squadrons and centuries of the cavalry, and to the companies of the infantry as far as their number sufficed.

Chapter XXVIII
Alexander Holds Rejoicings in Karmania on Account of His Indian Victories – List of His Bodyguards – Nearchus Reports to Him the Safety of the Fleet

SOME AUTHORS HAVE RECORDED, though I cannot believe what they state, that he made his progress through Karmania stretched at length with his companions on two covered wagons joined together, enjoying the while the music of the flute, and followed by the soldiers crowned with garlands and making holiday. They say also that food and all kinds of good cheer were provided for them along the roads by the Karmanians, and that these things were done by Alexander in imitation of the Bacchic revelry of Dionysus, because it was said of that deity that, after conquering the Indians, he traversed, in this manner, a great part of Asia, and received thc name of Thriambos (Triumph) in addition to that of Dionysus, and that for this very reason the splendid processions in honour of victories in war were called Thriamboi (Triumphs).

But neither Ptolemy, the son of Lagos, nor Aristoboulos has mentioned these doings in their narratives, nor any other writer whose testimony on such subjects it would be safe to trust, and as for myself I have done enough in recording them as unworthy of belief. But in the account I now proceed to offer I follow Aristoboulos. In Karmania Alexander offered sacrifice in thanksgiving to the gods for his victory over the Indians, and the preservation of his army during its march through Gedrosia. He celebrated also a musical and a gymnastic contest. He then appointed Peukestas to be one of his bodyguards, having already resolved to make him the satrap of Persia. He wished him, before his promotion to the satrapy, to experience this honour and mark of confidence for the service he rendered among the Malloi. Up to this time the number of his body-guards was seven – Leonnatus, the son of Anteas; Hephaestion, the son of Amyntor; Lysimachus, the son of Agathocles; Aristonous, the son of

Pisaeus of Pella; Perdiccas, the son of Orontes from Orestis; Ptolemy, the son of Lagos, and Peithio, the son of Krateuas from Eordoca – Peukestas, who had held the shield over Alexander, was added to them as an eighth.

At this time Nearchus, having sailed round the coast of Ora and Gedrosia, and that of the Ichthyophagi, put into port in the inhabited parts of the Karmanian coast, and going up thence into the interior with a few followers related to Alexander the incidents of the voyage which he had made for him in the outer sea. He was sent down again to sea, to sail round to the land of the Susia and the outlets of the river Tigris. How he sailed from the river Indus to the Persian Sea and the mouth of the Tigris, I shall describe in a separate work, wherein I shall follow Nearchus himself, as the history which he composed in the Greek language had Alexander for its subject. Perhaps at some future time I shall produce this work if my own inclination and the deity prompt me to the task.

Extract from
Diodoros Siculus

Chapter CVII
Kalanos, the Indian Philosopher, Immolates Himself – Alexander Marries the Daughter of Darius

WHEN THE KING HAD HEARD their story to the end, he ordered the leaders of the expedition to sail up to the mouth of the Euphrates. At the head of his army he traversed himself a great stretch of country, and arrived on the borders of Susia. About that time Kalanos, the Indian who had made great progress in philosophy, and was held in honour and esteem by Alexander, brought his life to an end in a most singular manner; for when he was three years over three score and ten (seventy-three years old),

and up till then had never known what illness was, he resolved to depart this life as one who had received the full measure of happiness alike from nature and from fortune.

He was now, however, afflicted with a malady which became daily more and more burdensome, and he therefore requested the king to prepare for him a great funeral pyre, and to order his servants to set fire to it as soon as he should ascend it. Alexander at first tried to divert him from his purpose, but when he found that all his remonstrances were unavailing, he consented to do him the service asked. Orders were accordingly given for doing the work, and when the pyre was ready the whole army attended to witness the extraordinary spectacle. Then Kalanos, following the rules prescribed by his philosophy, stepped with unflinching courage on to the summit of the pyre, and perished in the flames which consumed it. Some of the spectators condemned the man for his madness, others for the vanity shown in his act of hardihood, while some admired his high spirit and contempt of death. The king honoured him with a sumptuous funeral, and then proceeded to Sousa, where he married Stateira, the elder of the two daughters of Darius.

FLAME TREE PUBLISHING

In the same series:
MYTHS & LEGENDS